DESCENDANTS OF THE ECLIPSE

Laris Shae Dwight

ISBN-13: 979-8-9894538-0-1

Cover design by: Art Painter
Library of Congress Control Number: 2018675309
Printed in the United States of America

It took a long time for me to have the courage to publish this book. My best friends and my closest family supported me through it all, from when it was just an idea to a full book. Thank you all for being my critics, editors, and cheerleaders. I dedicate however successful this book may be to you all. You all know who you are.

CONTENTS

JESSAMINE

Chapter 1
1837

The sound of my frantic running disturbed the otherwise peaceful forest area, my body felt heavy and my footsteps even heavier. Carrying my young daughter in my arms was not making my movement easier, even worse in a dress. I had no clarity on where I was or where to go, with the moon as my only source of light, my surroundings added to my confusion. With my mind racing faster than my feet I stopped to catch my bearings, I looked around trying to find something, anything just to ignite a small sliver of hope. I started to readjust my hold on my daughter, my mouth was dry and raw from running so hard and I swallowed deeply as my spit was the only source of liquid I had. Small speckles of light caught my attention, my eyes wide. I stared bewildered till my brain sent a message that finally allowed my body to move from its frozen state. Run.

My legs were on fire as I ran as fast as I could, they screamed for me to stop but I ignored all the pain signals they were sending. Shouts from behind pushed me to run harder, I was sweaty and tired, but only one thought crossed my mind. *He will not have my daughter*. It was a thought that made me push harder and fueled me to keep going until I felt my ankle twist and I began to fall. Before I could fall on top of my daughter, I twisted my body to land on my back and as I hit the ground the air escaped me in full force. I laid there, with all the dangers around me, I laid there. If I didn't have air before, I certainly didn't have it now. Trying to ignore the pain and recover my breathing while my daughter was on top of me was not helping. Calming myself seemed to be the most impossible task. I picked my head up slightly to see what had caused my fall, seeing a rip in my dress made me grunt in frustration. I gathered all the strength I had to lift my upper body, but with both my own weight and my daughter's, I struggled. Finally sitting upright, I used my left hand to wipe the sweat from my forehead and my right hand to support my daughter. In a rage, I ripped what fabric I could from my dress to prevent me from falling again. "Damn it all being a bloody woman, stupid dress!"

"You ok Mommy?"

I instantly calmed down when at the sound of Rachael's voice, the guilt crept in. I had woken her up in a hurry when I heard men shouting her name in the saloon hotel we had been staying at. I rushed clothes onto Rachel, forgetting shoes in the process, and we escaped through the window where I had propped a ladder in case of emergency. I didn't know where all her bravery came from, when I was three, I was a spoiled brat and got anything I wanted. My ex-husband was a coward, so it surely didn't come from him. I had turned Rachael's life upside down and she never complained, she was concerned but calm and understanding, and I loved her for it. She wasn't like me or her father, she was just herself. Giving birth to Rachael at eighteen had been hard because of my ex-husband but raising her had been easy and I appreciated her for it.

"I'm fine darling, Mommy is just a little tired." I placed my hand on her cheek as reassurance, "I need to put you down for a second darling, will you be alright?" I asked her in a hushed voice. I knew the men were drawing near, their torches becoming brighter and chasing the darkness away. Rachael had shaken her head yes in response, so I let her slide off my lap before I tried to get myself up from the cold dirt of the forest floor. It took all my strength. Rachael pushed me forward letting out a childlike grunt. Suddenly, one of the men shouted,

"I heard something! This way!" I stood quickly, and the hunt began again. In a full panic, I picked Rachael up but when I stepped with my left foot I nearly fell, and my ankle throbbed in pain. I muffled my cries with every step I took, the pain surging through me, but it did not deter me from trying to move faster. I was reduced to fumbling, quick hops landing mostly on my good leg to stay ahead. "I see her!! Let's get her before Mr. Day gets US!!!" *Damn.*

I tried running again but the pain in my ankle was becoming intense and more persistent, so I pushed on with my fast-limping hops. The men were not far behind me, I could feel them getting closer without turning around to look, but the sound of water made me stop in my tracks. It was a strong current which meant it wasn't a lake. I kneeled to the ground switching Rachael to my left arm to give my right a break. I began to blindly feel around the dirt in search of the water, as much as my mind screamed to keep moving, my body was in dire need of a cool drink. I kept searching but all I felt was the ground ending in a cliff, and a sob almost escaped me.

"It's over miss!!"

The approaching torchlight only confirmed my fear, the river was probably a hundred feet or more below the cliff. "Come quietly Mrs. Day and go on back to your husband."

"That is not my name, and he is not my husband!!!"

Fear rose within me, making me press Rachael closer against my shoulder. There were 6 men surrounding me in a 'U' shape, it was excessive how many men were hired for this, but I knew my ex-husband would do anything to get us back. The man that was in the center of the 'U' formation stepped closer with the torch in his right hand and his left hand outstretched toward me, "Comes on miss, we's can't go on home without 'cha, don't make this harder than what it already is." he said creeping closer.

"Stay the bloody hell away from me!!"

"Or what?!" The man shouted back, making the surrounding space echo, and making me flinch in the process. "You're trapped with nowhere to go. Now comes on and stop actin' like a bitch!!!!" I was frozen in place with the inevitable choice, my only choice. I pulled Rachael away so I could look into her green eyes, we stared at each other as tears flooded my eyes. She shed tears of her own, I kissed her cheek and pressed her into me again.

"We're not going back, hold your breath sweetie..."

I turned around and made the ultimate leap of faith off the cliff, taking a deep breath of my own before submerging into the river's wild and strong current. I didn't know in what direction it was taking us, the water thrashed Rachael and I around. I was able to grab onto a rock allowing Rachael and I to catch our breath. I paused to look up and saw the torches hanging over the cliff. I knew they were looking for us, but the torchlight could not reach. The last thing I heard before I let the current take us away was one of the men yelling.

"FUCK!!"

TALON

Chapter 2

"Talon!!"

John had been yelling my name for over half an hour from inside the house. All I wanted was to be left alone to let my long hair flow with the wind as I rocked myself in the hammock at the top of the tallest tree near the house. I basked in the moonlight watching the stars create their constellations, but just before I closed my eyes, I dodged a rock that flew at me from below. (He found me.) I looked down and found the short Asian man standing on the porch of the house with his hands behind his back, I stared at him visibly upset. I loved the old man but there were times he tested my patience and limits on the things I let him get away with before he put me back in my place.

"Supper!!"

I grunted as I moved and steadied myself on the hammock, I then launched myself to the nearest branch. I grabbed it firmly supporting my body weight before swinging to a lower branch, then repeated this until I landed. After reaching the ground, I pulled twigs and leaves out my hair. Walking into my home, I saw that John had dinner on the table already, but he was nowhere to be seen. Feeling a bit victorious I walked lightly past the kitchen heading to the training room.

"Where are you going?"

With all the skills this man taught me, I'm still unable to sense him when I really want to. I released the air I was holding in order to sneak around, and relaxed and turned around to face my master. John had his peppered hair in a braid that cascaded all the way down to the back of his knees, his beard was peppered as well, and styled into a long thin braid that reached slightly past his collarbone. John had his hands behind his back which usually meant he was growing impatient, there's no telling how many times I've gotten the gesture since I was four, so it didn't bother me. But I decided to answer him just in case. "I'm just going to do some training John, I'm not hungry..." I said as I turned around.

"Talon! Grow up, you're twenty-three..."

"I'm fine John!!"

"You have let that woman kill your spirit for a whole year, when will you let it end?"

I rubbed my temple; I was annoyed by the whole situation and conversation. Sometimes I don't know why I try to go against John, or why I try to hide things when he already knew everything. John was like the overprotective parent I never had. My native mother is a blur in my memory and somehow John was able to get me to see my white father before he left this world. I remember when I first saw him, I was sixteen. I entered this house for the first time surrounded by unfamiliar and disgusted eyes. Though they thought they were frightening me, I just so happened to be wearing a Stetson, so when I revealed the undaunted eyes that the hat hid away, they were greeted by golden irises. They all backed away from me. *Now who is scared?*

I always had this thing about my eyes, sometimes my eyes and I got along, sometimes we didn't. There were days when they kept unwanted company away and other days when I wanted social contact, but people were too afraid. Anyway, John walked behind me, weaving through the crowd of people, and up the stairs to my father's room. I didn't know what to think when John opened the door, but I took off my Stetson anyway and loosened my hair from its ponytail, dusted off my clothes, and waited. John looked up at me with a perked eyebrow, at only sixteen I was already 6 feet tall to his 5'6. He opened the door allowing me to walk in first, only to see a pale man lying in bed weakened by illness. There was also a boy sitting in the corner with his books, three women standing huddled together near a window, and everything inside of me screaming that I didn't belong. The three women I assumed to be his daughters and wife, pretended they didn't see me, and the boy barely noticed me. But my father did. He tried to get up, forcing himself to lean against the bed's backboard.

"Come my son, come to me. Let me look at you."

My father patted a spot for me to sit on his bed, I didn't know how to feel. To me, John was my parent, teacher, and friend, but now I can see where I got my strong jaw from. I can see that my father used to be a man of strength and now his strength had passed down to me. I was very burly and only developed more muscle as I got older. Everything else must have come from my mother, because my father's eyes were brown, and his hair was short, black, and wet from the cold sweat he was having.

"Thank God!! He gave me a strong son to carry on my bloodline."

My father then looked toward his youngest son in disgust. He felt up my arm and then my face. The gesture was a bit rough, but I would never flinch or pull away. My father then smiled genuinely and deeply.

"Who would have known a savage woman would give me a man instead of a boy."

My father then looked toward his wife I assumed, then turned to John.

"Will you get everything set up Mr. Tao. Talon will have my name and my legacy."

This time my father's presumed wife finally snapped.

"Edward Adam Thomas what has gotten into you?! I've spent my

7

life having your children and taking care of you and this is how you think of us? All your children ever tried to do was make you happy, all their lives, and this is how you treat them? I let you move us from my home to this cold and lonely place in the Oregon territories for what? To hate us? To leave us homeless?"

Tears slid down her face, her eyes pleading for some kind of love or emotion from Edward. He then turned his attention back to John, leaving his wife completely broken, she dropped to her knees and sobbed.

"Tao make sure he has my last name, and he is in my will. It will not be long til I'm buried, and I don't want no one in his way when my time comes."

John bowed his head in understanding, and I said nothing. I did not know this man, but I could tell he was cruel, and I wanted to be nothing like him. I got up from his bed and bowed to him in respect, I then looked around at all the gloomy faces except one. My younger brother. I never knew his name, but he kept his face in his book, silent, and for some reason that bothered me. However, I said nothing. When I was finally able to exit the house, the air came easy, and I thanked the spirits I had gotten through without having my father's wrath upon me. A few days later my father showed me around and introduced me to many of the people in the town, he was very proud for reasons unknown. Then several days after that he was gone, and I felt nothing, but I prayed for the spirits to guide his soul to a better place and find peace. That's all I could do. Edward had left all his money to his family but gave me the house, the land, and his business which didn't sit well with anyone, but his will was done. I stood in front of the empty house not sure what to do, I didn't like it. Its aura was filled with sadness and anger. This made it hard for goodness to circulate so I tore it down and built anew for John and myself, making it bigger and better than before.

My mind returning to the present situation I said, "John, she is not killing my spirit. It's already dead."

I had no idea the repercussions of that statement until I felt a dreadful pain in my right ear. John was pulling my ear in the direction of the dining room, then sitting me down in the dining table's chair. Sometimes it amazes me that I have grown five inches taller since I was sixteen and he can still reach certain parts of my body. "You lucky I respect you, John," I said trying to make my voice sound threatening. I already had a deep smooth voice so trying to sound threatening meant dropping my voice lower.

"Talon, I taught you everything you know, so you don't scare me, and I'm not lucky you respect me. I'm lucky that you love me." John responded making me turn a shade redder than my skin. I took a deep breath, grabbed my hair that was up to my hind part, and braided it before I began to eat. I grabbed the chopsticks to my right and placed them in my hand for proper use, then stared at my bowl of rice and plate of fish. "I'm a monster, John..." was all I could manage to say as tears began to fall.

"Just because your outer shell is a woman does not mean you are not the man that I know and care for, Talon. If she couldn't understand that, then she was not your second soul." John said, picking pieces of the fish and placing them in his bowl full of rice. "Now enough of the wallowing, eat." We ate in silence with only the chopsticks clanking against the dishes, and I let John's words circulate through my mind. *Maybe John is right, maybe she was not my second soul.*

"I know I'm right," John said winking at me before taking his dinner in the kitchen, I stood stunned. He always had a way of doing that, which made me think he had a direct link to my brain.

"Thanks, John," I said, leaving the table and heading upstairs to continue wallowing alone.

I woke before the sun could grace the sky. I grabbed the shirt that I kept on the chair beside my bed and put it on over the bind that kept my breasts out of eyesight. Every day I would thank the spirits that I had apple size breasts instead of the boulders other women carried around. I put on my trousers before I got up and looked at myself in the mirror, with my golden honey eyes glaring back at me. I took a good look at myself. There was not much of me that was a woman, I had a strong manly face, wide shoulders, and big hands, and every part of me was muscular. Like I said, I am burly. Ever since John carried me away from my tribe, he had taught me his people's art of fighting, combined with all the physical exercise this made me who I am, along with farm work for six years. Anything feminine about me disappeared other than the small hidden breasts and lack of phallus. I took myself away from the mirror before I started to look back on the past again, and I practiced my training before I started the day.

When I was done, only slightly sweaty, I put my leather vest and boots on and left my room. I went to the bathing room where I had a jar filled with mint leaves and water that was made to sit and used to gargle and clean my teeth. I was letting my hair out of the braid it was in as I walked down the stairs, when I reached the bottom, I shook out my hair as if I was a wet dog then flipped it back. To my surprise, John was sitting at the dining table with tea. "Did you sleep well?" John asked me with no eye contact. I shrugged even though I knew John didn't see,

"I'll live," I responded, as I grabbed my Stetson and placed it on my head. "I'm going on patrol," I announced before going to the training room to grab my bow and arrows, then exited the house. I stopped before descending the porch stairs to wrap my quiver around my upper body along with my bow, and to take in the view of the forest and the sun trying to peak over the mountains.

Even though it was spring it was still cold enough for me to see my breath. I jogged down the steps and in the direction of the barn. The barn was the size of two barns, John and I had expanded it to fit more supplies and animals. But the most important reason was to fit my beautiful black Clydesdale named KoKo, who neighed as soon as I opened the giant sliding door. KoKo and I understood each other well, horses like him were not available in this country so when I had the opportunity to use the trading company Edward passed down to me, I wasted no time to import a baby Clydesdale from Ireland. I let KoKo out of his pen and placed a blanket over his back, I then placed the rein over his face. There were times I stuck to my native roots and rode bareback, I felt more connected to my companion instead of a saddle to separate us. I mounted KoKo and clicked my tongue on the roof of my mouth once and KoKo began to move forward, I didn't raise KoKo by kicking or hitting for him to move. I stopped KoKo in front of the house and stared at John through one of the windows. *John is never up this early. I'll investigate that later.* I made two clicks and KoKo galloped forward leaving a dust trail behind us.

Patrolling was either an eventful or uneventful chore. I would find campers, wanderers, and other natives passing through my land but as long they were gone before the day was over, I let it be. Unless of course they had thoughts to set up a home on my land, then I'd drive them out. I leaned forward against KoKo's neck and closed my eyes as the horse's sways lulled me to sleep. KoKo stopped walking and the suddenness provoked me to sit up and survey my surroundings. My eyes swept the scene, we were next to the river when I saw a figure lying by the edge. I started squinting trying to get a good view but when I couldn't I made a click and KoKo moved forward slowly. As I got closer, I was able to better see what the figure was, a woman. She was on her side with her back toward me so I couldn't see her face. I dismounted and walked closer creeping along the ground to make as little noise as possible. Before I could stop my movement, I heard a rustling sound, then a little head filled with dark brown curls and green eyes, popped up from in front of the woman causing me to try to grab for a knife I did not have. *Way to go Talon, forgetting your knives.*

There was silence between us before it was broken, "help..." was all the little girl said and it shook my whole world. I was speechless for a moment before I stood at my full height.

"Umm hello my name is Talon, and you are?" I asked as I introduced myself, I did not know what to think about the situation, maybe some reassuring words? "I'm not here to hurt you, I'm willing to help, just tell me your name?" I moved closer till I was right behind the woman's body and gave her my hand, she stared in a long pause until finally, she placed her hand into mine.

"Rachael" she said in a low but audible voice. I smiled brightly. Rachael already touched my heart with such little effort that it stunned me.

"Is this your mother?" I asked Rachael, and she nodded. I was prepared to handle many issues; John had taught me a lot about wound care, but nothing prepared me for what happened next.

After gaining some trust from Rachael, she allowed me to check her for injuries, it was a short process due to how little she. The small girl managed to come out with only a couple of bruises for her trouble, so I moved on to her mother. I flipped the woman onto her back to assess her then was frozen in place. *This woman is stunning!!* Her long black hair was some inches past her shoulders, she had an elegant square face and full pink lips. She was wearing a light blue dress that was torn at the edge, soaked to the bone, and had no shoes on. Still, her beauty shined like the sun in her tattered state. *Aren't you supposed to be helping Talon?* I mentally kicked myself for getting distracted, so I decided to keep my hands busy and started checking her pulse and for any broken bones before my eyes wandered elsewhere. I tried to feel her body respectfully, but everything I did seemed lewd, at least in my opinion. I nearly jumped for joy when I was down to her legs and was almost finished the inspection. Then I noticed her left foot was swollen and colored a purple shade. I turned my attention back to Rachael who was staring at me intensely, I gave her a soft smile.

"I will help you and your mother," I affirmed, while also inwardly panicking. I knew they would have to stay with John and I until the mother was healthy. A part of me tried to speak reason, I had a bigger responsibility than myself to take care of. I should pass them on to someone more capable, but I didn't trust anyone with this task other than myself, and I made more excuses in my head as to why I was the only one who should care of them. "I'm going to pick your mother up and place her on KoKo." I said to Rachael. I hooked my right arm under the woman's knees and my left arm around her back and lifted her with ease. A grunt of displeasure at being moved came from the woman, which made me chuckle a little. A light tug on my trousers grabbed my attention.

"What's KoKo?" Rachael asked with furrowed brows. I whistled and KoKo came trotting toward us. Rachael stared in awe when KoKo stopped in front of us.

"By the way Rachael, what's your mother's name?" I didn't want to call her 'woman' all the time and was annoyed with myself that I didn't ask sooner.

"Jessamine."

JESSAMINE

Chapter 3

      I was in eternal darkness before I saw torchlights coming toward me at a rapid pace. I began to run as hard as I could before a harsh realization occurred. *Where is my daughter?!* The torches disappeared, leaving me in darkness once more while hollow steps rang out. The uncertainty and nervousness caused me to sweat, I whipped around wondering where the bloody steps were coming from as they got louder like thunder. I shut my eyes tightly praying it would go away, the footsteps stopped abruptly giving me some bravery to open my eyes. All color drained away as I found myself in the room, the very same room my ex-husband would lock me in, hit me in, and do whatever he wanted in. I could have sobbed for the failed attempt to get away from this wretched life until his voice made all my tears hesitate to fall, "Come to me my dear, I'm glad you made it back home safely."

I turned slowly and found him sitting at a small table with a teacup hovering below his chin. *There he is.* His short brown hair, brown eyes filled with fury and anger, and clean-shaven face with the same menacing smile I knew so well. The sight of him made my tears finally flood over. I shook my head and grimaced. "No...." is all I can say, my feelings a mix between utter fear and anguish.

"Oh yes you tried to take my child away, how could you? We are a family, no?" He said still smiling and putting his cup of tea on its saucer.

"WE are nothing, she is MY daughter!! We don't need you!" I yell back trying to be defiant and unafraid, but he already knew he had me. The smile disappeared from his face, he then stood up abruptly and walked toward me. I backed up instinctively as he got closer. "You and Rachael belong to me! I own you both! I will always find you and you will pay!" he said with a vicious tone, foam forming around his mouth. He lunged at me.

I threw my upper body off the surface I was laying on so fast that it was dizzying. My vision had a hard time adjusting due to the pounding in my head and the ache that flowed through my body. Cold sweat was upon my skin, and I clutched my head with my hands feeling a small sense of relief. "It was all a dream. A bloody fucking dream." I said as I felt my body relax a little, allowing air to flow easier. When the pounding subsided to an almost muted state, I combed my fingers through my hair as I took in my surroundings. I was in a warm and tidy room with two windows, lit by lanterns that hung from the four corners of the room, everything was made of hand-crafted wood with unique designs. I didn't know what day it was, let alone the time of day due to the curtains being drawn. My mouth was parched and felt like desert sands resided in it. I whined longingly after noticing a jug and glass sitting to my left on a small table. Before I was able to reach for the jug, I threw off the covers that were on top of me, and panicking, I tried to get up. A terrible thought sent me into frantic terror. *Where is Rachael?* When I did make it out of bed gravity pulls me down once more, and that's when I notice the tight sling around my left leg "Oh bloody hell." Clarity hit me when I remembered my dress tripping me in the process of running for our lives.

I tried to stand up once more putting all my weight on my right leg. The dizziness came back with a fury, playing my brain like a drum with its pounding. I tried to fight through as I had more pressing matters to deal with, but my body and mind wouldn't hear of it. In my near-paralyzed state, I noticed a crutch leaning against the wall, I grabbed it and placed it under my left armpit. To my surprise, it sat comfortably, like it was designed specifically for me. Still reeling from the pounding headache, I moved forward toward the door I thought was the exit and opened it with my right hand. I looked to my right and stared down the hall to multiple doors, then I looked to my left and was greeted with nothing but a staircase. I stepped out of the room trying to be as quiet as possible, but this crutch was not helping, clunking against the hardwood floor. Then my heart began to race making it worse by causing me to shake a little. The realization that I did not know where I was or where my daughter was sent fear and panic that settled deep in my soul. I made it to the top of the stairs and looked down, they were a bit steep and maybe too much for me to handle in the early stages of my recovery, but my panic overrode my common sense as I descended the stairs.

I was able to complete one-fourth of my task to make it down the stairs when I caught a glimpse of my daughter laying on her belly on a bearskin rug, beside a huge figure with a globe in their hand. There was furniture and a fireplace, and Rachael had the biggest smile on her face. The light off to my right caught my eye, to the side of the staircase was a hallway. I looked over the railing curiously down the hallway, I observed closed double doors along the wall so I couldn't get a peek inside. When I looked further down the hall, I felt the blood drain from my face; at the end of the hall, a door was ajar letting light into the hallway. Weapons were aligned on the wall vertically inside the room, I was only able to see swords that led to axes. My attention was pulled from the room when I heard a soft but deep voice speak. "This is the country Uncle Tao comes from, they like to dance with dragons on their heads. At least that is what Tao told me." said the figure to my daughter. He suddenly rose from his belly standing up on his feet and turned to me. I was frozen in horror as his yellow eyes met my grey ones, "you're finally awake, good." the man said with a smile. He had hair that was so long it went beyond his rear end, and he was huge. I can tell he is full of muscle, not the natural kind that came easy for males but the kind you spend years working on. I could also see that he was Native which further frightened me that my daughter was beside him playing with the globe.

I descended the last remaining steps almost falling in the process, when I finally reached the bottom, I realized that my crutch was the only weapon I had within arm's reach. I took the crutch from under me and held it up ready to swing. Rachael finally looked in my direction and her face lit up in a gigantic smile as she ran up to me. "Mommy! Mommy!" Rachael screamed crashing into my left leg. I was trying to keep weight off the leg so that hug that made me whimper inwardly in pain.

"Rachael, get behind Mommy, you'll be safe," I said trying to sound calm and in control. Deep down I was far from that. The man seemed unphased by my threatening gesture as he stood there with his sun-kissed honey eyes locked on me. "Where did my ex-husband find you, hmm?" I asked, making my voice steady, I wound up the crutch as if I was going to swing a paddle. The man tried to suppress a giggle that was making his shoulders shake.

"Listen, I don't mean to laugh but I don't know your ex-husband. All I know is I found you and your daughter at the side of the river, and she asked for help, so I helped" he said shrugging his shoulders. I stared at him uncertain of his motives, I still held the crutch in my hand ready to swing as I looked around for an exit.

"Alright you helped us now let us leave." I countered, testing the level of his sincerity.

"First can we start with names?" he asked in a slightly annoyed tone.

"Why, so you can confirm your targets?" I shot back. The man rubbed his temple and sighed, undoubtedly becoming frustrated with me.

"If that was the case it would have already been confirmed with my employer who you were, considering Rachael already told me your name," he said crossing his arms across his chest. I made a scolding look toward my daughter, she gave me a defiant one back, I rolled my eyes turning my attention back to the man.

"If you already knew my name, why are you asking!?" I shouted unintendedly.

"For my own safety I would like to know if I have an outlaw that has been unconscious for a week under my roof!" he shouted back.

"A WEEK!!"

I turn my attention to the floor absorbing the information that was just given to me, I was in between incredulity and shock. When I turned my attention back to the man he stared back in amusement. "I doubt you'll see Jessamine Lunetta James on any wanted list." I scowled trying to get back to the situation at hand. The man smiled with clean white teeth.

"Beautiful..."

He whispered softly like it was meant for only me to hear, but I did not let myself read too much into it. "You know my name now sir, it would be proper to tell me yours," I said with rudeness that I knew was beneath me, but it annoyed me how this man had me flustered and unsure, qualities that weren't usual for me. He is easy on the eyes a quiet little voice said in my head, but I buried it before that small thought grew any bigger.

"My name? Talon Edgar Thomas and it would be polite to put the crutch down, I worked so hard to make it for you." He said throwing my own sarcastic remark back at me. I huffed in frustration and lowered the crutch back under my armpit. It didn't escape me that Rachael didn't like the way I was treating her new friend, but I knew I was doing the right thing to protect my daughter. When I put the crutch down Rachael went from a look of defiance to one of pure joy.

TALON

Chapter 4

Relief flowed through my body as Jessamine finally put the crutch down, her behavior was making me feel very defensive toward her and that was the last thing I wanted to be. No, I was not going to hurt her, but I wasn't going to let her hit me either. So, I stayed a respectful distance and waited till the situation was calmer. Tending to her had loosened the hold on familiar feelings I had tried to lock away inside of myself. The week had truly tested my resolve, between healing wounds, checking for fever, slinging her leg, wiping her down, and ensuring she was hydrated by opening her lips and gently pouring water into her mouth. It was too much, too much contact. After Lisa, I had sworn to stay away from any woman I found attractive enough to talk to and, so far, it's been easy. I made no eye contact and kept to myself when I was in town. But this woman washes up on my land, looking beautiful, with her cute daughter, and now she's in my house threatening me. *You could have given them to a more capable person.* I let my mind speak whatever logical sense it wanted; at the end I knew it wouldn't win against my determined heart. If these feelings ever seep into my soul, I'm a goner.

It didn't escape me that Jessamine thought I was a man, everyone in town and beyond thought so too. I know that her thinking I am a man is causing this tension between us, and as much as I wanted to reinsure her that everything is all right, I would rather be shot with a million arrows than confess that I am a woman. I know it's selfish but it's better this way. All my life I felt like a man, I lived as a man, and a man is who I am. The only thing that reminds me that I'm not, ironically, is when I get too close to another woman. When they begin to talk about having a family and living that happily ever after that I can't provide.

Placing all those dark thoughts at the back of my mind I leaned to my right to catch Rachael's attention, she was beside Jessamine and not behind her where she was told to be. "Rachael, Princess, would you like to go to the barn and play with KoKo?" I asked, knowing I would have to win with the daughter first before the mother. Rachael shook her head yes furiously then looked up toward her mother. I made eye contact with Jessamine next, making my body straight, and with a dashing smile I asked, "If you don't mind would you allow her to play with KoKo?" I watched Jessamine as an internal war brewed inside her. Jessamine looked very nervous, her eyes went from me to Rachael, once again to me then back to Rachael. At that time Rachael was pleading with her mom, pulling on the dress Jessamine had been wearing since the day I found her. "Jessamine it's okay, she's been with us for a week and no harm has come to her. Rachael has been nothing but helpful and a joy to have running around the farm." I assured her hoping it would give her some ease. I watched as Jessamine closed her eyes taking deep breaths, and when she opened them, she looked me straight in the eye. It sent warm waves through me, no one ever looked me in the eyes. People whom I consider friends looked me in the eye but never a stranger. *There's something about this woman that makes me want to take a chance one last time.*

I was pulled from my thoughts when Jessamine asked "Who's KoKo?" and I answered without hesitation.

"My companion." She gave me a puzzled look.

"Companion?" Jessamine asked puzzled.

"KoKo is a horse, but he is not just a horse but also my companion," I explained hoping that was a good example for her to understand. She looked at Rachael who was on the verge of tears then looked back at me.

"You promise no harm will come to her?" she asked, finally giving me a little bit of trust. I grinned deeply.

"I promise," I responded, and with a hesitant nod from her mother Rachael was off and out the door. When Rachael was gone, I tried to step closer to Jessamine, but with my step forward she stepped back. I huffed a sigh and swallowed my disappointment. "I thought that maybe you would want to refresh, after a week of not being able to bathe or relieve yourself on your own I'm sure you would want to try," I said sincerely praying the spirits will give me the patience to help her in her recovery.

JESSAMINE

Chapter 5

With Rachael gone, I didn't know what would happen to me, all the what if's swimming in my head were driving me crazy and making me anxious. Though I had married the craziest son of bitch I have ever known in this world, I couldn't help but be fearful of what other men could do. When Talon got close to me, I couldn't help but flinch and move away. His eyes, though a bit odd, showed he was sincere and trustworthy, but I had made that mistake once too many times to trust my own judgement. His offer to have me bathe sounded like heaven, I felt dreadful. I felt like I didn't get the chance to wash that night off my body and start anew. One thing is for sure, I was getting tired of the constant brawling that was happening within myself. Every decision felt like it was life or death, which it was, but living this way was becoming cumbersome.

"I can take you to the bathing room upstairs if you're willing."

Talon's voice snapped me out of my thoughts, and he gestured with his left arm up the stairs and stretched out his strong right hand toward me. I gave in, I would go upstairs, but I would not take his hand. I firmly gripped my crutch and turned around to the stairs behind me, "I don't need help Mr. Thomas I'm a big girl." I ignored his hand and started to walk up the stairs one by one. The stairs were wide enough for us to walk side by side, and even with my rudeness, Talon kept an arm behind me just in case I faltered. I felt the sweat starting to bead on my forehead. I didn't notice how many steps there were when

I was in a rush to find my daughter nor did I know how many steps I had slid down from, but with my left ankle nearly broken it seemed like there were more than before.

"I'm sorry Jessamine but you're making this a lengthy process" I heard Talon say before I was swept off my feet effortlessly, crutch and all, and cradled in his arms. He walked up the steps slowly. I assumed this was so as not to accidentally hit my ankle on the railing or wall. I was fighting furiously against the blush that was trying to appear on my face, but it was of no use. My face was as red as a beet.

We reached the top, finally, and Talon slowly and gently put me down and didn't let go completely until I had stabilized myself to stand on my own. I didn't get the full extent of how tall Talon was until I was staring up at him and my chin was horizontal, I could feel the fire in my cheeks simmer as I tried to take back some control of the situation.

"I told you I'm a big girl Mr. Thomas!" I said sternly. Before I could give Talon the tongue-lashing of his life, he put his hands up defensively and stopped me.

"I will never take the power of choice from you Jessamine, I did not pick you up to undermine you, just wanted to help." He said with a softened voice, his words piercing deep in my heart. (No one has ever said that to me, and I'm not sure if I can believe it, but I want too so badly.) I was staring deeply into his eyes; they were different yet reassuring and it was hard not to be mesmerized by them. "Is there something wrong Jessamine?" Talon's concern made me feel ashamed of myself, I dropped my head till I was looking at the floor. I swallowed the lump caught in my throat then looked back up.

"I'm fine, lead me to the tub will you please Mr. Thomas? I'm feeling quite unpleasant," I responded. *And a little embarrassed.*

Talon had given me a nod of acceptance, I wasn't sure if he

believed me, but I didn't care, I was going to shove these feelings down even if it killed me. We started to walk down the hallway I came from earlier; I was moving very slowly since the painful throbbing in my ankle let me know how injured I was. I noticed that Talon walked right beside me, even at this slow pace he met my stride. We walked past the room I woke up in.

"This is Rachael's room, I put her right next to you so you would worry less," Talon said, Rachael's room was exactly a door down from me. *Good to know for a snatch-and-grab escape in the middle of the night.* The next door down was opened for me by Talon, he stepped aside and let me go in first. The light from the sunset illuminated some of the bathing room through the two large windows, but from what I could see there sat a huge metal tub in the middle of the room, with a pump, coming from the floor and over the tub. On the other side of the room were shelves that held herbs and flowers in jars, a sink only a few feet from the door we were standing on the left, a long bench on the right, and four lamps in every corner of the room. "I forgot a towel for you and since it's getting dark you might need me to light the lanterns. You can sit on the bench and rest up. I'll be right back." Talon said closing the door behind him, then I was alone. *I must get out of here, no one is that nice. What if he is lying about everything?...* I gasped at my fearful thoughts, I knew I had to get out of here fast, something caught my eye as I surveyed the room. It was a green dragon statue with gold trimmings. I had a plan.

TALON

Chapter 6

I felt like I could skip down the hall after closing the door, but I knew I would make way too much noise. I jogged down the stairs massaging my cheeks to get rid of my smile, but I was caught red-handed. To my surprise, Rachael sat at the table with John beside her cutting apples. John met my eyes and had a smile reveal itself slowly on his face. Before he said something to make me want to jump off a cliff I said, "If I didn't know better, I would think you like being Uncle Tao." John chuckled.

"If I didn't know better, I'd think you liked playing doctor." John retorted, making me want to jump off a cliff anyway. "Speaking of, how is our patient doing? I heard she was up." John asked, placing all the slices of the apple he cut in front of Rachael. Rachael's hair was loose and flying around in all its curliness, so I walked up behind her, grabbed all her hair in my hands, and braided it out of the way of her food.

"I think she needs time to adjust to people being kind to her, I don't know where she came from, but it must have been bad for her to live with such distrust and fear." I finally responded to John's question.

I must admit I was quite curious about Jessamine and Rachael, where did they come from? What happened that had them floating in a river, and does it have to do with the ex-husband that she mentioned? I didn't know what or who was after them, but I knew whoever it was would have to get through me first. I rubbed Rachael's head then walked to the closet that was under the right side of the stairs. I grabbed two towels hoping it would be enough for Jessamine, I knew normal women would want a towel for their hair. Unlike me when I wash my hair, I just shake out the extra water and go to bed with my hair damp, either loose or in a braid. I went into the kitchen and got the matches out of the cabinet; I was about to go back upstairs when John called my name, stopping me. John's voice sounded like it was coming from the training room, so I peeked over the railing and found him at the door. "Yes, John?" I asked. John's brows furrowed and he seemed conflicted, his brows then relaxed, and he looked straight at me.

"Don't be afraid." He said with conviction. It was my turn for my brows to furrow.

"Okay?" was all I was able to say before hopping up the stairs two by two. I walked past the rooms toward the bathing room, I placed my hand on the knob and stopped. A full understanding of what John had said sank in, don't be afraid to love again, don't be afraid to trust again, don't be afraid to be myself. Don't be afraid. I hated it when John was able to get his message across with very few words.

I can be nothing but afraid, she cannot know my secret. I've been through enough heartache I can't take another.

Finalizing my decision, I knocked on the door with my right hand that was filled with towels, I closed my eyes and opened the door. I slowly walked in keeping my left hand outstretched ahead of me, "I'm sorry if you're indecent, I have my eyes closed I swear, I just need to …" My words were cut off by the striking pain in the back of my head, I didn't have control over my body as my knees collided with the floorboard and then it was just darkness.

JESSAMINE

Chapter 7

My breathing was now heavy and fast with exertion and fear. Talon laid unconscious flat on the floor; I couldn't believe this man weighed enough to break the floorboard with his knees. I looked at the dragon statue in my right hand and noticed a smudge of blood at the bottom, I was flabbergasted as I covered my mouth dropping the statue in the process. *This is no time to be feeling bad, time to get your daughter and move.* I turned but abruptly stopped when an Asian man a few inches shorter than myself stood in the doorway, he has salt and pepper hair that almost touched the floor and a chin beard that rested on his collar bone. *He must be Uncle Tao.* The man I had assumed was Uncle Tao didn't spare a look my way, I was next to the sink, my heart racing in my chest. I didn't know what to do, I didn't know what he was going to do, and I felt my life was more in danger now than ever. The man just stood there with little to no emotion on his face and he just stared, finally walking toward Talon putting two fingers along his neck. I couldn't hear it well, but I saw the movement in his chest when out of relief, he finally let go of the air he was holding. *Now is your chance, get out of here!* I let the need to survive pull me toward the door, grabbing the crutch, I leaned against the sink and limped slowly toward the door trying not to make a sound.

"We opened our home to you, treated your daughter as family, treat your wounds, and this is what you do?" the man said with a thick accent. His voice stopped me in my tracks causing me to flinch, and his dark brown eyes pinned me at the door frame where I was almost free. A small gasp made me look down beside me, Rachael then ran for Talon settling herself next to his head.

"Talon are you otay? Uncle Tao, will Talon be otay?" Rachael asked with tears in her eyes and wiping Talon's hair off his face. (So, the Asian man is Tao got it.) Tao then gave me a sideway glance with an arched eyebrow raised, looked down at the statue on the floor, back up at me, then to Talon's head. Tao then moved some of Talon's hair out of the way, looking closely at his scalp. Tao touched a spot with the fingers of his right hand and then showed it to me. Blood. Rachael began to cry, if John's words and accusing eyes weren't enough guilt, Rachael's cries for her friend to get up made it worse.

"Rachael Talon is fine, it's just a scratch he will be up shortly," Tao said rubbing Rachael's head with his left hand.

"I was just trying to protect Rachael and me, after everything we have been through, I wasn't sure we can trust you," I said trying to ease the guilt I was feeling, but Tao seemed unconvinced. "Look my name is Jessamine and I know you are upset..."

"Give Talon a chance," Tao said in a hushed tone interrupting me.

What did he mean?

"I'm bloody sorry, but my ex-Husband..."

"We know nothing of your ex-husband, and honestly, we care nothing of your past. All we care about is that you're safe and healthy, everything else will be figured out later." Tao said cutting me off.

Tao stood up and grabbed the matches that had fallen from Talon's hands when I knocked him out, he lit up the four lamps that resided at each corner of the bathing room. He then walked toward the shelves I had gotten the statue from and grabbed a jar with a green cream-colored substance inside, "This is the ointment we use to take care of wounds." Tao said holding it up for me to see then suddenly it was in my hand. "Come now Rachael it's time for dinner then bedtime," John said holding his hand out for Rachael to take. Rachael kissed Talon's forehead then ran to grab Tao's hand. They walked out of the bathing room hand in hand.

"Wait!" I shouted getting Tao's attention. "What am I supposed to do with this?" I said holding the jar in the air.

Tao stared for a moment before saying something that caused my jaw to drop.

"You made the mess; you clean it up." and left me with my daughter in tow.

Standing in the doorway of the bathing room I stared at the unconscious Talon. I was torn between feeling sorry and not sorry at all. Sorry for being a complete idiot, distrusting, and a level of crazy that would instantly find me in an asylum. Not sorry for protecting my life, my daughter's life, and our all-around safety. What's done is done, all I can do is make up for my mistakes and keep moving forward. I grabbed the towel that Talon was so kind to retrieve for me and pumped water on it from the pump over the giant tub. To my surprise the water was warm, usually the pumped water is cold due to the water being underground. I lowered myself to the floor using the rim of the tub to support myself. Once I was on the floor, I used the towel to wipe the back of Talon's head, most of the blood was dry and entangled with Talon's long hair. I had to move closer to see what I was doing. (He smells pleasant, unlike most of the men I have encountered.) That was a weird thought. I got up to wet the towel more, and by the time I went to sit back down on the floor, my leg was sending painful messages throughout my body telling me to stop moving. I cleaned the wound till I was able to see the small scratch on his scalp, I looked for the jar, and to my dismay, I had left it on the sink. I groaned loudly at my mistake. "Why bloody me?" I whined to myself.

A deeper groggier whine caught my attention as Talon's limbs started to move, a breath escaped me in relief. He pushed up from the floor, his hair cascading around his face. He then maneuvered his body, so he was sitting on his hind end. "Talon I'm so, so, so sorry. I was a fool, and I hurt you, and..." My rambling was hushed by a finger placed softly on my lips; Talon's hair was still in his face, but the light illuminated his eyes making it possible to see through the curtain. A shiver ran down my spine, numbing the pain. I didn't know where it had come from or why, fear? Apprehension? No, this shiver lit a fire I have never felt before but couldn't really place what it was. Interesting.

TALON

Chapter 8

"Jessamine, I understand, just lower your voice for me please I have a headache," I grumbled trying to keep the gruff from my voice, making it as soft and sincere as possible. I was mad, beyond mad, no one had hit me like that other than John and even then, I was lit ablaze. But was I mad about that? No. I wasn't mad that Jessamine nearly cracked my skull open. Nope. I was mad at myself for doing it again, for letting my guard down for a pretty face. I didn't sense her at all around me. John has trained me to see where there is no sight, his words not mine, and I was not able to see anything with this woman. I saw her shiver which made me remove my finger. "You shivered, are you alright? Are you cold? Do you need heat?" I asked concerned, Jessamine swallowed hard.

"No, I'm not cold just in a little pain, I'll be fine," she answered tucking her hair behind her ear. Fighting the urge to go to sleep, I couldn't help but berate myself. I should have talked more, I should have listened and made her more comfortable. I asked the spirits to give me patience, instead, they gave me eagerness to be close to this woman. I accepted her excuse, it took all the strength in me not to inquire further. I flipped my hair back getting it out of my face, looking around taking in what I missed.

"How long was I out?" I asked hoping me and Jessamine could dispel the silence that grew between us.

"You weren't out for very long just till the sun went down about an hour or less." She explained, looking toward the floorboards and then at me.

Two holes in the floorboards caught my attention, I pointed at the holes in confusion. "Did I do that?" I asked Jessamine.

"Technically you didn't, I did when I knocked you unconscious. I should be put away after what I've done to you." Jessamine answered putting her good leg against her chest. My heart warmed; Jessamine felt genuinely bad for clocking me so when I saw the healing balm, I got up slowly using the bench for support. I rose to my feet but the pain in the back of my head pulsated making me stagger a little bit, I closed my eyes to focus on controlling my body. "Mr. Thomas be careful; you should have let me help you!" Jessamine said, struggling to get up, but I kneeled in front of her placing my hands gently on her shoulders. *Way to go Talon all that effort to stand up. Now, where are you? Right back on the floor, and why? Because a beautiful woman is about to hurt herself.*

"Jessamine, I got it, please don't try to get up until I'm able to help you, it won't take long," I said trying to sound convincing. I knew she felt bad, but I wasn't going to let her hurt herself to appease me, though her effort was adorable.

My pleading fell on deaf ears, instead of calming, her face turned to anger. "Why do all the men think I'm some damsel in distress?! Bloody hell! For God's sake, I want to help you, but instead, you're turning it around like I'm some weakling. How dare you?!" She shouted causing me to flinch a bit in surprise. I shook my head and then looked her straight in the eye.

"Jessamine, stop looking for a problem when there isn't one. I forgive you, and I'm glad you're still here. That's all that matters, I'm okay and you're okay." I let her think about what I said and slowly her expression of anger dissolved into a sincere one. Jessamine then turned her face away. *I thought we were getting somewhere.* My ears perked at the sound of sniffling; my bones nearly left through my skin. I was losing my nerve; my well-practiced calm demeanor was withering away. Before I knew it, I was pulling her into my embrace, giving way to a rainstorm of tears. I did not know what was coming over me, this was putting me in a position of vulnerability, leaving me way too open. An openness I suppose I can afford, just for a little while.

When Jessamine stopped shaking and I was sure she had released it all I fixed her in my arms to pick her up. "Talon what are you doing? You're hurt." Jessamine tried to voice her objections but before she could pull away, I had her cradled in my arms and in the air. But I was frozen in place, my mind playing catch up with my heart. All of Jessamine's whining and protest muffled out as the realization consumed my attention. *She said my name.* No Mr. Thomas, but Talon. She stopped complaining when she saw me grin down at her.

"Why are you smiling at me like that?" she asked.

"You called me Talon," I responded confidently, with her face reddening.

"I'm going to sit you on the bench, okay?" Trying to put some distance between her and myself, it was time to close off all these emotions. It felt good to have them, but I knew it would be a waste in the end, lies were already between us and would benefit no one if I tried to invest further.

I placed Jessamine on the bench lightly so she wouldn't hurt her leg, I plugged the tub and then began to pump. When I was done the tub was about three-fourths to the top, I tested the warmth and to my surprise, it was hot but not enough to burn. (John must have heated up the water.) I went to the shelves that held the medicines and herbs we use for bathing, healing, or relaxing. I picked up the jar that had lavender flowers inside, I went toward the bath and dropped 2 stems in the water. I thanked the spirits that the dizziness didn't reveal itself again as I placed the jar back on the shelf and grabbed another containing aloe extract. When I was done, I turned to Jessamine who was watching me intently. "Will you be able to undress and enter the tub on your own?" I asked hesitantly, clearing my throat. Jessamine gave me a nod yes and I was out the door like a jackal, grabbing the ointment and closing the door behind me. I was startled by John, meeting him just outside the door as I closed it behind me. I was so focused on trying to put some distance between me and Jessamine that I hadn't sensed John at all. John tilted his head slightly to the side at me.

"You must be distracted or completely out of your senses from that hit in the head to be thrown off by my presence, after everything I've taught you," John said with his hands behind his back as usual. I scoffed at him as I opened the jar and dipped one of my fingers into the healing balm and felt for my wound.

"Why she have to hit me so hard?" I asked wincing at the sting on the cream.

John smiled at me which usually meant he was going tell me something I already should know and walk away. "Trust, my student, is not easily earned," he philosophizes then turns back around toward the stairs and behind the corner. I knew it. I stared at him furiously until he was out of sight and let out a sigh of frustration when he was gone. I leaned against the wall letting myself slide toward the floor and waited. While waiting, my mind decided to remind me of all the reasons why I shouldn't let myself get too close to this woman. Flashes of the moment Lisa found out my secret, her screaming that I deceived her, the name calling, me pleading with her to calm down, to not leave.

"I'm ready Talon."

I was brought back by Jessamine's sweet, accented voice calling me through the door. I had no recollection of how much time went by or when my tears began to fall, but I cleaned myself fast and thoroughly. I got up, dusting off my pants and opened the door slowly, closing my eyes. "You're not going to hit me again, are you?" I asked tentatively, I heard Jessamine chuckle a little making my heart flutter. *No way heart! Stop it, no more of that!*

"No, I'm not going to hit you Talon I'm... I'm going to trust you starting now." she responded in a stutter, I smiled.

"Are you covered Jessamine?" I asked, my voice dropping in deepness. "Yes..." she responded. Then I opened my eyes, I was frozen in place, and I gulped hard. *I did not think this through.*

JESSAMINE

Chapter 9

My bath was exactly what I needed, hot and relaxing. The lavender and aloe were a sweet gesture for Talon to make. He didn't have to go above and beyond for me, but I was appreciative of it anyway, it had been so long since I had a relaxing bath. My mood darkened when I started to think of the times with my ex-husband when taking a bath meant trying to wash him off my body and soak my bruises. I dipped my head under the water to wash my hair and the thoughts plagued my mind. Hoping when I bring my head to the surface the dirt and the horrible memories will trickle away, like water off a duck's back. I drained the water out and put all the weight on my right leg and used the sides of the tub to stand up. I was ready to sleep at this point, though I had slept for a week it wasn't a restful one. It was a healing sleep, all the energy I was gathering while I was sleeping went to repairing my body. I called for Talon and waited.

All I had on was a towel when Talon entered the bathing room. After convincing him I would not foolishly make the same mistake twice he stood solid in place, just looking at me. I felt perturbed, but I was unsure of why. Am I embarrassed? Am I feeling shy? Violated? It was something about the way Talon stared at me that invoked an intense feeling that was still unknown to me. "Talon? Hello..." I said waving my hand to get his attention, he finally snapped out of it and rubbed his palms on his pants.

"I'm sorry Jessamine I don't know what came over me." He responded clearing his throat, "You ready?" he asked, pointing his gaze to the floor. My brows furrowed.

"What are you going to do?" I asked puzzled. I thought he might just walk with me as I hobbled alongside him, to keep me safe from falling on my face, but he had a different plan in mind.

Talon once again picked me up sweeping me off my feet, with one arm behind my upper back and the other under my knees. "Talon you're hurt! Stop straining yourself!" I yelled but not loud enough to echo throughout the house. Talon gave me a knowing smirk.

"Aren't you hurt as well?" he quipped rhetorically. I opened my mouth, then shut it. I had no ground to stand on. He allowed me to grab my crutch and carried me in his arms to my room. As we made our way down the hall, we said not one word to each other. All that was heard were the slight creaking sounds of the floorboards with each of his steps. I wanted to break free from his hold, being so close to him was making my face color in a red blush. We reached my room, and to my surprise, the lamps were still burning bright. Talon placed me on the bed gently and hurried out toward the door. He stopped at the door. "You have new nightgowns, dresses, and anything else a woman might need in the closet." he said facing out the door. I raised an amused brow even though he couldn't see it.

"I see, so you were trying to keep us after all," I joked causing him to laugh, he turned around and walked a little closer to me. Talon's eyes were something mystical, the lights always made it seem like they were glowing, mesmerizing me.

"I don't know about keeping you, I might get a few more knots on my head," he said with a wide grin, but I didn't find it funny at all. I scowled.

"I said I was sorry Talon, what-..."

"Jessamine I was just joking I believe you won't hurt me again."

Talon interrupted me mid-sentence, "We went shopping for you and Rachael, I hope you like what we picked out. Again, Rachael's room is right next to yours, so you don't have to be worried. Goodnight." Talon gave me a smile, and before he was able to get far, I grabbed him by the hand.

"Question Talon..." I spoke in an almost whispery tone. Talon completely faced me making me look up at him. His hands were rough, soft, and strong all at the same time. It isn't the first time I noticed either; every time he touched me with these hands it sent shivers through me. Talon's brow was propped up high waiting for me to say what I needed to say, he seemed nervous.

"Why would you do all this? Why would you be so nice to a woman and child you know nothing about?" I asked. Though it sounded more desperate than I wanted it to, I needed to know. For a week this man had taken care of me and my daughter, and no harm came to either of us. I needed to know what he wanted in return. Talon shrugged at my question.

"Can't a human help out another human?" He responded.

"Not for nothing," I answered looking down at myself only covered in a towel. "The men I know would have taken advantage of me in this state." I gestured at my body.

There was silence between the both of us for what seemed like hours. I wondered what was going through his mind about what I had just said, I needed to know. I stared at the floor, all the memories, everything that happened still haunting me, I needed to feel secure. When I finally raised my head to meet Talon's eyes, there was nothing but warmth and something else I couldn't quite put my finger on. He flashed me one of his dashing smiles. "I'm not like other men, and deep down I'm a very shy person." We both had a light laugh. "Goodnight Jessamine."

"Goodnight Talon."

TALON

Chapter 10

It had been about a month and a half since Jessamine and Rachael entered my life and home, and from the look of their happy faces, it seemed like they were here to stay. At least I hoped so. They grew on me. It amazed me how smart Rachael was, she was a fast learner and had a stronger spirit than the average girl. Though I can see all the pain in Jessamine's eyes, she found the strength to smile through the darkness that loomed in her life. It made me want to learn more about this amazing woman and child despite my better judgment to keep my heart out of the equation. Having them around also widens my daily routine. I woke up before the sun, exercised, trained, got dressed for the day, and then prepared breakfast for my two guests. I shook my head at myself in a chuckle, usually, I left cooking and such to John. He was far better than me in these types of things while I patrolled the lands. But lately, John has been leaving his room later and later in the day. I was starting to get worried. I wanted to investigate this change but never really got the chance. Working on the farm and keeping an eye on the ladies took most of my attention.

One early Monday morning the sound of pattering feet filled my ears, but before I could look to see where Rachael was coming from, she had already laced herself around my left leg. Her presence frightened me for one specific reason. I was cooking and moving the pan off the stove. I closed my eyes to calm my fast-beating heart, but it was short-lived when I heard

Jessamine groaning in irritation to herself before entering the kitchen. I moved the pan of bacon out of the way so no one could get hurt. "Rachael my love, please, for mommy, put on the dress," Jessamine whined.

"No!" Rachael shouted hugging my leg tighter.

"Darling, we have to go into town, and Mommy would like for her daughter to look like a proper young lady for one day!" Jessamine shouted back. I winced at Jessamine's statement; it had stung quite a bit. I understood where Rachael was coming from feeling that way myself when John started to take care of me. I was enjoying my time with the bickering duo, even now. The shadows of my past emerged once again, showing flashes of Lisa, reminding me it could very well happen again with Jessamine. (I had trusted Lisa, I loved her, but she couldn't accept me. The way Jessamine is acting with Rachael at this very moment I fear I would stand no chance in the future.)

Jessamine's growl brought me back to the situation at hand, "Talon! Would you help please?" Jessamine pleaded. I looked down at Rachael and she stared up at me. Rachael was never afraid to look into my eyes like most people. While other people found it frightening and odd, it seemed she looked me square in the soul. Rachael was still in her underclothes when I looked down, her nose was scrunched in defiance. I then looked at Jessamine who held a red dress that I couldn't help but think went well with Rachael's brown hair and green eyes. Jessamine was out of breath after chasing Rachael around the house and shouting at her. Her leg had healed well enough for her to walk around without limping, and I feared she may agitate it.

I was torn. With all the commotion and screaming, I truly did not want to be in the middle of this feud. Though Rachael was her own girl she had traces of her mother intertwined within her. So, Jessamine was inevitably facing down her own stubbornness. "Rachael it is just for one day." Jessamine tried once again to convince the young girl, putting on a small smile to seem friendlier.

"No." Rachael answered sternly. I fought to keep my eyes on Jessamine's face instead of her breasts that were rising and falling with the rhythm of her breathing, an all-around distraction to me.

I finally decided to say something for two reasons. First because I needed to stay a gentleman, and second because I didn't like the conversation that they were having with each other. I took a deep breath. "What exactly is the problem?" I asked. Jessamine pinched the bridge of her nose with her eyes closed.

"Talon this is the first time in over a month we can go to town and just be normal. All I want is for her to wear a dress for one day, for me." She answered giving me a pleading look to help her. I turned my attention to Rachael.

"So, no dress then?" I asked Rachael, she pouted at me.

"No." Rachael snapped. I looked at Jessamine, who was staring at Rachael. I turned back to Rachael, who was staring back at Jessamine. Argh If looks could kill. I finally had enough of the standoff, the food was not getting done this way. I kneeled to Rachael's level and smiled.

"When we return home, I promise to let you wear your trousers," I said trying to appeal to her better nature, Rachael looked like she was thinking about it.

"No," she said again. Jessamine groaned in frustration; I held my hand up in the back of me to silence her as I kept my eyes on Rachael.

"Okay, I will do anything you want for a day, plus buy you some candy in town," I said to Rachael causing her to jump around in excitement. "Uh-uh, first you got to put the dress on till we get back home." Rachael deflated under my words but shook her head yes anyway. She sulked all the way out of the kitchen and up the stairs. I felt bad that I couldn't take Rachael's side, but I knew it would be easier to convince her than Jessamine.

I got up from my knee and dusted off my pants. When I turned around Jessamine was only a few inches away from me, my heart sped up in beats like a jackrabbit. She had her head straight, but her eyes searched everywhere else other than my face, "You are wonderful with her Talon." she finally said in a deeper tone than normal, still looking everywhere else than at me. I chuckled.

"Rachael makes it easy; I shouldn't get all the credit," I said looking at her even though she was avoiding eye contact with me. Jessamine suddenly looked me in the eye making my heart thunder in my ears.

"You know you spoil her, right?" she teased.

"You got what you wanted though!" I shot back earning a heart-stopping smile for the playful banter.

"Thank you, you didn't have to." She spoke. I waved my hand.

"You're wel-..." My words were cut to silence with the feeling of warm lips upon my cheek, my whole body stiffened and at that moment and I wasn't sure I was even alive. I felt nothing but her lips. It was a peck, a small kiss of gratitude, yet it made me into a fool. "Come..." I finally finished gaining some of my senses back slowly, Jessamine flashed another one of her earth-shattering smiles before leaving me alone in the kitchen. I put my right hand over my heart to feel a beat. (If she keeps smiling at me like that, I don't know if I'll make it to summer.)

"She might be the one Talon." I whipped my head toward the front door to find John standing there with his hands behind his back. It annoyed me greatly every time John would slip past my senses knowing I was distracted by other things, then rub it in later saying, 'You still have more to learn' with a cheeky smile.

"How'd you get there? I thought you were in your room." I said trying to get back to my forgotten task of cooking. John now sat in a chair a few feet behind me. He let out a deep breath of air which was a sign I knew he was going to say something I didn't like. I had ignored his first comment, what he said had added fuel to the already ignited flame in my heart, and extinguishing it now was going to be an even harder mission to accomplish.

"You should trust her, ease her in," John said grabbing an apple from out of his pocket.

"John I'm cooking breakfast. I just got done with the bacon, I'm about to cook the eggs," I announced after hearing him bite into the apple.

"I'm not very hungry Talon." He responded nonchalantly.

That's it!

I was enraged, not only did I want him to stop talking about Jessamine and I being romantic, but I wanted to know what the hell was going on with him. I decided it was time to ask.

"What is wrong with you!? You have been waking up too late or too early, you haven't been eating." I alleged trying to keep my voice low enough so Jessamine wouldn't hear, but loud enough to get the point across that I'm mad.

"All it is... is age, I'm getting old," John responded dismissively.

"No John this is more than getting old, you're-."

"Stop trying to turn this on me Talon. It's not about me, it's about you! You walk around keeping these dark thoughts because of Lisa!" he snapped interrupting me. "Like you're not good enough, and worse, like you were the problem! But guess what Talon, she is not the only woman in this wretched town! Jess-." A twanging sound at his feet stopped him from talking. I couldn't hold the anger back any longer, but John wasn't some stranger I could pound on. He was my master so all I could do was throw the fork I was using to scramble eggs at his feet, it was stuck into the floorboard still vibrating from the amount of force I used.

JESSAMINE

Chapter 11

I was so excited to finally get Rachael in the dress, it was a long battle, one I couldn't win by myself. My win was short-lived, when I was done putting Rachael's hair in pigtails and turned her around to admire her, I was greeted by a pout. "My Darling!! You look so pretty!" I said enthusiastically, hoping it would change my daughter's mood even just a little. I saw the water gathering in her eyes, I was starting to feel like shite now. "Rachael, I promise you can wear your trousers as soon as we get home," I said, still trying to keep the excitement in my voice. One stray tear from Rachael's face may force me to cave. I hadn't seen Rachael cry since she had been here in this house, and I wasn't going to have her start now. I threw my hands up exaggeratedly in surrender, "Fine, you can take the dress off, but you're keeping the pigtails." I spoke. Rachael smiled so big and wide I almost thought it would envelop her entire face. I stared at her for a moment as she fumbled with the buttons. It then dawned on me why Rachael didn't want to wear the dress, or any other dress for that matter. I was reminded by memories of my ex-husband making sure we were always dressed in our best. I didn't mind the dresses, I did whatever I had to do to keep peace, but Rachael did. At three years of age, she was brave enough to stand up to him and tell him no. But this meant a beating that I refused to have my daughter take, so I endured it in her stead. That was the first time Rachael had ever seen me hurt by her father, and I decided to get the divorce and leave once I was healed enough.

All because of a dress our daughter didn't want to wear. Living with Talon has been nothing but joy, and though that scared me some, I couldn't help but be relieved that the memories did not surface often.

While Rachael undressed, I gave myself a moment to think of good thoughts, my face went full blush when I thought of Talon, and I didn't understand why. It was as if something was pulling me toward him, something unknown and out of my control. With other people I'm reserved and stay to myself, with the situation I was in it was better for people not to ask too many questions. But with Talon it was different, three weeks ago proved that I would tell him anything my heart would allow.

I was helping to pick snowberries on one warm yet windy Wednesday, Talon had said something about picking more since he used them all on me and Rachael to heal us. But between farm work, Rachael, and routine exercises he never seems to have the time. So, I took it upon myself, it was a light task for me to do on my bad leg, plus it got me out of the house for some fresh air. In addition, I was learning something new every day with Talon. He had smarts in survival, and he knew how to do so many things, probably with the help of Tao. I was so sheltered both in my childhood and adulthood, I never got the chance to explore as I got older, being here was refreshing for me. I was picking the snowberries when suddenly, strong hands began to tickle me. "Bloody hell!" I screamed and jumped in surprise, nearly hurting my leg again and falling backward. A sigh of relief escaped me when Talon appeared over me holding the small of my back to keep me up.

"Sorry, maybe that wasn't a good idea." He grimaces sheepishly. My grey eyes met his yellow which always seemed to glow as the sun hit them at the right angle. I stared for a moment only to shake myself out of the trance and stand on my own again. I played with my hair, a nervous habit I do to avoid eye contact with people when I'm embarrassed.

"It's fine Talon, no worries, you got me good," I say, trying to be reassuring. I went back to the task of picking snowberries; the silence was odd, and I was starting to feel awkward.

"Jessamine, I don't want to bring back any bad memories, I really don't want to talk about this at all, but" Talon said with an audible sigh, "I need to know what sent you down that river. Again, I don't want to stir up any bad memories, but I need to know so I can protect you if anything comes to pass." Talon finished.

I stayed quiet. Talon's plea resonated with me in many ways. For one he knew I was still healing from the damage in my life, but he also wanted to protect me as well. Every word he said only made me surer that he was a selfless man, and at that moment I decided I would trust him with my whole heart. I thanked God for his patience with me, I know I was not an easy person to deal with in the beginning. But when I turned to him, I was a more open and vulnerable person, and all he did was watch me. He was sitting on a nearby boulder just waiting. "When I was brought to this land, I was only ten, it's amazing how I thought it would be an adventure, but now I think we should have stayed in England," I said in a soft tone.

"So, you're English? That explains your voice, I believe John called it an accent" Talon said, now enlightened. And why would your family come here?" he asked. I smiled at him.

"Yes, I am English or at least partly so. My mother was Italian, but England is where I was born. Getting back to the story, my father thought it would be a good idea to establish trading in the Americas and beyond. You see my father owned his own trading company. We were a wealthy family, which begs the question of why we needed more. I didn't know at the time, but my father was a very rapacious man." I finished trying to keep the pain that was creeping up on me at bay. When I looked toward Talon for that extra warmth he always kept in his comforting eyes, I was instead greeted with a puzzled look, a perked eyebrow, and his head slightly tilted to the side. I couldn't help but start to laugh through the pain. "What's with the look?" I asked through laughter, he remained slightly serious.

"It is not funny when I'm confused and ignorant. What is rapacious?" he asked in a light scolding tone and scoff. I held in the next wave of laughter.

"Rapacious means very greedy," I answered. Talon's brow furrowed.

"Why couldn't you just say that?" Talon asked, and at this point, I let go of the laughter I tried so hard to hold inside and Talon laughed with me.

"May I finish the story?" I asked wiping a tear from my eye, Talon shook his head yes.

"Oh but try not to use any more big words so I don't interrupt you." He responded with a chuckle. I took a deep breath trying to gain some nerve again to continue, I grabbed one of the berries and popped it into my mouth.

"You know I have a feeling these are best cooked," I mumbled, still chewing on the berry. Talon arched his brow high. I knew I was side-tracking, but I was beginning to think Talon's eyebrows had their own set of muscles considering he raised them either individually or together often. "I know I'm getting off topic, give me a minute, this is hard to speak of. It's like regurgitating!" I shouted in frustration. Talon's features softened to another confused look.

"What's re-."

"Don't ask!" I interrupted holding my hand up, with that Talon stayed quiet. "So, off we went to North America at my father's behest or command, my mother was not okay with his plans. She never wanted to leave Italy, but she had me, and my father said he would take care of us. So anywhere he went she went, and I went along with them. We weren't alone on our trip, just in case we had any legal or unwanted problems my father's lawyer came with us along with his son, Elias." I paused to swallow the lump that was collecting in my throat, before it robbed me of all speech, "When we were young, he always used to tease me, he picked me flowers, followed me around, and I thought he was going to be the perfect man when he became one. I guess being in a strange land where you know only one other person, makes them seem like they're better than gold."

I felt my legs lose their strength as if the pressure of my past were squishing me from above. My shoulders shook uncontrollably as my tears forced themselves to fall down my face, my body was enveloped by a warm and comforting hug and my head pressed onto a shoulder. With my tears of pain numbing my awareness I didn't notice during my fall that Talon had eased me to the ground. I swallowed deeply again, I pushed away from Talon, his comfort would be my strength to finish my story. Talon gave me a questioning look but allowed me to be free of his grip, I placed my hand over my heart as if it was going to mend the tear that my pain flowed from.

"You don't have to continue if it's too much, and sorry I didn't mean to invade your space," Talon nearly whispered, offering the olive branch that any other day I would have taken just to avoid feeling I was less than human. For some reason, his tone sounded sincere, but his eyes said something different. When I looked up at Talon his eyes told me if I gave up, I'll always be broken.

"No, I'm fine, you need to know right? Don't worry about the hug it was just unexpected is all." I responded.

"When I was fourteen my father and my mother were killed in their chariot on the road, they said it was a robbery that went wrong. Four years after being made to come to this outlawed land and I lost my family. I was left to the care of Elias's father and the maidservants of our household. For some odd reason, Elias's father felt it was important to be taught how to cook, clean, mend, and make clothes, all the things to be a good wife. When I reached the age of seventeen Elias began trying to woo me on an everyday basis, day by day he continued to make these romantic gestures. You know, bringing me flowers and small gifts, eventually, I gave in to his efforts and started to flirt back. Now that I think about it, I was young, impressionable, and naïve to think he loved me. I should have known what it was when he kept pressuring me to wed right away and I wasn't even eighteen, it all happened so fast." I told Talon as I found the strength to get to my feet. Talon stayed on the ground staring up at me, "The night of our wedding was a cruel one, gone was the man so loving and kind, he-... Let's just say Rachael was not conceived by love... Or willingness." I finished.

I stormed off after that, leaving the berries and my haunting past behind me with Talon, hoping it would suffice Talon's need for knowledge for the time being. At least until I was ready to share more. I felt bad I wasn't strong enough to keep going, leaving Talon with a slew of unanswered questions, but I exhausted my will to keep the conversation going.

Rachael hopped in front of me bringing me back to the present. She had her trousers on proudly with untied worn boots, still wearing her pigtails. "Mommy I'm ready!" She said smiling gleefully. I tied her boots, tucked her untucked shirt in her trousers, grabbed her hand, and headed out of the room.

When I opened the door two people's voices echoed from downstairs, John's voice was very faint, but Talon was loud and clear. Rachael and I moved slowly toward the top of the stairs, Rachael was about to step down, but I stopped her and placed my hand over her mouth when a thud sound, as if a knife was thrown at a piece of wood, caught my attention. "Talon when you were a child neglected by your tribe, I took you in my care. I educated you, trained you. I couldn't be any prouder of what you have become and whom you have become, but you have frozen your heart to keep love from growing." John said in a huff. *Love?*

"As much as I care for you and appreciate everything you have done, you couldn't be more wrong. I'm a monster. No one is willing to care for a monster in this world." Talon responded solemnly. I covered my own mouth with my free hand, I didn't understand the conversation and I didn't understand the conflict in my mind and heart. My heart told me Talon was far from a monster and was the gentlest and kindest soul I'd ever met, while my mind raced about what kind of monster Talon thought he was. I've lived and laid next to a monster and even met many of them face to face, I knew after our exchange in the bathing room that Talon wasn't one of them, but it didn't stop my mind from making assumptions anyway. My heart was untrustworthy after everything. A loud bang on the table snapped me out of my thoughts.

"Talon! You are no monster, you let a silly girl who, in her nineteen years of life hasn't yet seen the world, label you something that she doesn't even understand! Without her father she would know what true monsters were and-..."

"No monster Talon! No monster!"

Focused on eavesdropping, it didn't occur to me that Rachael already had left my side.

TALON

Chapter 12

I felt my heart nearly leap out from my throat when Rachael ran into the kitchen and hugged my left leg at the knee, "No monster Talon! No monster" Rachael yelled looking up at me and pouting with her bottom lip. I picked up the small human, hugging her tightly against my chest. It amazed me how this little one could change my mood in an instant.

"She is only three years old, yet she sees more than you. Wise beyond her years." John said as he walked up to us and stroked Rachael's hair with a smile. He then turned around and walked out of the house knowing I was glaring at him. If my eyes were truly like the sun, he would have melted already. I turned my attention back to Rachael in my arms.

"I see your mother let you wear your trousers," I said giving her my brightest smile, Rachael shook her head yes then wrapped her little arms around my neck.

"No monster..." Rachael said again but in a whispering voice in my ear, I released the breath I was holding when Rachael embraced me and began to chuckle.

"Okay, all right, you win little lady, I'm not a monster, but I am a tickler." I started to tickle Rachael. We laughed so much that I didn't notice the silhouette leaning against the door frame.

"I think you've burned your eggs."

I turned my head toward the sound of Jessamine's voice, her

words registered in my mind and my smile dropped. I whipped my head toward the pan on the stove with eggs black as coal. I put Rachael down and rushed to remove the pan from the stove and dump it in the pail of water with a sizzle. I was frustrated with myself but when I looked at Jessamine, I saw nothing but amusement, she chuckled with her arms folded across her chest, which made me huff out a laugh in return.

How do these females disrupt my senses?

I leaned over the bucket with the cooled pan floating at the top, I grabbed the rag that hung at the rim of the bucket and began to wash the pan. A soft gentle hand caressed my right forearm causing me to look into the silver-lit eyes looking back at me. I enjoyed, loathed, and feared the feeling I got when we made eye contact, it gave me a false hope I knew it was foolish to let bloom. "How about I make breakfast? You seem to have a lot on your mind," Jessamine said with a smile. I shook my head slowly to say yes and walked past her and Rachael, heading toward the front door trying to put as much distance between me and Jessamine as possible. I stopped as I was late to respond to the words that came out of Jessamine's mouth. *Wait, a lot on my mind?* I was frozen in place at the realization. *She heard everything.* I turned around slowly.

"Jessamine…" My voice was hesitant.

"Hmm." She hummed at me in response, turning toward me with a smile on her face that made my knees weak. I did my best to shake off the effects.

"Did you happen to hear anything before coming downstairs?" I asked, trying to control my body from shaking.

"Of course, silly!" She answered with enthusiasm. I nearly shit myself. My whole body was tense to the point it was starting to hurt. "Something about you being a tickle monster and a whole bunch of laughter." Jessamine finally finished. I relaxed my shoulders and allowed air to circulate through my body,

"Is that all?" I waited for an answer with bated breath with a dash of skepticism "That is all Talon." She reassured me with certainty. I shook my head in acceptance.

"I'm going to pack the wagon while you cook, is that okay?" I asked rhetorically, I didn't wait for an answer and left through the front door.

I took in the brisk spring morning air as I stood on the porch, the weather had warmed up since a month ago and I was enjoying the cool yet warm winds. It made it easier to do farm work when it wasn't too hot to wear me out, or too cold; making my muscles feel stiff. The sun was gracing the sky with its glorious glow, lighting my surroundings in a dark blue with orange streaks. I unbraided my hair giving it a chance to breathe and ruffled it to loosen the curls, then pulled it toward the front. My hair was in the middle of my thigh meaning it grew about three inches from a month ago. I tossed it behind me and trotted down the stairs of the porch. I jogged toward the barn but stopped when I witnessed John practicing with a sword near our personal garden at the side of the house, he looked very focused, but his movement seemed stiffer than normal. I shoved my concern at the back of my mind for the moment because I was still mad at him, it was a weak excuse, but I really didn't feel like talking to anyone.

The wagon was parked next to the barn. It had four wheels to support the weight of the items that would be placed inside, and a bench seat to fit more than one person at the reins. While anyone else would use the horses to move it into place, I on the other hand would grab the pulling rods and use my strength to pull it in front of the barn. Most of the things that needed to be packed into the wagon were in the barn, so I started there, after making sure I put a rock in front of the wagon wheel to secure it before it spontaneously rolled away. I opened the barn doors and greeted all the animals especially KoKo. "Hey boy, you ready for some exercise?" I asked him while stroking his neck with both of my hands and leaning my forehead against his. He huffed his greeting back slightly bucking his head against mine. I pulled away from KoKo and started my task of gathering crates to pack the items I was going to sell to the general store. I had sold to the general store for almost six years, the owner always got special treatment because he was my best friend's father. Jonah had joined the army; I hadn't seen him in four years, but he often wrote to his father and wished me well. Mr. Kale always loved me as the second son he never had, which meant he got a discount from me. I sold to no one else but the general store and due to my trading business money wasn't an issue. It just made me feel a little more normal to thrive and survive like everyone else, or at least look like I do.

I packed eggs from both the geese and the chickens, dried meat, an assortment of vegetables, sacks of flour, a barrel of butter, two cold jugs of milk, shipped-in fabrics, sacks of sugar, a crate of jarred beans, a crate with jarred fruits, fishing nets, two sacks of rice, sacks of cotton, a crate of jarred dried fruits, a sack of salt, a barrel of dried fish, and a sealed barrel of fresh fish. I was about to load another barrel until I saw I had no room left in the wagon, I groaned in frustration, I was trying to ease my mind through physical labor. I had been so focused on lifting things and keeping myself busy that I did not notice how much I had filled the wagon. I put the second dried fish barrel back in the barn, I then wet my face from the water barrel nearby, cleaning myself from sweat. I unlatched the door to KoKo's pen allowing him to walk freely. I went to the back of the wagon and closed the hatch so nothing would fall backward. Then I grabbed KoKo's reins and harness to hitch him to the wagon and placed them on the seat. I looked to see if John was still practicing but he was gone, I shrugged and continued what I was doing. I rubbed my hands on the ground picking up dirt and covering my hands with it. I removed the rock that was wedging the wheel before I propped myself in between the two pulling rods and began to haul the wagon.

I struggled for a bit, slipping on some loose dirt, but when

I got a good footing, I was able to gather momentum and slowly pull the wagon to the front of the house. I had to turn toward the wagon to catch and stop it from rolling, I slid again because of the dirt but I was able to stop it from moving. Next, I found another rock and placed it at the wheel, then I sank down to sit on the ground with my back leaning against the wagon opposite the house. My breath was not steady. Concerned, KoKo walked up to me and nudged my head. "Hey, boy. What am I going to do?" I said, talking to KoKo and clasping my hands on his face. "My heart is a traitor. I thought I was done with love and feelings. Now that Jessamine is here, I can't control myself. I lose all my senses and Rachael gets to me every time. What am I supposed to do? Reject her?" I said in a loud whisper to KoKo.

"Talon!! Breakfast is ready!" Jessamine's sweet voice rang in my ear. I sighed releasing KoKo's head and got myself up from the ground. I dusted off my bottom and grabbed the reins I had placed on the seat. I hitched Koko to the wagon, patted his neck, and headed inside hoping I could keep myself together. I doubted it.

JESSAMINE

Chapter 13

I let out the air I was holding when Talon left the house. I was stumped when Talon asked me about my knowledge of his conversation with John earlier, and I was more surprised at myself when I played it off and it worked. It didn't escape me, the sick look Talon had when he thought I knew something, the image burned itself in my mind. I thought it was best I should mind my own business, but I was starting to care for the sensitive giant, who was kind enough to help a woman and her child. *I never met a man such as him, what kind of monster does he think he is?* Getting back to the task of making breakfast, I grabbed eggs from the basket Talon had sitting on the counter. I found a large bowl that was in the cabinet and began to crack the eggs inside the bowl, getting grand idea to make omelets with bacon. It had been so long since I cooked anything, all the priming and prepping in my youth was for absolutely nothing. I never cooked in Adam's home since we had maids and servants, funny enough he didn't want me anywhere near anything that could be used as a weapon. I didn't realize then, but now that I think about it, it made some sense. Before I could dwell on my past once more, I seasoned the eggs with salt and pepper before checking on Rachael, "Rachael stay here, I'll be right back." I informed her before I went out into the hallway toward the pantry.

On my way to the pantry, a light caught my attention, and I looked toward the door that led into the hallway. The pantry's double doors were just about six feet away from the cracked open door, I stared at it with intense curiosity. I was no longer afraid of what was inside, I knew these men wouldn't hurt me or my daughter, but it felt better to know what was in there. I bypassed the pantry toward the cracked open door, I clasped my hand over the nob and took a deep breath. "It's just a door." I tried to convince myself before swinging the door open. I was in shock at first, stunned to silence at the door. Then my shock turned to wonderment as I took in the assortment of different weapons that aligned the wall. I walked in toward a circular blade that caught my attention on the opposite side of the room. When I was close enough, I was able to see that this weapon was a matching pair. They were quite large in diameter, at least twenty inches if measured from one side of the circle to the other. It had a hand grip part where someone could grab and wield them, with a rope attached to the grip on each of them. I reached out my hand to touch them.

"Chakras..." a voice behind me said, startling me. I placed my hand on my heart, it was beating a fair amount trying to get the blood and air to flow normally. Realizing it was John, I relaxed myself.

John was in the doorway with a huge smile on his face holding a sheathed sword in his hand. Panic rose in me. John, sensing my growing anxiety strolled into the room, passing a table and chair set, and placed the sword on a stand that stood at the window. This gave me a chance to really look at my surroundings. There were different types of weapons that covered the four walls, most of them unknown to me. When I looked behind me opposite the window, I saw a standalone closet. When I looked at John who had already sat down behind the desk, I caught him staring at me. "I didn't mean to intrude..."

"My child, please do not worry, our home is your and Rachael's home." John said reassuringly, cutting off my rambling before it began. I let my nerves settle, and seeing John smiling at me made the guilt for sneaking into the room fade.

"What was I looking at?" I asked, turning my attention back to the circular weapons.

"I called them chakras earlier because it is easier to say than Feng Huo Lun which translates to Wind and Fire Wheels. Chakras are from India; they are used to throw while Feng Huo Lun is used for melee combat." John explained. I shook my head in both understanding and fascination, I placed my hand on the blade careful not to touch the sharp edge.

"They're very interesting." I mused, turning my attention back to John.

"I'm glad you found it interesting, maybe one day you will learn to wield them," John said with a perked eyebrow. I shook my head 'no' with a polite smile.

"No, I don't think so, I'm a woman and most importantly I'm a lady. No woman would be caught dead conducting herself in that type of manner." I responded with my voice at the end in a whisper. I wasn't convinced by the words I just said, it was a practiced response, something I trained to perfection.

John stared at me for a moment before he huffed a chuckle "If you told that to a woman like Empress Wu Zetian, I'm sure she would have a different opinion." John said.

"Wu Zetian?" I asked, John nodded.

"She was the empress of all empresses, who ruled China alone with no emperor beside her," John answered. I looked at him flabbergasted. My top-notch education did not prepare me for the information that was just presented, I was hesitant yet eager to know more about the woman he was talking about. Before I can ask him to continue, he begins to talk again, "I taught Talon to wield every weapon in this room; some Talon was good at, others Talon was not so good at. The Feng Huo Lun not so good." John and I laughed. I heard a grunt come from John when I was finally able to see from wiping the tears out my eyes from laughing. John was leaning against the table in front of him with one hand and the other grasping at his chest.

"Tao, are you alright?" I said rushing to his side, but he stopped my pursuit when he threw his hand in the air.

"I'm fine child do not worry, just getting old. You should finish what you were doing, so you can head out and enjoy the town." John said in rushed breaths. I wanted to stay and help but he shooed me away. I walked out of the room closing the door behind me, fearing for his well-being.

I went into the pantry and grabbed the bacon, cheese, and green peppers, closing it when I was done. I had the sitting feeling of guilt as I walked back into the kitchen, it didn't feel right to leave John to his own means, but with him dismissing my help what choice did I have? I hurried and finished making three omelets and called Talon into the house. A smile crept onto my face; excitement filled my being. First, this was my first time really cooking for someone. Second, this was another way to thank Talon, and third, I couldn't get rid of the butterfly feeling happening within me. Talon walked in giving me a soul-shattering smile, he rubbed Rachael's head and then sat in a seat at the table. I grabbed the plate with an omelet already on it and placed it in front of him while trying to hide my blushing face from his sight.

TALON

Chapter 14

If I wasn't in love already, I was now, figurately speaking. After years of rice, deer, fish, and chicken on repeat, I had something different this morning and it was all thanks to Jessamine. Usually, my food was separated into different dishes, never cooked altogether. Also, it was rare we had pork, and only got it for our guests. I sat back in my chair rubbing my stomach. "Jessamine that was incredible!" I praised with pure satisfaction in my voice. Jessamine smiled.

"Thank you, I'm glad you liked it. Though I already knew you enjoyed it when you asked me to make two more." She said removing the plate from in front of me, I had an impulse to grab her wrist before she went too far. I could tell she was a little put off by the action, she whipped toward me first looking at my hand on her wrist then at me. I took my hand back giving her an apologetic look, she looked less troubled, and her tensed shoulders relaxed.

"I'm sorry I wanted to say something and look you in the eye when I said it. I didn't mean to make you uncomfortable in any way." I used a comforting tone. Jessamine smiled at me.

"No, it's my fault. I shouldn't have responded that way, what was it you needed to say?" She asked gazing intensely at me.

"You did a good job with everything," I said, staring back just as intently.

"Good job Mommy!" Rachael cut in excitedly. Jessamine stared at both of us with a tear in her eye.

"Thank you, Rachael. Thank you, Talon." She sniffled out.

I got up, took the plate from Jessamine's hands, and patted her shoulders, "What are you doing?" Jessamine mumbled, drying her tears. My brows furrowed.

"I'm going to clean the dishes..." I respond, walking to the buckets full of water and grabbing the rag. Jessamine approached my side looking very concerned. I looked at her raising a brow "What?" I asked puzzled.

"Talon it is not a man's duty to make tidy." she said firmly. I looked up from the bucket and smiled at her.

"You cooked so it's only fair that I clean," I responded. I was nearly done and started on the frying pan when it occurred to me that Jessamine was still standing in the same spot staring at me. without looking I asked, "Did I do something wrong Jessamine?" I looked up and found her sorting out her thoughts and conflicts, I knew she was going to have a hard time breaking her etiquette. I noticed the upper-class women were always held on some type of pedestal; my father's daughter was the same. They didn't live like they were upper class, but my father's wealth said otherwise. His daughter said nothing to me the day I went to go see my father, the women stood primed with their backs straight, giving me no eye contact. No strand of their hair was out of place, they were perfect to an outside view, and maybe to them they were better than most, which is why I paid them no mind. They would live their lives as expected of them and always be boring. I would rather be a war-torn relic than a perfectly preserved one.

"I'm just a little surprised is all," Jessamine finally said before walking away from me and going up the stairs. I followed her until she was not visible, both me and Rachael looked at each other and shrugged.

After all the tidying up was done Rachael and I waited in

the wagon, it had been almost half an hour since Jessamine went upstairs. I hoped she was not too bothered. I noticed both KoKo and Rachael were getting antsy with Rachael bouncing on the seat next to me and KoKo marching in place with impatience. I started climbing down to get Jessamine myself until she decided to grace us with her presence all on her own. My jaw went slack as she came out. The front of each side of her hair was wrapped in a ponytail to contain the rest of her flowing raven hair, some stray strands lingered in front of her face, but it added to the allure. Earlier she just left her hair loose which I was used to seeing because every day was the same style, but this was different, it allowed me to see the shape of her face more clearly and made her eyes the main attraction. She also switched dresses; she normally wore those puffy dresses that made women look like they were flowing on air instead of walking. John had picked those dresses for her when she was unconscious, stating that we shouldn't give her too much of a culture shock. But the dress I chose for her myself was a slim dress that showed her figure but was also loose enough for her to do work and be comfortable in. A more humbled-looking style but not in material, I paid for the best.

"Why are you staring at me like that Talon?" Jessamine's question caught my attention, allowing me to finally close my mouth.

"Pretty mommy!" Rachael cheered, clapping her hands. I smiled at Rachael and then looked back at Jessamine.

"She beat me to it." I pointed at Rachael over my shoulder. We both laughed and when I looked into her eyes they sparkled in the light, igniting another war within myself. One side of me saying I'm in too deep and the other side saying to go even deeper. I climbed out of the wagon deciding no one would win and it would be easier just for today to be neutral and go with the flow. I hoisted Jessamine up onto the wagon bench with ease, then climbed up myself. Making sure Rachael was comfortable on the sack of cotton I set up for her in the wagon, I clicked my tongue twice and we were off.

I leaned against the backrest trying to get comfortable during the ride, I held the reins in one hand as KoKo rarely needed guidance but just in case I still held on to them. When I looked at Rachael, she seemed bored with the ride just as much as I was. Yeah, there was beautiful scenery but that was only interesting for so long. I held the reins up toward Rachael and her face lit up with excitement, we both looked toward Jessamine for approval and when she shook her head yes Rachael hurried to climb over the backrest and settled right between us with the reins in her hands. "What kind of horse KoKo is?" Jessamine asked, stealing my attention from Rachael, I smiled excitedly.

"KoKo is a Clydesdale," I answered proudly.

"Is he native to this land?".

"No, he is native to Ireland, I had him imported when he was just a little one," I answered.

"Imported? That must have cost a lot of money?" Jessamine asked in a curious tone. I didn't want to talk about the trading business that I inherited for several reasons. The two main ones were that her father was a trader and was very greedy, she might think all traders are like that. The other being that I try to avoid talk about money and wealth, it's very unbecoming. So, I just shook my head yes in response. A pregnant uncomfortable silence unfolded between us; I didn't mean to seem so put off by her questions. She had answered mine without much of a fight even though it pained her, so I tried a different tactic.

"I got KoKo because I was growing too big for regular horses, I looked funny. My legs dangled too much." I said with a chuckle, and it did the trick because she smiled in return.

"Well, I'm sure he is big enough for you now." Jessamine teased. I let go a sigh of relief that the tension was gone and enjoyed the rest of the ride.

After a little over forty-five minutes, we were strolling into town. People always stared at me whenever I came to town. It was as if there was a division amongst the people, one group sees me as no threat, another group only acknowledges me because they knew my father, another feared me due to my eyes, then the last just couldn't stand me and held their nose in the air. Today was no different, except there were a few extra eyes and they were not on me. I whistled to KoKo; he knew when I whistled once to park in front of the general store. Once we came to a full stop, I jumped out of the wagon and jogged to the side Jessamine sat on and held my hand out for her to take. Jessamine gave me her hand allowing me to help her off the wagon as ladylike as possible, on the other hand, Rachael leaped into my arms making me catch her into a hug. I unhooked my money pouch from my waist and held it for Jessamine to grab. "Here, why don't you and Rachael go around and buy some things for yourselves," I suggested. Jessamine seemed timid to take the pouch, I raised a brow and waited then I rolled my eyes; I was starting to get a little impatient. "Jessamine it's all right, take it and go shopping. Do womanly things. If you need anything I'll be here at the general store. One more thing before you go, don't let no one bully you, not anyone."

Jessamine finally took the pouch from my hands absorbing the words I just said to her. "Are you sure you don't need help with anything?" Jessamine asked me, looking concerned.

"Jessamine, go and enjoy the day, the both of you. Buy yourself something you would like, buy Rachael something. Toys, candy-."

"Candy! Candy! Candy!" Rachael said over me hopping around in excitement. I smiled at her, Rachael's pigtails flailing around were making me laugh.

"How much money did you give me?" Jessamine asked.

"Jessamine, live a little and stop worrying please, I beg you, enjoy the day and I'll join you when I'm done." I gave her a firm pat on the shoulders. I looked around to find the usual lowlife pest staring at Jessamine with lustful eyes, I composed myself from making a face that Jessamine and Rachael would notice but it was becoming increasingly hard. I watched as Jessamine grabbed Rachael's hand and walked toward the tailor's store. The tailor's store was across from me, and though I wanted to make sure Jessamine and Rachael were all right I couldn't help but look at the gang of idiots standing in front of the brothel house three buildings in front of me. *Let me hurry up and finish the deliveries, just in case.*

JESSAMINE

Chapter 15

The town was not very big, but it was enough for people to fill their daily needs. I could see the general store, tailor, church, railway, and pleasure house so far. The town stretched for about a mile with buildings aligned on both sides of the road. When we first got here, I was extremely nervous, I worried if my ex-husband was still looking for me and if he had sent people to find me. I was unsure of how far from where Rachael and I had fallen to where we are now, but the nervousness stayed with me anyway. It didn't help that when Talon assisted me out of the wagon the people around were staring, I didn't know if it was me that they were staring at or Talon. If they were staring at Talon, I couldn't blame them. Talon was a towering figure, with an eye color that is not common, and let's not talk about his chiseled and strong body. *Focus Jessamine, Focus!* I chased away the thoughts I was having and quickly switched to another. I couldn't help but think for an intimidating figure Talon was nothing but kind, gentle, and thoughtful. What eventually snapped me from my thoughts was a coin pouch being held in front of me and it looked heavy.

I stared at the pouch, then looked at him, then stared back at the pouch. I wasn't used to being given money, at least for me to spend in my leisure. A part of me thought that this was all happening too fast, I wasn't used to this type of care and tenderness. I keep waiting for Talon to become controlling and abusive, but nothing ever happened. I was stuck in my own daze after Talon said it was all right for me to take the pouch. His last words really didn't register with me when I turned around and tried to decide what shops I wanted to go to first. I chose the tailor shop since it was right across from us and without looking back grabbed Rachael's hand and walked forward.

Walking into the tailor shop, I first noticed that it was larger than expected with one side toward the left having wall shelves full of shoes, and to the right were shelves of blankets, ponchos, hats, scarves, shawls, and socks behind the counter aligned on the wall. There were mannequins further into the room on the left with men's suits and others with dresses. Straight ahead of me from the entrance and next to the stairs was a curtained room I reckoned was for trying on clothes.

"Howdy miss." The man whom I assumed was the tailor greeted us from behind the counter. He had a clean face, with slicked back hair, a white button-down shirt tucked into black pants, a black vest, and a measuring tape hanging around his neck. His grin made me feel sick and uncomfortable, but I waved my hand hello instead of speaking. A sharp intake of breath from Rachael caught my attention, she then ran excitedly toward the shoes leaving me to follow behind her. I couldn't shake the feeling I was being watched by many eyes. I peeked over my shoulder before giving Rachael my full attention. To my surprise and horror, the tailor eyed me up and down and he was not alone. Men peeking in from outside the shop and stared through the window at me. More noticeably there was a particularly chubby man who looked at me with dirty teeth and a beard that expanded up his jawline and into his hair.

"Mommy! I want it!" Rachael squealed, bringing my attention back to her, suppressing the urge to shiver inwardly. When I turned back to Rachael, she was holding a pair of brown leather boots with fur at the top. I smiled at her; in the past, she could never get everything she wanted. We would have to go out with a henchman of my ex-husband and anything I wanted to get for Rachael was a no until he himself went and approved, which again was usually still a no. I smiled at my daughter.

"Sit down and let me see if they're your size," I told her lowering myself to the floor with her making sure my dress wouldn't be caught under me. I took one of the boots and pressed it against Rachael's foot and luckily enough the boot was about three-quarters of an inch bigger than the boot she was wearing. They were big enough to give Rachael some time to grow into them before she would need new ones. Satisfied with the results, I grabbed the other boot, making sure they were a match, and hauled them to the counter. I would have loved to stay and look around but having so many eyes on me was starting to unnerve me and made me want to get back to Talon where my daughter and I were safe. Besides, I also didn't want to waste all the money Talon gave me in one place. "How much are these boots, good sir?" I asked the tailor. I looked for Rachael making sure she was in sight, content that she was looking at hats I turned my attention back on the tailor. The lewd look he gave me was starting to frustrate me. "Price! Sir..." I yelled then calmed my voice at the last minute, I didn't want to alarm Rachael and I could already tell after I had raised my voice that she was concerned.

There is nothing more annoying than being gawked at when I'm on my last nerve. From the very beginning, this tailor had only said one thing to me when I walked through the door. After that, all he did was stare at me. If he was like those men who try to flirt with you while looking at you in lewd ways, I might have not been so mad. But he completely ignored my words and looked at me as if I was an object to be admired. "The boots are a half an eagle or silver peso miss, that is unless you're trading something." The tailor finally said with his eyes on my cleavage and a stupid smile on his face. I huffed. I didn't want to spend the money I had so frivolously, but it was best we left and quickly. I tried to keep the pouch hidden from sight; I did not want anyone to know exactly how much money I had. I gave the tailor the half an eagle coin, I tried to place the coin on the counter, but he moved fast enough for me to place the coin in his hand. He held on to my hand a little longer than necessary when I tried to pull it from his grip, but he wouldn't let go without me yanking it free forcefully.

"Come Rachael," I said grabbing the boots and walking away before the tailor could say more. I extended my hand out for Rachael to take, and watched the men scatter from the window as I walked toward the exit.

"Y'all come back now you hear." The tailor said with a small chuckle before the door could fully close behind me.

I stood in place trying to calm my body from shaking, Rachael tugged on my arm and when I looked down at her she had a familiar look of concern on her face. I smiled at her to assure her I was fine. "Where should we go next?" I asked her, wanting to distract her from the current situation.

"Candy!" Rachael exclaimed excitedly jumping up and down.

"Alright, alright but first let's put your boots in the wagon," I suggested as we walked toward the wagon. Even though I had a smile on my face I was very aware of the eyes continuing to watch over me, it started to get to the point that even passersby were noticing me because the feral beasts were eyeing me. I put the boots into the wagon when we finally arrived. It really was just a short distance but with so many people looking at me I felt like everywhere I arrived safely was a relief, like a soldier who leaves his fort. Outside of his fort anything could happen, but when he is in his fort the security eases those fears away. That's how it felt reaching the wagon.

I looked around to see if I could spot Talon and I was shocked that half the wagon was already done. *He never ceases to amaze me.* I looked around for Rachael and found that she was playing with KoKo, I hadn't realized that she and the horse were so close. I couldn't quite put my finger on why, but I had a feeling that Rachael and I were going to be longer residents of the farm and the horse knew that. Then again KoKo must be so bored just standing there that I'd think he'd pretty much do anything.

"A pretty woman like you, shouldn't be all alone in such a dangerous place." A voice startled me, causing me to literally jump around to see who was making me hit my back against the wagon. I got a good look at the man that snuck up behind me and much to my dismay he was the same chubby man that was looking at me through the window at the tailor shop. I didn't think that my disgust could get any worse, but to my unpleasant surprise, it did when his breath reached my nose. He was much fatter in person, with dark brown hair, his teeth even more stained than through the window, and on this warm day, he still wore a heavy coat making him smell of sweat and a recent romp at the whore house.

"Umm, sir please excuse me I have to be on my way." I tried to reason while trying not to inhale too much and smile at the same time. I attempted to be polite, and I didn't think he was getting the message since he stepped in front of me blocking my path.

"You gots' yourself a pretty voice there ain'tcha."

This man was moving way too close to me, every time he spoke, I had to hold my breath. Panic manifested itself and not being able to breathe was causing me to become dizzy. Focusing was becoming a hard task. "Rachael honey, let's go," I said pushing myself past the man. I grabbed Rachael trying not to slow my walking. I was stopped by a group of men standing in my way, I did not let my resolve falter at the sight of these men, but I was starting to get nervous.

"Mommy...?" Rachael whined to me tugging on my arm. I looked down at her, she looked very unsure of the situation.

"She's got a little girl with her Dan. Where's your husband?" one of the men in front of me asked.

"Excuse me!" I shouted pushing through the crowd of men again. Hoping I was free from the situation I walked a little more calmly. Pain ignited on my left wrist, and with a strong piercing pull, I was face to face with the chubby stinky man once more.

"Who do you think you are missy?!" The man yelled, twisting my wrist harder. I heard KoKo neigh loudly, nickering and stomping his feet. He felt exactly how I did, helpless. KoKo was still hitched to the wagon, it didn't make it better that Rachael was beginning to cry making KoKo rise on his hind legs but was hindered by the restraints. The traffic of people stopped to stare. The fact that they didn't step in for a woman in distress told me this man was important or rich. "I'm gonna teach you how to respect a man..." the chubby man said raising his hand above his head. I braced myself for the hit, but then I realized something. *I can't always depend on Talon or any man to come fight my battles for me.* Then Talon's words, which had escaped me in my daze earlier came back to me with renewed focus.

"Don't let no one bully you, not anyone."

TALON

Chapter 16

I was finally able to drop the three sacks of sugar in the corner where Mister Kale told me to put them. Mister Kale was lucky he was a fifty-five-year-old man who just so happens to be my best friend's father. Otherwise, me holding more than one hundred pounds of sugar for twenty minutes, while he figures out where he wanted to put it would have been a problem. I wiped my forehead of sweat, my arms felt like I just got done doing four hundred push-ups. I glanced out the window for the thirtieth time looking for Jessamine. (Maybe the girls are still at the tailor.) I was already half done with unloading the wagon and wanted to hurry and free my time for the two ladies. I was already having a bad feeling, and though I tried to quell the overprotective nature I was developing, it did not help when I took a good look at the tailor store to find horny beasts gathered. I took two strides toward the door. "Thank you, Talon. You've been a big help as always son." I turned to Mister Kale when he spoke to me, I looked back toward the tailor and found most of the men dispersed. With a sigh of relief, I turned my attention to Mister Kale hoping some small conversation may ease the tension in my shoulders.

"No problem, Mister Kale, I'm always willing to help. I must apologize for not being able to show up two weeks ago, circumstances held me." I apologized leaning my elbows on the counter, Mister Kale gave me a stern look.

"Talon now, I told you about calling me Mister Kale. Call

me Bill. Been telling you that for years now, and about your circumstances you're here now and that's all that matters with more and more people coming from the east and south I'm going to need extra supplies."

I gave Bill a toothless smile. "Have you heard from Jonah?" I asked, I missed my friend and with everything going on I felt I was going to need his bright look on life.

"Oh, that boy is alive, he's my youngest, I worry about him the most out of my four kids, yet he's the sanest and well-adjusted one," Bill answered with a chuckle. I watched as Bill opened a small box and handed me a Double Eagle coin, then he walked toward his back room. I rolled my eyes with a smile; Bill was the type of man who always like to give me extra for my troubles. KoKo's loud neigh echoed from outside, and before I knew it, I was outside the general store checking the surroundings. KoKo was on his hind legs as if he was trying to break free from the wagon restraints. I dashed around the wagon looking down the road, some men were grouped together and when I saw Rachael's tear-stained face I was engulfed in rage. KoKo calmed when he saw me but was still visually upset at the situation as he pounded his hooves on the ground. I walked at a brisk pace contemplating my plan of attack, I mentally counted the group of men. *Eight.* I closed my hands into tight fists, I then gathered my hair into a bun so it wouldn't get in the way. I couldn't just attack right away, with Jessamine and Rachael still in the way it would be hard to fight around them if they were not fast enough. I would be in a defense stance until it was safe enough to turn into an offensive one.

A fat man that was obscuring my view of Jessamine raised his hand over his head, I knew who the man was which only fueled my anger more. "Dan!! Don't you dare!!" I yelled in a near roar, Dan turned to see where my voice was coming from. I was now a few feet away from him when I noticed his eyes squeezed shut like he was in pain. He then dropped to his knees clutching the package between his legs, he yelled out in pain.

"Don't you ever put your hands on me! Ever! Or I'll make sure I do more than kick those disgusting things you call testicles!" Jessamine huffed out in satisfaction at the damage she had done. My chest filled with pride for Jessamine. She was changing, I didn't know if she knew the influences that were growing within her, but I could think about them later. Shaking myself out of my new-found feelings I needed to take advantage of the minor distraction and Jessamine's short-lived freedom. I charged at them, with one swift movement I grabbed the man that was on the far side of the group on the right next to Rachael by the arm and flung him over my shoulder making him land hard on his back. The men decided Jessamine was less of a threat than myself, I had a height advantage over all of them which made it easier to use my long limbs to keep them at a distance. I started to bounce to get a rhythm, and one of the men brave enough to come at me threw a punch toward my face. I dodged to the left avoiding the swing, but grabbed his shirt to bring him close to me and kneed him in the stomach, finishing him with another knee in the face. *Three down, five to go.*

Suddenly two of the men came at me all at once, pushing me till I hit one of the beams of a building. The impact wasn't enough to sway my focus, but with one of the men propping his forearm against my neck and the other punching my abdomen, I was taking a bit of damage. I tightened the muscles of my abdomen so I wouldn't feel the punches as much, and now I'm pissed off. *They're too close.* I thrust my fist into the chin of the man that was holding me by the neck so hard that I heard his teeth chatter and chip. As for the other man I hit him in the neck causing him to lose air and choke. Before I could finish off the man that was missing a couple of teeth, another man attacked me with a knife aiming it straight at my chest. I deflected it by twisting my body out the way and chopping him in the back of his neck. Being back-to-back with him I reached behind me to grasp him by the chin flipping him over my shoulder, making him land on his feet in a daze, and finished him off with a spinning back kick. I ran toward the chipped toothed man, lifting my right leg in the air and with all my might I collided my heel into his shoulder. I aimed for the shoulder, for had I connected to his head I probably could have killed him. *Two left.*

I approached the remaining two, and I brought myself to my full height. The men finally decided to turn and run. I calmed myself taking slow deep breaths, I took in my surroundings, and the altercation had gathered a crowd. When I looked at them some stared back, some flinched away, and others diverted their eyes. In this moment, I cared very little about what they thought of me, none of them had the courage to stand up for Jessamine and I don't feel bad for what I did. Soft hands caressed my arm, being that I was so tense the gentleness caused me to flinch away. Jessamine did not relent in her action and gripped my hand in reinsurance, I looked down at her with still the heat of battle in my eyes. "Are you alright?" I asked with gruffness in my voice. Jessamine looked down but shook her head, yes, but that wasn't good enough for me. I placed one of my knuckles under her chin and made her look at me. "Are you alright?" I asked again, my voice deeper than before. She looked me directly in the eyes, I saw the tears gathering almost tipping over the edge.

"I am now." she responded in a shaky yet confident voice. Satisfied, I released her chin and allowed my muscles to ease.

"Talon Thomas!!!" I whipped around at the sound of my name, to find Dan Jr. finally getting up from his meeting with Jessamine's knee. "You red-skinned bastard!" Dan Jr. spat with venom. I've known Dan since my father paraded me around town. Dan Jr. and I were always at odds, and this was no different. One thing is for sure, he knew just exactly how to get under my skin, by insulting my people.

"You still haven't learned to treat ladies with respect, have you Dan?" I said in a cool tone. I looked at Jessamine to make sure she was safely behind me then turned my attention back to Dan.

"Mind your own business ya red skin! She's gonna pay-."

"The woman and the child are my business and you have harmed them," I yelled louder interrupting Dan. I could tell Jessamine was trying to see from behind me, but I tried to make sure not to put all my attention on her. Keeping Dan in my sights was my primary task, he was always unpredictable and irrational. I needed to be the barrier between the girls and Dan.

"I said move God dammit!! That bitch is gonna pay for kicking me in the nads!!" Dan yelled, his face was getting redder and redder by the minute. When I didn't respond to him, he growled in frustration, he reached for his revolver and took aim at me. I narrowed my eyes at Dan, another thing that gets to me is when people point guns. "You freak..." I heard Dan say in a whisper cocking his gun.

BANG!!!

JESSAMINE

Chapter 17

I was startled by the gunshot and all the color drained from my face to the realization that Talon had been shot. I rushed in front of Talon searching for the bullet wound as I held back sobs. Gentle hands collapsed over my shoulders, I looked up at the giant man, "I'm all right." Talon assured softly. It was all I needed to let the tears fall from my eyes. Talon used his thumb to wipe my tears. I wanted to lean into his touch, but I restrained myself. Rachael hugged Talon's leg allowing her to do the things I wanted to do for her and myself.

"Where did that shot come from?" I asked trying to reel my emotions back. I saw Talon point to the chubby man whom Talon said was named Dan, but he was joined by an older, slimmer, and cleaner version of himself. The older gentleman had a gun in his hand, he was waving the gun around in an angry fit yelling at Dan. Me and Talon watched as the two men put on a mini show. Dan suddenly yelled back to the older man, he was yelling and pointing his finger toward us with his face very red. He then pointed to the men that Talon had fought with earlier as if making his point that he had to shoot him. As much as I just wanted to grab Rachael and Talon and leave, Talon stood rooted in place with Rachael still latched on his leg. Reluctantly, I stayed by Talon and waited. The men continued to argue inaudibly, it was then Dan raised his voice to the older man, again making the man reprimand him with a slap in the face with his free hand. This caused Dan to stumble a little.

The older man then combed his fingers backward through his short, white hair as he walked toward us, I felt the sudden shift in Talon's demeanor. "Talon, I'm so very sorry for the trouble my son has caused." The man said looking at Talon. Seeing him up front, he had a snowy goatee on his face and had the same brown eyes as Dan, I thank God he was more pleasant to speak to than Dan. He had a well-kept appearance, good teeth, and his breath wasn't intolerable. Turning his attention to me I flinched backward a little, and he gave a toothless smile. "I'm also sorry to you, young lady for my son's manners. I failed in raising him. Edward had all the luck when he had a son like Talon. Speaking of manners, where are mine? I'm Daniel Senior. You can call me Big Dan, Big D, BD anything you like to differ from my Junior." Daniel Sr. went on until he was done, he then grabbed my hand and kissed it. I fought the urge to pull my hand back, I didn't want to be rude, but I also didn't want his lips on the back of my hand, but everybody was calm, so I played along.

"Daniel, I don't want no more problems. Let's just move on from this and all will be forgiven." Talon said with a steady yet strong voice. I looked at Talon, I could tell he was being cautious with his words. Talon was staring intently at something, I traced with my eyes where he was looking. *Daniel's gun.*

Daniel also caught what Talon was staring at, "Oh I'm sorry, let's put this away shall we?" Daniel placed his gun back in the holster on his waist and gave a smile to Talon, Talon nodded back. Daniel and I made eye contact once more, "All is forgiven, and with that maybe you can grace me and my son at our ranch what do you say?"

"Though that sounds quite lovely, I regretfully decline. Thank you, but no. Besides you hardly know me, and it just wouldn't be proper." I answered, gathering my best smile to lessen my rudeness. Daniel stared at me intently as if he was trying to find a way around my words, he threw a smile on his face, and with a stiff nod, he gathered his son and walked away. People who were watching the drama had found nothing else was going to happen and decided to disburse. It infuriated me that people were such cowards, what's worse was I had been raised to be like them. A person who shouldn't stand in the way of people who had money, that's when I vowed to raise Rachael to be brave, kind, and know the difference between right and wrong. *Like Talon.*

Gentle hands grabbed my wrist, I was so lost in watching the Dans walk away that I whipped my head toward the touch. Talon examined the wrist that Dan Jr. had in a tight grasp. "You should have your wrist looked at," Talon suggested still looking all around my wrist where purple and blue painted itself. "I'll be alright Talon I've had worse." I tried taking my arm back, but I could not beat Talon's strength, Talon finished inspecting me and made eye contact. His eyes told me he was concerned and not to fight him, but he still felt the need to say it anyway. "Please, for me, go see the doctor. I don't have any ointments to help right now, and I would at least like to know if anything is broken or wrong."

"You didn't have a problem finding broken bones when you found me," I said with a sly smirk, that managed to get Talon to smirk along with me. *Are we flirting now?* Talon gave me a pleading look.

"I had time to inspect your wounds when I took you home, even before then by the side of the river I had time to really feel for broken bones. Please, the doctor could check you fast, by the time you are out, and I'll be done at the general store."

I gave in to Talon's demands knowing that in all truth I just didn't want to be left alone at all right now. I did not have anyone I could trust by my side, and Rachael betrayed me by deciding to go with Talon to unload the rest of the wagon. After Talon told me where to go, I watched as he placed Rachael on his shoulders and headed back to the general store. I walked down the dusty road still feeling some eyes on me. When I made eye contact with a man that was staring too hard, he immediately dropped his gaze.

I guess Talon's display today worked to some effect.

I reached the doctor's office which was all the way at the end of the road adjacent to another road that led to a chapel. Outside the shop read a sign that said Doctor; confident I was where I needed to be I opened the door and went in. When I walked in, I saw a counter and a door leading to a room with beds inside. Before I could really take in more of my surroundings a man came through the doorway. He looked like he was in his thirties, skinny from what I could tell, brown hair that was cut close to his scalp and a clean-shaven face.

"Ah, I didn't hear someone walk in. Please sit at the table." the man said gesturing to the table opposite the wall with glass cabinets behind it. I was able to see different pills in jars, beyond there was a wall with a counter.

I sat down at the table, and a minute later he joined me. Sitting across from me, he was a fair-looking man and not horrible on the eyes. "I'm sorry I wasn't in front to greet you, I heard there was a commotion on the road and was just getting ready to take in anyone that was injured. Anywho, my name is Doctor Dean, how may I be of service?" Dean said, visibly trying to calm his nerves in my presence. *I'm not that pretty for these men to get flustered around me, at least I don't feel like I am.*

"I just need you to check my left wrist please, that is all." I responded, trying to get out of here fast. He grabbed my wrist and felt around it. I winced at every manipulation of my wrist, and by the time he was done I was ready to slap him.

"No broken bones it's just bruised, allow me to check your pulse please." the doc said. His eyes furrowed for a moment as he dug his two fingers deeper into my uninjured right wrist.

"Hmm, I see." he said getting up abruptly and heading behind the counter.

"What is it, Doctor?" I started to panic. The Doc started opening and closing different glass cabinets pulling out various things. "From now on, you'll have to be careful of your stress levels, try not to take part in any hard labor, and be watchful of what you eat." My jaw hung slack at his words. The Doctor came back with a bandage and wrapped my injured wrist, I started to chuckle nervously.

"If I didn't know better those sounded like instructions for pregnancy, instead of a bruised wrist." Dread was starting to kick in slowly, but I still plastered a smile on my face.

"They are." The doctor smiled back.

TALON

Chapter 18

There was an awkward silence as I drove back home, Jessamine sat quietly beside me making me wonder what happened when she left my side. To think, I was so excited to see her again. After getting everything done and spending time getting Rachael whatever she wanted, which was of course candy, I set out to get a gift for Jessamine. I didn't have long before Jessamine got back. Luckily at the general store Bill had a simple yet pretty bracelet that he was willing to trade for one sack of cotton. I waited at the wagon with the bracelet behind my back. I stood slightly nervous, I knew today had been rough on all of us and maybe a gift would lighten her mood. My respect for Jessamine grew today; in the face of danger, she stood her ground and fought back. When Jessamine finally came into view my smile slowly faded as I noticed she looked rather disturbed. Before I could ask, Jessamine raised her hand to keep me silent, "Let's just get home." was all she said before I helped her up into the wagon and I decided to keep the bracelet a secret for now.

I looked to see what Rachael was up to in the back of the wagon, she had enough space to do anything she wanted now that it was mostly empty. Instead, she used the remaining cotton sack for a bed and took a nap. I couldn't take the silence anymore; it was more worrisome than boring. Jessamine barely looked me in the eye since the ride started and I was starting to panic. *Why she is so quiet? What does she know?*

"Jessamine, what's wrong?" It came out a little sterner and

rougher than I wanted it to. She hugged herself, remaining silent. With the sun going down it was getting a bit chilly and the only quilt available was being used for Rachael. I cleared my throat trying to gain some courage to ask Jessamine to do something I wasn't quite comfortable with. "If you are cold, you can... umm... snuggle closer to me." There I said it, and all I could do was wait for the result. After a minute of waiting Jessamine scooted closer to me leaning her head onto my shoulder. My heart felt like it was about to burst out of my chest, I never let anyone other than John come this close, let alone touch me. The only times I had ever broken that rule was when my secret was revealed and now.

"Well, I thought you were great back there. No woman I've met is brave enough to stand up for themselves against men." *Except for myself.* "Rachael is going to grow up just as brave as you are and with my help, she'll know more than just kicking in the phallus." I was starting to feel like I was talking to myself, but seeing Jessamine smirk just a little made it all worthwhile.

I hoped that if I kept talking enough, I could probably get Jessamine to tell me what was wrong. Jessamine's warm presence near my body sometimes made it hard to think. "I can't wait to watch Rachael grow up." My eyes went wide, the words so fluently came out my mouth I could not stop them.

"Are you saying we could stay forever?" Jessamine whispered just loud enough for me to hear. I smiled knowing the truth that I was about to spew. We looked at each other at the same time, with my yellow eyes meeting her silver ones.

"I wouldn't have it any other way." *Now all you must do is hide your secret forever.*

I stopped the wagon in front of the house and hopped down giving KoKo a pat on the neck as I made it around to Jessamine's side. KoKo huffed his appreciation. I offered Jessamine my hand, leaving her side had made my body feel cold. Jessamine slowly grazed her hand over my palm before taking a good grip on it. I helped her off the wagon and when she tripped, I was there to catch her. We stared into each other's eyes with my arms around her upper body holding her up. I was lost in those moonlit eyes. An urge awakened inside of me, a surge of arousal and need that was starting to grow all on its own. I pried myself away from her with all my strength. *This is starting to get unbearable.* I heard a whisper of thanks come from her and all I could do was nod. I started to climb the wagon thinking it would be better to distract myself with someone else. I slowly and tentatively dug my arms around Rachael so she wouldn't wake. Satisfied with a good grip I lifted her to me; it was early in the evening, and she still had time to sleep before supper.

When I reached the ground, I couldn't help but catch the odd look Jessamine was giving me, it was like a look of wonderment or admiration. "What is it?" I asked with a perked brow, she didn't answer at first. It was like she was trying to find the words to say. Jessamine walked closer to me, placing her hand on my biceps.

"You're good with her, you would be a great father." She replied, and the compliment made a warm fuzzy feeling grow within. I knew I never would have children; I had only got the blood curse for four years of my life until it was gone. I wasn't attracted to men at all anyway even if the bloody curse had stayed, so having Rachael around has been the spirits' blessing to me. If not forever, at least for a little while. The screen door creaking open stole my attention, John greeted us arms opened wide.

"Ahh, my three favorite people are home, I was starting to-... what happened my child?" John's brows creased in worry pointing to Jessamine's wrapped wrist. Jessamine and I exchanged knowing glances at each other sighing in unison. John looked at the two of us, perplexed.

"John why don't you take Rachael, and Jessamine can fill you in on our little adventure today," I suggested handing Rachael over.

"Where will you be?" Jessamine asked, her voice filled with

concern.

"I'll be back, I'm going on patrol."

I made the poorest excuse ever, then rode KoKo hard and fast trying to ease my spirit. I was happy I had remembered to bring my bow, arrows, and knives this time. With the rumors going around that more Easterners were heading over I had to be prepared to protect and defend my land. I clicked my tongue once as smoke filled my nostrils. KoKo stomped nervously in place. Still trying to get the direction of the smell I rubbed KoKo's neck, though it comforted him very little. I searched the area while still sat atop KoKo and squinting through the trees I saw that a faint light shone. I dismounted KoKo patting him twice on his body as a signal to stay, I bent my knees and lowered my upper body to sneak quietly. Inching closer to the light I had to scout the area, from what I could see the smell and light were from a campfire where a few men sat around. I couldn't tell how many men there were, but I could see guns, both pistols and rifles. I really couldn't get closer because the tree didn't give me enough cover. I could crawl closer but being on the ground wouldn't give me a good advantage just in case I was caught. I looked up with a smile, the intertwining tree branches were the best I had to spy without getting caught.

I waited for the sun to set further to hide in the night's shadows. I pulled my knives out and readied myself. I leaned my forehead on the tree, and I asked for forgiveness for the damage I was going to do to it. I didn't have a rope to cause less suffering, and this was the best plan to stay safe. *This day couldn't get any worse.* I jumped and plunged my knife into the tree using my upper strength to pull myself up. I only needed to climb til' I reached a thick branch that would support my weight. I grunted very little and tried not to make too much noise with my knives digging into the tree. I finally reached a thick branch and rested a bit. Between trying to be quiet, the force to climb and stab, and the strain in my limbs, I was quite winded. After catching my breath, I stepped on the thickest tree branch. I barely made a sound as I approached from above making sure I was still masked by enough darkness. There were three men sitting around the fire, they were worse for wear like they hadn't had a bath in days, and they smelled it too.

"Saw a house about a mile or two up the road, wanna check there?"

"Did you scout it out first?"

"A little but nothing happened for more than four hours so I got tired."

"Did you even look inside the house?"

"No boss..."

The third man rolled his eyes and scoffed.

"You got something to say, Fred?" a man I assumed was the leader asked.

"Yea, I do! It's been over a month, and we haven't found the woman or the child! I got a family needing me, Herb!"

The man called Herb stared at Fred for a minute before spitting the tobacco out of his mouth in a large amount. "What do you think Mr. Day gonna do to us when he sees us empty-handed, hmm? Do you think he'll let us go with a slap on the wrist? No..."

"We are only three men against a vast land, there's no way we'd find them now." Fred says, visibly upset.

"Fine we'll check this house up the road first, and if there's nothing, we head back."

The men shook their heads in agreement as they pulled out food from their sacks to feed themselves. Anger, alarm, and anxiousness coursed through me. As much as I wanted to hop down and take care of this it wouldn't have been wise to do it now. The best plan was to wait until they were ready to sleep, the big question was how I would get rid of them. If I kept them alive and they returned to their boss, Jessamine and Rachael would be assumed dead to him and they would be free. The fact that they wanted to check the only house within fifty miles or more made my hair stand up, I had to make a decision that would affect somebody else's life other than my own. Was I ready to put my life on the line for a woman and child I'd only known for almost two months? I really didn't know who her enemy was to make them my enemy, but he hurt Jessamine and anyone who hurts someone I care about is my enemy. *They should have gone home.*

JESSAMINE

Chapter 19

"Sweet dreams, darling." I kissed Rachael goodnight on her forehead after tucking her in. The sun had already set, and dinner was had without Talon, which left me to tell John about our horrible day in town. I would have worried, but my pregnancy plagued my mind. I knew how it was conceived and the thought of that made me feel filthy all over again. It had been over two months since Rachael and I had gotten away from my husband's men. It had been 3 months since I left my husband and it seemed he haunted me even without me being in his presence. Well, what I said was too harsh, I will always love my daughter. Despite all the hell I have gone through she was the blessing that God gave me, not a "gift" like my ex-husband seems to call Rachael. I nearly shuddered when every morning he would say 'Where is my gift to you this morning?' As if it amended all that he had done the night before. Now I'm pregnant with another "gift" of his. As much as it was against my belief to take a life, I could not thrust this child onto Rachael, John, and Talon. Not like this. I was doing so much thinking I didn't realize I walked myself into my room and closed the door. So much was happening all at once and this day has been nothing but bollocks. I sat on my bed facing the direction of the window. Talon had been nothing but good to me and Rachael without knowing the risk. Of course, with Talon taking on eight men today I didn't know what I should be more afraid of. Should I be afraid that Talon is a man against an army, or should I be afraid that Talon would take on the challenge of leaving bodies in his wake? Talon was still a mystery to me, but I knew he was a man who would do anything to keep the people he cared for safe. Which is why I must do the same for him.

I silently cried and when I could no longer cry silently, I covered my mouth with both hands. After running out of tears I reached into my dress pocket and pulled out a cloth that was bundled together, unraveling it to reveal a pill. I sighed heavily to myself; I knew what this pill was used for. All the brothel girls used it to get rid of their problems. The doctor warned me that it may be too late and cause damage that may be unrepairable. I popped the pill in my mouth, anyway, filled with sorrow and regret I swallowed it.

"What have I done? How-." My crime was too great for me to bear but suddenly I felt a small prick in my neck and before I knew it, I vomited. My vision was blurred with tears, I was slouched over, and between my legs I drooled onto the floor all the excess saliva from my mouth.

"That is not how you solve your problems, Jessamine..." I heard John's voice from behind me. A searing pain burned my throat from the force of the vomit. John then put himself in my line of sight.

"What did you bloody do to me?" I questioned, trying to gather my energy to be mad. John kneeled so he could look at me eye to eye.

"You have betrayed my hopes and expectations of you. I had suspected you were with child when you arrived, but it was too early to tell, which is why I hadn't mentioned it to Talon yet."

"How could you know when I just found out today?" I asked, still trying to keep the anger in my voice. John smiled at me.

"When your leg was healing and I'd checked your pulse every time, I felt the second heartbeat growing stronger each time. I thought you knew but was just waiting for a time to tell Talon."

"Well, I didn't know, so now what? I assume you won't let me get rid of it." I said staring at the pill I threw up on the floor. John tossed a towel on my lap and used another towel to cover my vomit, taking the pill from my view.

I stood up from the bed tears streaking down my face "I can't throw this baby onto you and Talon this way, it is not your responsibility. You are already harboring me without knowing the risk, I can't live with myself to let this happen. I-."

"You don't have permission to make choices for us, we helped you and your daughter without asking for anything in return!" John was beginning to shout.

"This is not the kind of 'thank you' I had in mind, John!" I shouted back.

"The least you can do is trust us, the people who are risking their lives. We made our decision and regret nothing." John stared me down.

"John, you don't understand." I tried to reason.

"Your past? Everyone's got one, there are slaves in the East who must choose between the whip to their backs or escape to freedom to a future that is not guaranteed. Thank God, the spirits, the deities that you and your daughter made it out alive. Fán shìdōu nán yì." John said in finality.

"What does that mean?" I had to ask, knowing I already had frustrated John enough.

"It means, all things are difficult before they are easy. Tell Talon as soon as you're ready and don't ever bring the Portuguese poison in this house ever again."

I was rendered speechless for some passing moments. I was about to say something, but John put his finger up to keep me silent. "Did you hear that?" John asked, his brows furrowed. I tried to listen to see if I could hear what John was hearing, but nothing came to me.

"John, I don't hear anything." But John ignored my ignorance and opened the nearest window wide. Sticking his whole upper body out the window, I approached next to him trying to concentrate on the sounds. At first Frogs, crickets, and the streaming water filled my ears. Suddenly a man's scream echoed around the forest, "What or who was that?" I asked.

"I don't know but-." A loud shot rang out cutting our conversation short and startling me half to death. "Get the first aid ready just in case," John said before disappearing from my side.

I paced the kitchen; I didn't know how much time passed by and I was beyond the point of worry and panic. Waiting was torturing me, I didn't know what was going on, all the sound stopped and nothing but the normal forest silence filled the air. *I'm so stupid, I should have been more honest. What if I never see him again, what if he's dead?* Okay, I really needed to calm down, I was getting ahead of myself. The thought of losing Talon caused a slight pang in my heart. I'm finding myself thinking about Talon more often as the days pass on, slowing myself down from these feelings is becoming harder. I decided that maybe I should sit. I have always been a sucker for a kind and sweet man, thinking about it now, that's how I got into the mess with Elias. With Talon it seems his kindness is genuine, every time he interacts with me it's as if everything I do or say matters. I am not used to this treatment, I'm only twenty years of age, so there is plenty of time to learn new things.

Who am I kidding, what man would want to love a woman with a child and one on the way that aren't his own blood? A woman could only dream.

The door swung open in a loud slam against the wall, I jumped from my seat going from startled to concerned very quickly. "John would you please stop treating me as if I'm going to die!" Talon whined while using John for stability. I rushed for Talon and gasped when I saw his right thigh bleeding.

"Is it serious?" Before I could do anything, Talon placed his clean left hand on my cheek.

"I'm fine, just do me a favor. Remember this always. As long as I am alive you and your daughter will remain safe and alive. Just remember that please?"

"Harrumph…" John cleared his throat; we turned our heads toward John who was raising a questioning brow at us.

"Sorry to have ruined a moment, but we do have a wound to take care of." John smiled teasingly. Talon's hand dropped from my face and though it was gone the warmth remained.

"I'm coming old man!" Talon yelled as he limped toward the kitchen. Rendered speechless due to Talon's vow I decided that I should go upstairs before my cheeks got any redder. When I entered my room, an odor bombarded my nose. I pinched it shut to keep me from smelling. Then I realized John and I completely forgot to clean the vomit on the floor. *Great…*

"Are you going to tell me why you resorted to violence?" John's voice caught my attention on my way to get a bucket. He didn't sound enthused.

"Those men were after Jessamine and Rachael; I couldn't just let them be." Talon's revelation made me nearly gasp out loud.

"Is that why you made such a declaration to Jessamine?" John's teasing made me flush one more time.

"I just wanted her to know that she is safe here and… Ouch! Geez Tao that hurt!"

"Shut your mouth, the girls are sleeping" John scolded with a chuckle. "I think it's about time we put up that fence we've been planning on for years," he said with a sigh.

"Ugh, that's going to take forever," Talon whined.

"All to keep the girls safe and unwanted people off our land." John retorted.

"Ha-ha very funny," Talon grunted.

I left from the top of the staircase and headed toward the bathing room to get the bucket. For once my heart was at ease and I felt truly safe. I took a deep breath letting my worries go and though I was picking up a rude habit of eavesdropping, it was the best thing I ever heard.

TALON

Chapter 20

The bullet graze I received was cleaned and wrapped, and I growled inwardly. The work we must do in the upcoming months is going to wear me out. In addition, I won't have time to do the things I want to do. I still debated whether I was stupid or a fool. Being stupid is something you don't mean to be on purpose, being foolish is knowing you are about to do something stupid and doing it anyway. I could have left the men alone. Let them come to the house, lie to them and tell them what they seek they will never find on my land, and it would have been over. A deeper truth lay within me though, I wanted them men nowhere near Jessamine and Rachael.

John went to bed after he was done complaining that he was too 'drained'. I was starting to become more alarmed around John. Something was going on and my attention was being pulled in so many directions I could not fully focus on what it was. I sat in the kitchen and just contemplated, there was nothing more for me to do today.

* * *

Weeks went by and no other men showed up on the property, I guess it was safe to say we were ok for now. So, I allowed myself to relax, at least as much as I could. Something was going on with John. I was starting to see him work less and Jessamine, I felt, was avoiding me. Every time I would talk to her, she kept conversations between us short and never looked me in the eye. I thought everything was okay between Jessamine and me, that maybe we were more than friends. A thought I kept to myself and only indulged in at night by going to sleep with a smile on my face. But I couldn't help but feel bothered by the distance. It helped that Rachael always wanted to be around me, she tried to do everything I did which was nothing less than adorable. My leg was for the most part healed, allowing me to get back to exercising the way I normally would.

I was practicing much later in the day than usual, dressed in clothes that I wore to do work around the house since I didn't give myself time to practice before work. The work clothes were too stiff to practice in, but I did it anyway, trying to save time in changing. I started with the slow and precise movements of punches and kicks. I executed a high kick holding it in place, suspended in the air for as long as I could, I needed that muscle to stretch. A light sheet of sweat started to form on my head. My thigh muscle still needed to be stretched so I moved my leg in the air till it was flush with my chest. My leg was starting to hurt but I pushed forward. From the corner of my eye, I could see Rachael with her leg propped against the house, I turned my head to get a full view and she was trying hard to look exactly like me. I couldn't help but smile at her effort. I decided to test her resolve further.

I put my leg down and started making punch and kick combinations but kept an eye on Rachael. I didn't want her to hurt herself, but I also didn't want to miss what she could do. For a three-year-old, she was able to keep up, in her own way. When I finished with a jumping kick Rachael tried to do the same and ended up falling on her bum. I laughed out loud jogging up to Rachael and picking her with one swift motion off the floor. I couldn't help it, I squeezed her into a tight hug without it hurting, then raised her above my head. "Oh, little one, if I can I will teach you everything I know. You'll be a formidable woman when you grow up." I hugged her once more, taking in her glowing smile.

"How can you teach her everything, when I haven't taught you everything that I know Talon?" John approached me and Rachael with a smile.

"Tao!" Rachael screamed in excitement, reaching out to try to hug John. I let her down and she collided with John's leg. I inhaled a breath of courage.

"John I've been trying not to pry, but I could no longer hold back to ask. What's going on with you? For weeks you haven't been yourself and-."

"Not in front of the child." John snapped but he was still calm and looking me straight in the eyes. Arguing in front of Rachael was not an option, I never want her to worry another day in her life. So instead, I turned toward the barn and gritted my teeth, grumbling unheard insults. I know John will talk when he is ready. He'll give me the run around with his unsolvable riddles and I'll mentally go insane trying to figure it out all for one answer.

I finally reached the barn letting out a long sigh, I massaged my eyebrows from the permanant crease I might have gotten from being so frustrated. I crossed my arms across my chest leaning against the barn door frame. "Is something wrong Talon?" I nearly left my skin at the sound of Jessamine's voice. When I fully took in the scene, Jessamine was holding the chickens', ducks', and geese's feeding bag. It seemed like every day she was starting to glow and become more beautiful. If that was natural, it was one hell of a talent. "Talon... did you hear me?" her sweet voice nearly made me shudder. *She's already getting tired of you so keep it short and simple.*

"I'm fine..." I started to walk out of the barn.

"Talon, talk to me..." Jessamine pleaded; her voice filled with worry. I fought to build my willpower; Jessamine had a way to beat it into submission, but I needed the will to walk away if ever the day came, I truly had to. My shoulders were tense, and I kept my back toward Jessamine because if I looked her in the eye, I knew I would lose.

"Is it something I did?" Jessamine asked.

I finally turned around brandishing a smile. "Nothing out of the ordinary, just looking for my axe." She gave me a skeptical look as if she didn't believe me.

"Are you sure?" Jessamine squinted at me.

"Jessamine I'm fine!" I covered my mouth with my hand surprised at my own stern response. I turned and walked away, I took long strides hoping it would put enough distance between us and the painful memories that were trying to play in my head. I went into the garden that was at the side of the house. I looked all around the garden for my axe, trying to make my excuse plausible. "Where's my damn axe?!" I asked myself as if I yelled loud enough, I'd have the answer.

"Looking for this?" Once again Jessamine startled me, making me spin my whole body around. Jessamine was holding my axe. I calmed my face trying to hide all my emotions.

"Thank you..." I mumbled. When I reached to take the axe, Jessamine moved it away from my reach. My brows furrowed in puzzlement. "Give it to me please." I kept a growl at bay, but it took a lot of effort.

"Not until you tell me what's wrong!" Jessamine moved the axe behind her, her accent becoming presently thicker and stronger.

"There's nothing wrong! Jessamine I'm-."

"After all this time, now you want to be dishonest. I can take you hiding things, eventually, you'll tell me. I could accept if you said, 'I don't want to talk about it right now.' But lying?" Jessamine's voice was cracking under unshed tears. I was feeling quite perplexed. Anger, sadness, the painful memories all flooded my mind all at once.

"It seems y'all are having a little issue." I thrust Jessamine behind me at the sound of Daniel Senior's voice.

"Daniel, what are you doing on my farm?" I pulled myself into my full height arching a skeptical brow. Dan Jr. came from around the house and stopped next to his father, with a cheeky smile. My blood started to boil.

"I believe not too long ago I extended an invitation to the young lady over here." Daniel pulled his pipe out of his pocket and lit it. "That day of that awful misunderstanding." He blew out some smoke. I looked from Daniel to Dan Jr. suspiciously.

"I don't remember the lady saying yes..." I retorted.

"Ah-ha, let us try again, shall we?" Daniel tried to step around me, but I stepped with him. Blocking his approach.

"You are on my land..." I said in a low growled voice.

"Ah yes, of course." Daniel took a long inhale of his pipe and blew the smoke in my face. I stood unfazed at his gesture.

"I gave you my answer. But if you'd like a proper response, ask, so you can leave." Jessamine remarked stepping in sight but not close enough that Daniel could reach her.

"So much for trying to be pleasant," Daniel said in an audible mumble. He took off his hat with his free hand and placed it on his chest. "Me and my son here would like to invite you over to our ranch to stay. It seems you're the first woman to ever catch my son's eye for the long term and he wants to wed." He took another puff of his pipe. "I know he's quick-tempered. But he is the best you can do around these here parts. You don't want to be seen around with a savage; people will start to talk." Daniel criticized in a provoking tone.

"They already are." Dan Jr. pitched in to help his father's case. I knew what they were trying to do, they wanted to get a rise out of me so if I'd make the first move, he will have the right to defend himself, even on my land.

"You need to leave, now..." Every second was becoming harder to contain my anger.

"I'm still waiting on the lady's response." Daniel countered.

"You don't need one, because she is engaged. To me." I declared with all the confidence I could muster. Daniel's brows furrowed; I could tell he was surprised but kept it hidden.

"Is this true?" Daniel tried to look past me.

"You don't need to ask; you need to leave!" My composure was gone. Daniel straightened up and placed his hat back on his head.

"Well, if that's the case Talon we're sorry to disturb you and your family," Daniel said emptying the burnt tobacco on one of the growing cabbages. He turned around and walked away and Dan Jr. followed.

"By the way, please do send us an invitation, will you?" Daniel said waving a backward hand and laughing a cynical chuckle. I didn't allow myself to loosen up until I was sure Daniel and Dan Jr. were long gone. I heard a thud on the ground and Jessamine pushed past me, she had thrown my axe to the floor and was stomping away.

"Hey, what's wrong?" I asked, but no answer followed. I chased after her but not fast enough as she stomped up the porch stairs and into the house slamming the screen door behind her. I entered soon after, trying to stop her while she was close enough, I grabbed her by her upper arm. Then a sudden sharp sting on my cheek made me let go to hold my face. "Did you just slap me?" I rubbed my cheek in disbelief.

"How could you do that to me? Say those things?!" Jessamine snapped, rubbing her right hand.

"What did I do?" I asked holding on to my cheek still.

"How dare you just claim me, as if I'm some bloody property?!" Jessamine yelled. I went from perplexed to full of anger.

"I did it to protect you! Unless you want to go make more Dan juniors in the world! Two is enough!" I defended. but another sting to my other cheek caught me off guard. "Stop doing that!" rubbing both my cheeks at the same time.

"You can't make decisions for me Talon! I am a woman with her own voice!" Jessamine pointed hard at her chest. I scoffed.

"So, you were going to go be his wife? Fine, go to him then." The moment those words left my mouth I wish I could have taken them back. In a fight between two people, I was taught you must play fair. Well, I didn't at this moment. Tears started to gather in Jessamine's gray eyes. I opened my mouth to take it all back.

"Talon, I may be your guest, but you do not control me..." She spoke before me in a trembling voice.

"You're more than just my guest Jessamine!" I countered, my frustration showing.

"Yes! I am more, I'm now your wife-to-be!" Jessamine snapped back.

"I said what I said to protect you from them we're not-."

"We must get married now you fool; they want an invitation as proof of our union! I had no say at any point in that conversation to help!" Jessamine exclaimed, cutting me off.

"You think they would have declined? That they would stop? They'll keep trying, maybe even kidnap you. So, I'm sorry if I took the initiative to protect you! Why can't I do that for you?!" I questioned; I was having a hard time understanding.

"Because I have to learn to do it on my own, that's why." Jessamine's voice was starting to crack again.

"I'm sorry Jessamine I truly am, but that's not the world we live in. I understand you more than you know, these days women are at the bottom of the barrel. Hell! Horses get treated better than some women. I'm standing beside you, you're not alone." I was trying to sound convincing hoping it would reach through her.

"I still have to try Talon!"

"Why?! Why must you do it alone?" I needed to know.

"Because I'm pregnant and it's my responsibility, not yours!"

JESSAMINE

Chapter 21

It was my turn to cover my mouth the moment the words left it. We both stared at one another for what seemed like a stolen moment in time. I slowly removed my hands. "Talon my point is Rachael and this baby are my responsibility. If I can't protect myself then I can't protect them." My tears finally broke through and down my cheeks, the clog in my throat made itself more prominent as the anxiousness of waiting for Talon's response made me impatient. "Say something…" I pleaded. I had never seen Talon like this. His sun-bright eyes were piercing through me as he stared in silence. "Say something!" But Talon did not flinch at my sudden exasperation. I wanted to shake him, but with his size and strength, it would be impossible. Talon suddenly turned his back on me and proceeded to walk down the hall toward the weapons room. "Talon what are you doing?" I asked franticly trying to keep up with Talon's large strides. "Talon, talk to me please?!" I was beginning to beg. Talon threw the door open slamming it against the wall, I heard clanks of metal drop to the floor after. He grabbed a side bag, stuffing small jars of creams, bandages, and salves. "Talon what are you doing in here?" I whined; his silence was only breaking my heart.

Talon then strapped a leather holster around his upper body, attaching a hatchet and two large knives to it. Talon then walked behind the small desk and grabbed a quiver full of arrows wrapping it around his torso. Talon let his hair loose out of the braid it was in, he then grabbed a bow off the wall so forcefully that other weapons fell. Before I knew it, Talon was facing me and visibly angry.

"Excuse me." The tone sounded more of a demand than politeness. I was becoming more upset with Talon; I couldn't put my finger on why. A part of me felt quite foolish being angry at a man that only wanted to help me, while another part felt disrespected.

"Talon, I asked you a question that you haven't answered." My ire becoming impossible to contain.

"I'm sorry Jessamine but there is nothing more I can say. Other than I need to be alone." He spoke calmly. I placed my hands on my hips still standing in his way. An uncomfortable silence fell between us, neither of us backing down. Someone gracefully clasped my shoulder, when I looked beside me, John was there. John let out an audible exhale looking back and forth between myself and Talon.

"Let Talon go child. He'll be back." John finally broke the silence. I was reluctant, I didn't want to end Talon and I's disagreement with him leaving, it just didn't feel right. John smiled at me deeply. *If he thinks his smile will reassure me then he was the daftest man today.* But I was able to see that holding Talon against his will in his own house was not ladylike. As much as I didn't want to, I moved out of the way of the door, and much to my dismay Talon briskly walked past us leaving a mint lemon smell behind. I jumped, startled, as I heard the screen door slam. I rushed to the window in the kitchen, Talon was walking into the forest with his long hair caressing his bottom.

"I can't believe I bloody let you talk me into letting him go like this!" I screeched, turning to John. Right now, I was fully aware of how insane I sounded. My emotions were all over the place and I had to wonder if it was me or the baby that was the cause. When I turned back to look out the window Talon was gone, and my heart broke.

"Talon is the sort of person that needs their own space for deeper enlightenment," John responded nonchalantly. I rushed toward the door needing to get to Talon but before I could open it fully John slammed it shut holding the door in place. "Allow Talon to release some stress and you should do the same. Not only for yourself but for the baby you carry as well." John pleaded with his eyes, though his face stood stern. A defeated sigh escaped me, I had to admit to myself that my lackluster approach to our situation had caused Talon to leave. The fight between my past, present, and future was becoming more out of control each day.

"I'm going to take a nap..." I said quietly. "If you don't mind, look after Rachael for a few hours please?" John gave me a nod and with that, I ascended the stairs.

"I hope you don't regret the words said today." he said. I scoffed at John's sarcasm. *I already do.*

✻ ✻ ✻

Ten bloody days had gone by, and Talon was not home yet. *How long does he need to de-stress?* Every morning since his departure I tended to Rachael getting her dressed and ready for the day, a task that I had grown lenient toward since Talon was always up before me.

"Where's Talon?" Rachael would ask me every morning and every time she asked, I would sigh and reply, 'He'll be back soon darling.' And nothing more. I started to hate myself for lying to Rachael, her growing sadness had not gone unnoticed by John and myself. John tried hard to distract and entertain Rachael, but nothing was comparable to Talon. She always tried to emulate him and without him, she was disinterested in everything. Sometimes at night I stared above the tree line toward the stars begging for him to come back. I was sorry, and I just wanted things to go back to the way they were before I opened my big trap. I had taken advantage of Talon's kindness in allowing me to speak freely. I wasn't used to that kind of freedom and in the end, it hurt one of the few people that cared for me unconditionally. With that realization, tears rolled down my face every time.

I did all the chores meant for me like feeding the animals, cleaning up the house, tending to Rachael, and other small tasks. I wanted to do as much as I could before the inevitable was to occur, for once I felt like I was really contributing to a home instead of just being there and being seen. In a few months, I will feel like nothing but a vessel for another life to come into this world. Another realization of Talon's absence was that my bath time was met with lukewarm water, I was informed that Talon and John had made some sort of boiler that is attached to the pump upstairs. Though very impressive the boiler needed to be manned by someone and lately John seemed a bit less productive than usual. When I see him, it is only because he made his presence known. Leaving meals for Rachael and me but none for himself. Feeling so depressed in my own right, I haven't even gathered the courage to ask John what ails him. Even KoKo shared his disappointment with me. One day while brushing him I tried to hug his snout, but he turned away from me with a huff. "Oh, not you too "KoKo!" I whined while trying to get KoKo to look at me but to no avail. I huffed and stomped my foot out of frustration, "Fine you beast, have it your way!" I threw the brush across the barn frightening some of the geese and headed for the exit. KoKo let out a laugh like neigh, "Oh shut up you twat!" I yelled clearly angry with myself for arguing with a horse.

I'm going mad.

* * *

I sat at the table early in the morning thinking how the twenty horrid days without Talon were becoming unbearable, it was almost pure torture. Some of the housework that Talon usually did was left undone, no laughter filled the house, and my comfort and safety were nonexistent. I finally had to admit to myself that I missed him, and it seemed as if Rachael was near bloody suffering. Of course, John was unbothered by Talon's absence, I suppose he was used to Talon just wandering with no food or water or a warm place to sleep. True enough I didn't understand why Talon was so angry. Yes, we argued and yes things were said, but it was not worth leaving for days without a word. I nursed my green tea pondering these things when a knock sounded at the door. I looked at my pocket watch, it was fifteen before ten. My brows furrowed in disbelief that I had been sitting in my thoughts for nearly two hours. The knock came once more, forcing me to get up from my seat. "I wonder who that could be so early in the morning?" I whispered to myself as I walked to the door. I hesitantly opened it and tried to identify the being on the other side of the screen.

"May I help you?" I asked the slender-bodied woman with auburn hair draped around her shoulders, her bright green eyes contrasted with her blue full-length dress and white blouse. Looking at her, I felt a little self-conscious. I only now noticed that in the days before I wasn't really caring about my looks, but of course, I didn't think I was much to look at.

"Hello! I'm terribly sorry for comin' by unannounced, I had to gather quite the amount of courage to walk up to this very door." the woman said with an accent very familiar to me. I blinked in confusion for a moment before opening the screen door.

"And you are...?" I perked a brow.

"Oh, I apologize, my name is Lisa." I stepped fully outside. We gave each other a short and timid handshake with even more timid smiles.

"Is Ta...Talon home?" Lisa stuttered; her eyes drawn to the floor. I was put off balance by her question.

"What do you want with him?" I said with a nip. (Talon is gone for 20 bloody days and he has some daft girl looking for him?)

"Nothing in particular honestly, Talon and I used to be close friends at one point... Rumor is Talon was getting married..." I couldn't help but notice Lisa was choosing her words carefully. I crossed my arms over my chest.

"Whom may I ask is spreading gossip about Talon's private life?"

The only people who know are...

"Daniel Jr. has been talking about it all around town. Saying not-so-nice things about Talon, that he is domesticating like a savage shouldn't was one of them." I narrowed my eyes at her. Silence hung between us.

"Well, I'm quite parched from the long ride over here, can you spare some time to allow me a drink?" Lisa smiled a bright smile, putting an effort to end the silence between us. I smiled in return trying to shake the bad feeling she emitted.

"Sure, I just made some tea," I said leading the way into the house and Lisa followed. When I arrived at the table, I pulled out the seat and offered it to Lisa. I grabbed my already cold tea and brought it with me to pour a fresh cup. I poured tea for Lisa, then took our cups back to the table and sat at the opposite end from her. Another uncomfortable silence ensued as we sipped our tea.

"This tea tastes different... in a good way that is, never seen it this color before." Lisa spoke again, ending the silence between us.

"Yes, it is indeed different, when I first arrived here, I wasn't used to its light taste after drinking many teas that were darker in color. John Tao... You know who Tao is right? Since you and Talon were friends?" Lisa's face turned disturbed for a second before fixing itself back to its façade. I noted it.

"Well, of course, I'm quite familiar with John..." Lisa played with her fingers. "Speaking of the old man, is he here?"

"Yes, he may be tending to my daughter at the moment," I responded still sipping on my tea.

"Daughter? Yours and Talon's daughter?" Lisa's eyes furrowed.

"Unfortunately, no, but I count myself a lucky woman. I'm twenty of age, a woman with a three of age daughter, yet Talon was still willing to make an honest woman out of me. I count my blessings in that, being with his child now..." Inside I grimaced at how easily that lie came out of my mouth.

"You're with child?" Lisa nearly shouted in shock. I unconsciously placed my hand over my stomach, for the first time I was a little protective of the child.

"Yes, I am. Is there a problem?" (There could be many things she could have asked me. Where did I come from? How did I end up here? Clearly, I have an English accent. She used to be friends with Talon, is she upset she missed out? Who is she to Talon?)

"That could not be Talon's child," Lisa said with Infallibility. "It is simply impossible!"

"I don't have the slightest idea of what you are talking about, but I don't like it. The child I carry is Talon's, I have no doubt about it." I said confidently.

"You're lying," Lisa said in a small snarl. I could tell she was getting irritated. She sat more upright in her chair with tense shoulders.

"For someone who doesn't even know my name, you are bold enough to call me a bloody liar and think to get away with it?" I asked sternly and warningly.

"Then you must know." Lisa rose from her seat planting her hands stiffly on the table. I looked at her hands and then at her face, I was visibly getting angry.

"I think it is time for you to leave Miss Lisa, I'm sure your thirst is quenched is it not?" I said more suggestively, trying to keep from being rude. *Always be a lady, Jessamine.*

"I don't think you understand, Talon is a freak. I've kept this secret from everyone in town, but not from you. The truth is...."

"Whatever the truth may be, that is for my future husband to tell. Not you" I cut off her rant before she could get ahead of herself. I was already out of my chair and the suddenness made me a little dizzy, I was starting to physically feel the stress.

"Look, all I want to say is that you shouldn't be in the dark as I was. I prayed for many days after finding out the truth, no woman should ever be forced to live that kind of lifestyle. Holding this secret in so long has shattered parts of my soul." Lisa finished her dramatic speech placing her hand over her heart. I rolled my eyes.

"Darling, if your soul is shattered by a meager secret then you're not ready for this horrid world we live in. At only twenty I've been hunted, raped, and tortured all while raising a daughter. My deepest apologies if I don't share your sentiment, but if Talon's secret is all I must deal with then I think that'll do." I said with finality. Lisa looked appalled for a moment before turning to a face of contemplation. Pattering feet caught my attention as Rachael ran into the kitchen. "Good morning!" Rachael shouted, colliding herself into my leg giving me a tight hug.

"Lisa, it has been a long time," John said smoothly as he sauntered into the kitchen behind Rachael with his hands behind his back. He placed himself firmly next to me, and though he did not show it I could feel he was not happy to see Lisa. "Are you here to see the future Mrs. Thomas or Mr. Thomas?" He said as if he had the upper hand in the situation.

"Well hello John, it has been a while, hasn't it? I was just here to see Mrs. Thomas and-..."

"That is funny. When you announced yourself, you asked for Talon." I cut in crossing my arms over my chest.

"Rachael why don't you play in the barn with KoKo, I'll be out there in a few," John said lightly leading her to the door. As soon as he was sure she would make it to the barn he turned his gaze to Lisa. The look he gave her even sent chills down my spine; I have never seen Tao so serious. He walked back to my side where he stood before. "Lisa, I told you never show your face on this farm again. So, why am I looking at you?" I could see Tao's fist tighten behind his back. "Haven't you done enough damage to Talon's mind? Here to cause more?"

"I'm just here to make sure the future Mrs. Thomas knows what she is getting herself into, nothing more," Lisa said playing with her fingers.

"I have a name you know! It's Jessamine! Being Talon's bloody bride doesn't take that away!" I looked at both John and Lisa, clearly frustrated. "I'm a damn person you know." I pointed toward my chest.

"Mrs. Thomas is your badge now, not what defines you. Understand child, that badge will protect you." John said, still staring at Lisa. John took a deep breath from his nose. "It's time for you to go. We have things to do here and I'm sure your father is worried." I looked in puzzlement at Lisa and then toward John.

"Who is her father?" I asked. Lisa stayed silent as her knuckles were turning white from how tightly she gripped her hands together. John placed a coy smile on his face.

"Ahh, I see, so you want to reveal other's secrets but keep your own. Jessamine, meet Lisa Henry, Daniel Senior's youngest daughter." My eyes were wide for a moment before my shock subsided. I lunged at Lisa, but John restrained me, without hurting me or the baby.

"Calm yourself Jessamine she isn't worth it. Think of the baby." Slowly my body relaxed and John's grip on me loosened.

"You have luck unforetold. If I were not pregnant, I would be burying you. Your brother acts a complete arse and your father supports him. Yet you walk into this house and call my husband a bloody freak!" *So much for being a lady.* "Whatever secrets you have kept, I implore you to keep silent still. If anything slips, I will start and finish what I wanted to do to you. Now leave my home!" I pointed toward the door that was still left open by John earlier. Lisa left in a hurry, leaving me and John standing at the table. "I overdid it this time," I said taking a seat in the chair, breathing steadily to get air flowing into my body.

"A life depends on you my child, show some restraint next time," John said filling up a glass of water and handing it to me. I felt a kiss on my forehead, causing me to look at its source in utter amazement. "You did well." John complimented, rubbing my back to soothe me. I relished the comfort for a long moment taking gulps of the water. A sudden scream made me choke on the water in my mouth, fear set in, and I raced to the door.

"Rachael!"

TALON

Chapter 22

Seeing Rachael through the tree line was a sight to behold, she was walking out of the house and heading toward the barn with John keeping an eye on her till she was safe at her destination. I had lost track of how many days had gone by. Being away I was able to work out my frustrations, live off the land, and sharpen my skills that have gone a bit weak due to becoming a caretaker. (And soon a husband and father.) I had felt bad about how things ended between Jessamine and me, we should have acted better about the situation. I let the morning breeze fill my lungs as I waited for John to go back inside the house before heading straight to the barn. A carriage with a driver was parked outside the house, it looked familiar, but I couldn't really place where I had seen it before. I would have gone into the house to see who had graced us by coming by, but I thought better of it and continued to the barn. Rustling leaves and the sound of grass being crushed made me look out toward the tree line, "Talon!" The tiny voice seized my attention. Rachael was barreling toward me and when she was close enough, I collected her into a huge hug. Rachael's tiny arms squeezed tightly around my neck, but I didn't mind. I had missed her as much as she seemed to miss me.

Running steps off the porch caught my attention, I felt like my pulse had stopped and my spirit left me. I begin to breathe heavily, and my surroundings blurred. *What is Lisa doing here?* My legs were about to give way as I watched the carriage trot off down the road. Remembering I had Rachael in my arms had forced me to fight through my dizziness. My mind was miles away and I had not realized Rachael was talking to me. Her scream and a roar penetrated my ears, a hard pressure occurred in the middle of my back. Before I can fall on top of Rachael, I place my right hand in front of me and roll out the way to get a good look at my assailant. A bear stood tall on its hind legs roaring at me.

How did I not know a bear was nearby? How could I allow myself to get so distracted?

"Rachael!" I heard Jessamine scream from the house. I held on to Rachael tightly with my left arm with only my right to defend myself, the bear roar swinging its arms wildly. Rachael cried in my arms, refusing to look at the animal that had attacked us. The bear lunged and in reaction, I kicked straight up in the air right in the bear's jaw. With the opening I created, I dashed toward the house. The bear recovered much faster than I expected. Not wanting to lead the bear right up to the house I tried to run in as fast as I could around trees. "Rachael!" Jessamine was screaming hysterically.

"Stop screaming woman!" I yelled out trying to concentrate on not tripping. I still had loads of stuff I was carrying, and it was weighing on me, along with carrying Rachael.

I was running toward the porch; John must have known what I needed to do because he held his arms out at the bottom of the porch stairs. As I passed by, I tossed Rachael into his arms. I quickly stripped my side pack off, threw my bow and quiver to the side, and unsheathed my knives. When I thought I was at a safe distance I turned around to face my opponent. I was against killing animals without purpose, I tried to think of a way to get rid of the bear away from the house to a safe distance. The bear was panting from chasing me around. "Please go!" I shouted; the bear roared again rising on his hind legs once more to swing his claws at me. He stepped too close, and I punched him in the side of his nostrils. My shoulder collided with the bear trying to wrestle it to the ground. I almost had it down before a pain ignited across my back and before I knew it, I was laying on my back, knives knocked away from me. I was keeping the bear's mouth away by having one of my hands on the top of its mouth and the other on the bottom trying to shut it. I avoided the bear's claws reaching for my face, I punched it over and over to get it to give up. The bear lunged its head with his mouth wide open. In the last attempt to protect my face, I thrust my forearm into its mouth. Painful pressure was building on my right forearm, I closed my eyes trying to mentally numb the pain.

The bear let out a blood-curdling roar, its grip on my forearm loosened, and blood trickled from behind its head dripping onto me. The bear collapsed on top of me, I looked up to find Jessamine shaking and panting. I looked for the cause of the bear's death, to find my axe buried deep into the back of its neck. I grunted, lifting the bear off me and it fell on its back, I pulled myself into a sitting position. Placing my hands behind me to keep me up, even though my right forearm burned in pain. Jessamine kneeled next to me with tears in her eyes. We looked at each other eye to eye for what seemed like forever until Jessamine threw herself onto me in a hug. I was shocked and felt a little unsure of the embrace, I timidly wrapped my right arm around Jessamine's upper torso while my left held both of our weights.

"Don't you ever leave me like that again Talon! I was so worried." Jessamine sobbed on my shoulders, her small breaths tickling my neck.

"I didn't go too far." I tried to be reassuring.

"I don't care! I couldn't see you; I was clueless about your survival! You just left for twenty days without a care!" Jessamine yelled, starting to pound my chest.

"Hey! I do care!" I yelled back trying to gather what I really wanted to say. "What you said that day hurt, all I want to do is be there for you, Rachael, and now even the baby. That's all! Is that so wrong?" Jessamine pulled arm's length from me, staring at me intensely as more tears flowed. I used the cleanest part of my hand to wipe some of her tears away.

"Why?" Jessamine asked, her grip tightening on my shoulder. "Why would you want to do that for me?" Jessamine tried to shake me. "I have done nothing for you, you could be in danger because of me. all I have given you is grief. So, why would you want to be so committed to our lives? For a child not of your own blood, for a baby whose breath has not yet been taken." I sighed at Jessamine; I knew she wanted answers. Answers I couldn't give her, not yet. I can't ruin things, not now. My heart sank.

"I wish I could tell you, but I fear I can't." I breathed out audibly, Jessamine raised my head up to meet her grey moon eyes.

"Tell me Talon..." Jessamine said almost pleadingly but demanding.

"Let's worry about Talon's wounds first Jessamine, we all have lots to talk about. Some tea and a clear mind will help." John interrupted, approaching with Rachael in his arms.

"Wounds? What other wounds other than this." I raised my right forearm for everyone to see. Rachael's worried gasp made me hide it from her view, to ensure her I was ok I smiled. It seemed to ease her a bit.

"This one," Jessamine said casually, and a searing pain shot through my entire left shoulder.

"Ow! Geez!" When I looked where the pain was coming from, a third of Jessamine's pointer finger was sticking into a puncture wound.

"That's for leaving without a word for nearly a month." Jessamine extracted her finger, wiped the blood off on her dress, grabbed Rachael from John, and stormed off toward the house.

"All you had to do was tell me where it was!" I yelled so she could hear me. I was speechless, I looked at John with a flustered and confused face.

"I quite agree with what she did, you deserve it greatly." My whole face scrunched up; I made a questioning gesture with my arms, but it was ignored. John was already walking back to the house. "Hurry I need to stitch you up, get you ready for the work you so kindly skipped out on." I clicked my tongue and pinched the bridge of my nose; the move caused another sting in my shoulder, and I hissed. I got up carefully off the ground and dusted off my hind side with as little movement as possible. I turned my attention toward the lifeless bear, I put my hands together in prayer.

"Shash, your death will not be in vain. I will use your body for a good purpose, then give you back to the earth. I forgive you." With that I turned toward the house, walking to the inevitable awkward conversation that was going to take place.

When I entered the house, a pressure gripped my knees and when I looked down Rachael had gathered both of my legs into a hug. "Are you ok Talon?" She asked with a worried look. I smiled at her ignoring the throbbing happening all over my body.

"I'm fine princess, don't worry," I hoped by stroking her head I could put her at ease. My heart sank when I saw tears rolling down her face, I kneeled and engulfed Rachael in another huge hug. "It's all right, it's all right."

"Why you go somewhere?" Rachael asked through her tears. I felt my heart sink; I felt guilty. I didn't have enough experience to know that Rachael would miss me so much, married or not I had somehow affected this child. I meant something to Rachael. I hugged her tighter.

"I'm sorry..." Was all was able to choke out as my throat formed a lump trying not to cry. I managed to calm the crying child into a smile. I promised to teach her the bow so that she can come with me the next time I go, much to Jessamine's dismay when I looked at her over Rachael's head. I let Rachael go and she ran upstairs.

The wounds on my back were starting to feel like hot iron, I winced at my pain as I walked into the kitchen. To my surprise, Jessamine was in the kitchen with the creams, clean wraps, a sterile needle, thread, and mashed snowberries with herbs.

"You got everything ready for John I see, you've learned a lot." Jessamine smiled at my statement.

"I have learned a lot and I'll be tending to you. I'm going to need you to take off your shirt and... Hey where are you going." Jessamine yelled after me, chasing me as I stomped away going toward the stair. Jessamine grabbed my left forearm to stop me or at least slow me down. Knowing her condition, I stopped and turned to her.

"I'm not taking off my shirt," I growled with clutched teeth. Jessamine gave me a confused look.

"Talon, you need to get stitched. Your wounds will fester if I don't clean and treat them." Jessamine tried to pull me back in the direction of the kitchen, but I didn't budge. "Talon let me..."

"I said no..." I interrupted her.

"No? That's all you have to say? How about explaining to me why you won't let me take care of you." Jessamine demanded, "I don't care about your damn secrets, I just want to help you!"

"Listen, there are things I just can't say and do! I wish I could Jessamine, but I can't..." I stared intensely, hoping I could conjure her understanding. Jessamine looked at me with the same intensity.

"My apologies Talon, but that excuse is not valid anymore. Especially when some twat walks in this house and claims she knows something about you that I don't!" Jessamine's voice was filled with aggravation. The weight of her words caused me to get dizzy again, my breathing became rapid. I placed my hands on Jessamine's shoulders.

"What did Lisa say to you...?" I said in a near whisper. I was seeing multiples of Jessamine and was trying to keep my balance as my legs felt like noodles. Shivers started to tremble throughout my body, it was taking all the strength I had left to keep my body upward.

"I didn't allow her to tell me anything." Jessamine professed. She looked toward the floor before looking back at me. "Talon, I'm going to be your wife soon. We both need to start to be more open and honest with each other."

"So, she didn't tell you anything?" I confirmed ignoring her words. My muscles were visibly getting tense.

"I told her I'm waiting for you to tell me, about everything. Even about her." Jessamine squinted at me. The air suddenly started to fill me, and I sighed in relief. I released Jessamin's shoulders and stood up straighter. When I got a perfect visual of Jessamine, I saw she was scowling at me.

"We are getting married due to convenience, to keep you and Rachael safe," I said sternly crossing my arms at my chest.

"Oui! Is that all this is Talon? Just a convenience? You go above and beyond for us and that's all this is?" *No.*

"That's not what I'm trying to say." I tried to explain.

"So, what are you trying to say?" *You and Rachael are the best thing to happen to me.*

"That I'm here to help you, Jessamine, you and Rachael have my protection." *You put your foot in your mouth.*

"I trust you with my whole being, even after your affirmation of our attachment. Why can't you trust me...?" Jessamine sounded hurt. Jessamine's eyes then fluttered closed, and her body headed to the floor. In fast reaction even with my wounds, I caught her, lifting her in my arms before she hit the floor. Jessamine lay limp in my arms, her head leaning against my chest. My wounds were hurting, including my right arm which was holding her upper body.

"Hey..." I whispered close to Jessamine's ear. "Jessamine hey...

I'm sorry, okay? You are right I must trust you, just give me time." I tried nudging her head with my nose but nothing. "John!!! I called out in a panic. I ran two by two up the stairs. "Jessamine please..." I whispered some more to her. I reached the top of the stairs, then turned to my right toward Jessamine's room. I made it to her room and placed Jessamine in her bed softly and carefully. "This is all my fault..." I said to myself, "you're pregnant, you must be tired, and I should be doing better for you." I grabbed her hand into mine. "I never had to take care of more than one person... just give me some time." Satisfied at my words, even though she couldn't hear me I got up to leave.

"I'll give you as much time as you need." Jessamine's groggy voice made me turn slowly in shock. Looking at Jessamine, she had a smile on her face before her eyes fluttered shut again. I slapped my hands against my face trying to cover my embarrassment and quickly exited the room.

She just had her way with me.

JESSAMINE

Chapter 23

I woke up to the sun leaving the sky, its orange and red glow being the only source of light in the room. I stretched my body, loosening my stiff muscles. I couldn't remember how I ended up in my own bed. I thought hard only remembering Talon and myself having a profound discussion before I was pulled into darkness. I slowly got out of bed. I looked at myself in the mirror that leaned against the wall. I noticed a couple of blood stains and speckles on my skin and dress, I thought it better to bathe myself and change clothes. I chose a new dress that was given to me when I first arrived on the farm, grabbed my undergarments, and headed for the bathing room. I closed the door and placed my clothes on the bench. I started to pump water into the tub and placed my hand under the falling water to check if it was hot, to my surprise it was. The hot water reminded me that Talon was home. Weeks of lukewarm water to bathe in had made me edgy because I couldn't relax and let the water wash over me. I pumped the water till the tub was almost full, I placed lavender, mint, and some of the soothing cream into the water. I undressed and went in. I mulled over the events of the day. (Lisa, Talon coming home, Talon almost getting killed, killing a bear, arguing with Talon, and blackness.) "Wait... I killed a bear?" I said to myself in confusion and wonderment. I played everything again in my head, at the time I wasn't thinking that I was attacking a bear, I was thinking Talon was going to die and I had to do something about it.

When did I gain such courage?

I pondered this. I've never been a brave woman. As a child everything scared me; the dark, any rattling even in broad daylight, I was a mess. I thanked the heavens Rachael was born much braver than me, but today I had faced danger unflinchingly and came out on top. Why?

"What is happening to me?" I asked myself another question I had no answer to. I loosened my wet hair from the braid it was in and went under the surface. The water surrounded me, filling me with calm. When I needed another breath, I only put my nose and mouth above the surface. When I collected enough air, I submerged myself again letting another wave of calmness consume me. I opened my eyes to clear blue surroundings, my mind felt open, and I was looking at the events with much clarity. 'Learn to love and trust again...' A disembodied voice flooded my mind. I flung my upper body out of the water. *What the bloody hell was that?!* A yelp caught my attention and when my gaze met Rachael on the floor I sighed in relief.

"Sorry mommy..." Rachael squeaked. I wiped my eyes and composed myself.

"It's quite all right darling, I'm the one at fault, I apologize. I didn't mean to startle you." I tried to piece together what had just occurred, it was like I was really in the ocean, just floating without a purpose. It felt so real.

What was that voice?

"Dinner is ready Mommy," Rachael informed me.

"Thank you darling, I'll be out in a hurry." I assured her and she ran off. "Honey, wait!" Rachael turned around, "Did you... say anything earlier?" I asked sheepishly.

"No Mommy." Rachael answered, then she skipped out of the room, closing the door behind her.

Walking down the stairs, I tried to dry my hair as much

as possible with a towel. When I reached the kitchen, it seemed everyone was waiting for me to arrive. No one had touched their plates yet. My gaze fell upon Talon who was smelling like variations of herbs instead of his mint and pine, his right forearm was bandaged, and I could tell through the lumps of his shirt he was quite bandaged up. "My apologies for keeping you all waiting." I took my seat across from Talon. John patted my hand with a smile, I gave a smile back even though the things running through my mind were nothing to smile about. Everyone started to eat, including myself, silence ruled all of us as the sound of chopsticks and silverware hitting plates filled the air. *Am I going mad?* I kept pondering that thought as I tried to replay what happened to me in the bathing room. I looked up to see sunlit orbs staring at me. Talon's stare was so intense, but it showed good intention, almost loving. I didn't want to get such childish dreams muddling my head. Talon already does enough, including marrying me and becoming a father. *Learn to love and trust again?* I scoffed out loud and everyone looked at me with puzzled looks.

"Is something wrong child?" John asked, concern masking his face.

"I'm all right, just tired." John gave me a skeptical look. I got up from the table wanting to avoid explaining myself. "Will you excuse me?" I declared without waiting for an answer.

I'm hearing voices and talking to myself out loud. I'm going mad.

I shook my head at myself heading to my room.

❋ ❋ ❋

It didn't take long for things to feel normal, at least for me. Talon was back and Rachael couldn't have been happier.

Our days went on as if Talon never left, we all did our work for the farm, and it went a lot faster now than when it was only me and John. Everything was the same except for one thing. I found myself staring in Talon's direction, a lot. When I was outside gathering the produce in the garden, my eyes would wander toward the hulking figure swinging an axe at a tree. I watched immersed at how Talon's muscles flexed every time he attempted to take a swing, how his body was able to take the impact of the tree, how his hair fell loosely around his shoulders wet from sweat and... I shook my head out of the trance.

Okay calm yourself girl, it's just muscles... placed on a perfect physique.

"Stop it, Jessamine!" I scolded myself, somebody had too. Talon was a very attractive man not in just looks, but everything about him seemed as if he was born from good intentions. He was kind, wise, helpful, and a great defender. I saw his respect and compassion toward nature. The night of the bear incident, I watched from the window as Talon had bowed all the way to the ground in front of the bear before he skinned in. I turned away since I couldn't watch the gruesome act. But those yellow sun eyes are what start the many cases of fluttering in my stomach, which in denial I blamed on the life growing inside of me. Then something unsettled me terribly, I've never been really attracted to any man in my life. I liked my ex-husband hoping it would grow into love but was never attracted to him. I tried to think back before the time when Elias revealed his monstrous ways. I tried to think about how I looked at him, how I felt when he touched me. I shuddered violently as nothing but the horrid years I spent with him drowned any good that possibly happened. I closed my eyes and all that came were thoughts of Talon. "Oh no..."

I dismissed everything I was thinking and feeling, for the moment. We were in the summer months which made the weather a cool warm day. My body though, felt like a hot hell fire. I picked up the produce I harvested and took it inside the house.

I placed the basket on the table, and due to my distraction, I picked one cabbage. *Really Jessamine?* I let out a sigh, shaking my head at myself.

"Is something wrong?" I let out a startled gasp at the sudden voice.

"I'm quite alright you just startled me, that's..." I couldn't finish my sentence right away. When I turned around, I knew what to expect but was not quite ready to expect it. There Talon stood with his button-down shirt sleeve folded all the way up to his shoulder, sweat glistening down his collarbone, his perfectly shaped arms... "You just startled me that's all, can't be sneaking up on a pregnant woman like that."

"You're right I'm so sorry, I should have been more thoughtful. Still getting used to the idea of a baby." *Ouch that stung.* I must have made a face because Talon quickly grabbed my hand. "In a good way I mean! Even though a marriage after your ex-husband is the last thing you could possibly ever want, I'll try to be the best for you and the children." I didn't have the means to respond. Between Talons words and his touch, I was too incapacitated to speak. So, I didn't. I let myself just revel in the moment, my heart racing. My body heat went past hell and into a bloody inferno. "I actually came inside to ask your opinion." Talon interjected in the moment. I raised a brow.

"Opinions are like arses Talon."

"Everyone has one?" He finished flashing me a bright smile, and I chuckled. *Why am I'm so awkward.* "I wanted to ask; well, I was thinking maybe if you think it would be a good idea... if umm... well, we should set a date for... you know for us to be wed, before... you get bigger. Not to say you're not beautiful, just it might be... you know with your growing belly... easier." Talon gave a nervous but shy chuckle with a lopsided grin. I could not help but laugh loudly, Talon's shy and innocent nature always made him tiptoe around with his words when it came to me.

"I think you are absolutely right. I want to be pretty as possible when I become your wife. Unhindered."

My heart needs to stop talking.

"I have something else to share with you. I hope you forgive me for throwing all this on you." Talon gestured between us. "It was a brash thing to do, you were and are right. You should have had a say, a choice in the matter and…" I placed my finger lightly on his lips to shush him, a move that sent small shivers down my spine.

"It's all in the past now. What's done is done. Besides you are a worthy husband to have, any girl would be blessed to have you. I'm blessed to have you." I assured trying to convince him. Talon gently removed my finger from his mouth and collapsed his hand over my own.

"A good husband would hold no secrets and fully give himself to his wife. Those things I cannot do for you, and you deserve it the most." Talon lowered my hand back to my side before I could respond, he headed toward the door. Then he paused and turned around.

"When things clear up you might meet someone. If he protects you, Rachael, and that baby, you are free."

"Ha! We'll see Talon, but it's not bloody likely." I retorted rolling my eyes. Talon shrugged.

"If I were that man, I wouldn't pass up that opportunity. But I digress, men are stupid."

"Does that include you too?" I asked seriously, I was already playing a dangerous game with my heart, and I needed proof that I wasn't alone before I took the plunge. Even if it was as small as a dust particle.

"Yes, it does…" Talon replied softly. "I'll get back to work." Then he was gone, my jaw hung open.

He really likes me.

Late in the afternoon I decided that I wanted to do

something special. I wanted to cook dinner for us. Since I've been here, I have only cooked breakfast while John tended to lunch and dinner. We always had nearly the same dinner every night. Rice, sometimes fish, chicken, rice, pork, rice, beef, more rice, and vegetables. I was growing tired of rice. So, to have varieties I decided to make mashed potatoes with steak and carrots. I had to be honest I was quite nervous to make the attempt; my cooking skills weren't very utilized in my past marriage. I had learned to cook breakfast, lunch, and dinner recipes since I was fourteen. Had to learn how to sew and make clothes, and above all other things to be a lady due to my father-in-law's request. I realized I was very excited to be cooking for Talon, since the first time I cooked for him, he seemed he enjoyed my food. I found a big pot and filled it with water, I grabbed wood to heat up the stove and once lit I went to the pantry. I gathered potatoes, peeled them, then put them in the boiling water. I then went into the ice box located behind the house in the ground, there were stone steps that lead underneath to a door. I opened the sealed door and entered the iced lined cavern. "Great only venison." I huffed. I grabbed six loins of venison, three for John, Rachael, and myself. The other three for Talon, if he liked it, I'm sure he would want more than one. I grabbed a skillet and placed them on the stove as I seasoned the meat with salt and pepper and one by one cooked each piece. By the time I was done cooking carrots and mashing the potatoes I heard hard thuds and yelling. Curious, I walked out to see what was going on. I stepped out onto the porch to hear the sound from the direction of the barn, Talon and John were sparring with each other.

I stood transfixed at the skill the two were exhibiting. While Talon displayed a skillful yet aggressive attack, John, due to his age and experience posed a simple defense and offense, allowing him to time all his movements using his shorter size as a counterpart to Talons massive size. I happened to spot Rachael who was sitting on a tree stump, clapping her hands in joy for the show the men were giving her. I giggled to myself as I walked up to the men. "Isn't there work that needs to be tended to, gentlemen?" I perked an amused brow at the two. As soon as I stopped speaking, Talon turned to me. In that moment John put himself next to Talon and used his arm to push Talon backwards at the same time kicking Talon's leg out from under him. Talon's body slammed to the ground with a hard thump, I covered my mouth in both concern and trying to keep laughter at bay. Mostly laughter.

"What have I told you about being distracted by beautiful woman?" John giggled. Talon flipped upwards landing on his feet and dusted his clothes off including his hair that hung loose around his shoulders.

"You never taught me that, that's why I get distracted now!" Talon said with a small growl. "Shouldn't you be cooking John?" Talon asked as if trying to rid someone.

"No, he will not be cooking today, because I already have." I looked down shyly. When I looked back up Talon and John gave me amused looks.

"Really?" Talon and John echoed one another. My eyes squinted at them.

"Yes, I cooked something special! Which reminds me for the next meal I cook, I wanted to ask if we can plant parsley and cilantro?" I gave a pouted lip. Talon gave a puzzled look with his head tilted slightly to the side.

"Why are you doing that with your face?" Talon asked pointing toward his own lips.

"Isn't that what a wife does when they want something from their husband?" I answered pushing my bottom lip further out, making a bigger pout face.

"No, that's what children do." Talon retorted.

"Then shall I show you how a woman gets what they want?" I teased bringing our bodies very close. I could tell my teasing was getting to Talon, his cheeks went rose and he tried to lean back from me.

"Ahem." Talon and I both turned to the sound of John clearing his throat. "I'm going to take Rachael for a walk, we'll leave you to it." John gave his hand to Rachael and started to walk off.

"John! Please don't go!" Talon pleaded, but all he got out of John was a wave of the hand without a glance back.

"Talon I could use your help with something, only someone with immense strength can help me with it." I lower my voice seductively. Talon audibly gulped and I suppressed laughing out loud. A feeling was growing within me that made my heart swell, I never experienced being a woman, being flirtatious and free to mingle. Everything in my life was rushed and even though me and Talon were soon to be married, he did not push me into anything I didn't want to do or take advantage of me. It was refreshing. I was making my own rules and in control.

"Wh- what do you need me to do?" Talon stuttered and I gave a coy smile.

"I need you to set the table."

"That's it!? That was all you tortured me for?!" Talon shouted. I slapped my knee in laughter, Talon's face was beyond cute and very frustrated. We walked toward the house together with my arms wrapped around one of his.

While Talon was setting up the plates, I placed the food upon large platters to sit in the middle of the table. If Talon liked it, I knew he would want more, and I didn't feel like getting up every time he was done.

I already sound like his wife.

John and Rachael walked in a few minutes later. "Thank you, John, for taking Rachael. I hope she was not a bother." John shook his head.

"Not at all child. As usual, she is the best. Being with her reminds me of the younger version of Talon, a time when I was also young enough to keep up. With her fierce determination, she will grow up to be a strong woman, but her thoughtfulness is like you, she will also be a wise woman." I smiled at his words; my only hope would be that Rachael becomes everything he predicts.

"Umm, Rachael's great and all, but can we eat now? I'm hungry." Talon whined. I rolled my eyes at the grown man and John shook his head while letting out a sigh as we set ourselves at the table. John and Talon served themselves while I served Rachael and then myself. We all ate in silence; it made me smile to see Talon nearly suffocate eating my food plate after plate. I could tell John felt odd using a knife and fork but gave me a smile nonetheless to show me his approval. Rachael had food all over her face, and I also enjoyed my creation. My gaze lingered too long on Talon for a moment, my mind went back to our earlier discussion. Though Talon had made it clear that this marriage was an arrangement for my best interest, day after day our relationship was becoming more to me. Tapping on a teacup followed by John standing from the table grabbed my attention.

"I think you two should wed the Sunday coming," John announced. I spit the water I was drinking, Talon dropped his fork, and Rachael smiled as if she knew all along. Talon Looked at me, his face growing serious. Talon turned his attention back to John, his brows furrowed deeply. "This Sunday?" John placed his hands behind his back and very confidently replied.

"Yes."

TALON

Chapter 24

I was barely able to sleep for two nights after John's proclamation because it was more of a demand than a suggestion. I knew we were to wed soon; I knew after my so-called display of chivalry there was no way to back out of this, and as I drove the wagon to town to get Jessamine measured for a dress and to make deliveries at the general store I had to wonder. *What kind of idiot am I?* I wanted to pull my hair out, I wanted to scream, but instead I sat motionless next to Jessamine as KoKo pulled the wagon along the rocky dirt road. *I'm going to have a wife...* That's it, I finally let it settle in my brain what was happening. A growing fear started to emerge, but not fear of being wed. The fear that I might be compelled to do something irrational, like kiss her. *Yup! That's a great idea Talon after the boundaries you placed.* I grunted inwardly.

"Talon are you alright?" Jessamine's voice flowed through my ears like a sweet smell to the nose.

"Hmm, Yeah, I'm fine! Why?" I responded then placed an assuring smile.

"Because you grunted, are you in some sort of pain?" Jessamine asked her features becoming concerned.

Good job Talon, let her know how you really feel.

"Nothing at all just a hard bump from the wagon that's all." I tried to sound convincing. I knew she didn't believe what I said but I was glad she left it at that.

We entered the town without another word and stopped in front of the General Store, I leaped out of the wagon and stretched my arms, I walked to Jessamine's side of the wagon and held my hand out. Our palms touched sending shivers from my head to my toes, and hiding it took more effort than usual. I helped Jessamine off the wagon and then turned my attention to Rachael. I signaled Rachael to jump into my arms and I caught her in midair bringing her into a hug that made us burst into laughter. I turned to Jessamine as I held Rachael in my arms, her eyes sparkled in what seemed like admiration with a wide grin. I didn't know why Jessamine was looking at me that way, but what I did know was that she was more radiant than ever. I didn't know if it was Jessamine's natural beauty, the pregnancy, or my growing fondness for her that was making her glow in such a way, but it looked good. Jessamine's smile faded as she took in her surroundings, she looked up to me grabbing my collar to pull my head down. "Dear, I think we are being watched," she whispered in my ear; another shiver traveled throughout my body. I fought through the shiver and looked around us. Men and women whispering to one another, pointing, and staring at us. A hairy face and dirty teeth caught my attention in front of the brothel house, Dan Jr. and his company stood there and like the other folks around us, he stared with daggers in his eyes. Dan Jr.'s face was red as if it was building pressure. I smiled at him and tipped my Stetson in his direction before I placed Rachael on the dirt ground.

"Jessamine, you and Rachael be careful, please. I'll be done quickly to join you both." I caressed Jessamine's cheek. In return, she clasped her hand over mine, closing her eyes for a moment.

"Darling, do what needs to be done, apparently John sent my measurements to the tailor, and they must get around my baby belly. This thing won't stop growing." Jessamine looked down and rubbed her stomach. I used my knuckle to lift her head to look at me.

"You're beautiful either way." Then suddenly I placed my lips upon hers, the kiss was light and short. I had pulled away quickly not sure how she would react, my heart was pounding as if it were dynamite going off over and over.

Why are you such an idiot Talon?! Why did you do that?! Remember the boundaries?

I guess my heart didn't remember. I stared at her trying to read her face, Jessamine smiled deeply at me. "Uhh... I... well." I stumbled on my words trying to figure out what to say, I nervously started to adjust my pants as if they weren't the right fit. "I... Umm... I should start... yea." That was all I was able to get out. Jessamine said nothing to me but smiled, and her smile was unmoving.

"Come on Rachael," Jessamine called out and began to walk toward the tailor.

If people were staring at me, they were going to get a show because I wanted to slam my head against the wagon a few times.

What the hell is wrong with me? I kissed her! Okay no more sly stuff, remember you have secrets to keep, a heart and soul to protect.

Of course, my heart doesn't agree, it thought the right thing to do was to kiss my soon-to-be wife. I slammed my fist against my chest above my heart. "I will not think foolish things, it would be stupid to." I gathered myself together and headed to the back of the wagon to unload the goods. I took the baskets of corn out first, setting it down near the general store entrance. Mr. Kale stepped outside his shop with a grin.

"What you got for me boy?!" Mr. Kale's booming voice echoed out, I smiled as I climbed up the wagon and began to tug at a heavy barrel I fitted in a corner and lead it to the edge of the wagon.

"I got butter for ya," I replied, embracing the barrel into a hug and readied myself. I took a couple of good deep breaths before I lifted the heavy barrel and walked slowly toward the general store. I stopped to adjust my grip and took a couple of deeper breaths then continued until I was in the store.

"Now how did you know I needed that, Talon?" Mr. Kale smirked as if he was so clever. I was heavy in breath, so I leaned against the beam the butter barrel always stayed in. I picked up the butter sign that read 'out of stock' and held it up to him; Mr. Kale burst into laughter.

"You know my stock too well son, we've been doing business for so long that I don't need to make an order no more!" Mr. Kale kept laughing and shaking his head. A rustling noise caught my attention from the open door to the back room, I immersed myself in listening.

"Pa, we need more stock or we gonna run out before canning season start and..." The sight of me caused the small man with blonde hair, a clean-shaven face, and ocean-blue eyes to smile wide. "Well, I'll be a monkey's ass; Talon is here!"

"Jonah!" I yelled excitedly; both of our arms were outstretched wide to embrace each other in a hug. I towered above Jonah by over a foot. While I was 6'5, Jonah still seemed the same height as before he left for war. When the hug ended, I held Jonah by the shoulders, and he held on to my elbows.

"Wow, Talon! You've got taller and stronger; I wouldn't stand a chance in one of our tussles." Jonah felt up and down my arms and I shook my head at his silliness.

"Talon just carried a barrel of butter by himself." Mr. Kale added, making me feel a little blushed. "Reminds me when I was a young lad." Jonah and I smiled at the old man. Back when we were younger and I had first met Jonah, we would watch Mr. Kale work all day and try to help in between. He couldn't do what I did right now but had good endurance.

"Well, I'm sure you can unload that wagon by yourself, but why don't you let a good ole friend help you?" Jonah said slapping my back.

We worked together for an hour unloading the goods and even delivered the fur I had for the fur trade company. Jonah got us both a cider and we relaxed together in the wagon, taking a break from the heavy lifting. I looked toward the sun. "It's about two hours past noon." Jonah took a swig of his cider.

"Talon, why it seems like you are waiting for someone or thang?" Jonah pierced me with his green eyes.

"When did you start saying thing as thang? It's odd." I made no eye contact. Jonah took another drink.

"Don't go changing the subject now, what's going on?" Jonah sat at the wagon's edge, swinging his legs, waiting for me to speak. I sighed.

"Jonah... I'm getting married this Sunday." I admitted finally.

"That's great! You found a woman to accept you! Why do you sound so... somber? Yea, somber about it?" Jonah looked at me puzzled. I took a big swallow of my cider. "She doesn't know?" Jonah whispered so only I could hear, his brows furrowed deeply.

"We are getting married for convenience, nothing more," I said knowing he was about to lecture me in some way.

"How is that so? You..."

"Talon!" Jonah was interrupted by Rachael's excitement. Jessamine, who was not too far behind her, was carrying a box. I tried to relieve Jessamine of the cumbersome item but was subdued by Rachael wrapping her little body around my right leg, I had to balance myself so I wouldn't fall from the abrupt stop. I gave Rachael a quick squeeze, so she knew I noticed her.

"Jessamine, let me help you with that." I held out my arms to take the box, but Jessamine didn't hand it over.

"Talon, I love your chivalry, really, I do. But though I may be with child, you don't have to be at my beck and call. You nearly hurt both you and our daughter in the haste." Jessamine held a smile on her face.

"I was just trying to … our daughter?" *Did I hear that right?* My jaw dropped; I didn't know what to say.

"A snake is gonna make a nest in your mouth if you don't shut it. Howdy! I'm Jonah." Jonah stood next to me waving at Jessamine.

"Oh, Jessamine, this is my truest friend, Jonah. Jonah this here is my wife to be, Jessamine." I picked my leg into the air with Rachael still attached. "And this little one is Rachael, our… daughter." I almost stumbled on my words. "Now dear let me help you please?" I grabbed the box from her hands, and she let it go freely.

"You can have it, but no peeking. It's for our wedding day." Jessamine warned, my body almost stiffened at the word 'wedding', but I kept moving. Being in watchful eyes allowed me the strength to keep calm and flow like a river, our marriage could not be seen as less than what it was.

At this point I can now say I'm a father.

I placed the box in a safe place in the wagon so it wouldn't get damaged. "Talon I'm in need of rest soon," Jessamine announced. I shook my head yes to convey I understood what she was trying to say. "If you don't mind Jonah, would you like to join us for dinner? I would really like to get to know my husband's friend other than John. Maybe tell me some stories of Talon's youth." Jessamine said, rubbing her stomach absent-mindedly.

"Well, I'd be delighted to come to dinner. Let me just go get my horse and I'll ride with y'all home." Jonah Responded.

"You mean your pony." I teased.

"Wait now hold on good friend, my horse might not be KoKo. But he's the fastest son of a… horse I ever owned, you wait and see." Jonah countered playfully before heading around the general store. It had dawned on me that Rachael was still quite attached to my leg.

"Umm, Jessamine. Mind helping me with Rachael?" I asked, not quite sure what to do.

"You know she does this when she wants your attention. She missed you all day I just don't seem to have the heart to take her away." Jessamine made her face look sad. I scowled at her; she was doing this on purpose. I let out a breath before taking Rachael off my legs and into my arms, Rachael's small arms wrapped around my neck. I started to rub in circular motions on her back with the assistance of small bounces, and suddenly small snores emerged next to my ear.

"I guess it's nap time. It is late in the afternoon." I climbed up into the wagon and made a comfortable spot for the little girl. After Rachael was settled, I jumped out of the wagon,

"You spoil her, you do realize that right?" Jessamine said when she sauntered up next to me. I shrugged knowing that she was right, and it would only get worse.

JESSAMINE

Chapter 25

Talon and I watching Rachael sleep was one of the most blissful moments of my life, other than Rachael's birth. Leaning against Talon's shoulder I felt safe and secure, and slowly I started to fall. Not physically, emotionally. I couldn't keep the smile off my face when Talon placed his lips upon mine, I didn't expect it either. His lips were soft and sent sparks through me. I had never felt a man's lips that were so soft. After the conversation we had, I thought we would never cross the line of a platonic relationship. I thought that even though my heart was growing for Talon, it would be unrequited. That wonderful kiss gave me hope that maybe I would experience this complicated thing called 'love'. My body felt warm everywhere until a cold shiver took its place, and a daunting thought entered my mind. *What if it was just an act?* "Miss Jessamine!" Before I could explore that thought I turned to the sound of my name being called. Talon did the same.

"Why Jessamine it is good to see you!" Finding who the voice belonged to, Doctor Dean walked over hastily to me.

"Oh, hello Doctor, good afternoon," I responded with a small curtesy. I could see from my peripheral a puzzled look on Talon's face, he wasn't used to me doing such mannerisms. I usually observed formal courtesies because they made conversations short, sweet, and impersonal. Which was good for me because I didn't want anything to do with this doctor. It was just something about him, all too quick to give me pills to kill the life inside of me as soon as he saw I was unhappy about it. Doctors are supposed to preserve life, not take it away. When Doctor Dean finally reached us, his walk slowed as he approached, and I caught him staring at my stomach. He pointed.

"I thought you-."

"No, I changed my mind," I said cutting him off. Me and John kept that secret of that night from Talon, but now I think we should have told him so he wouldn't hear it from someone else. Doctor Dean's brows furrowed, but they were not for me. Doctor Dean was Looking at Talon. Not sure what was going on I looked up at Talon who raised a brow toward the slightly smaller man in height.

"May I help you...?" Talon asked, but it sounded more like a statement. Suddenly the doctor grabbed Talon by his shirt with both hands.

"I've heard about you savage! About what you've done!" Talon stood calmly as Dean visibly spat in Talon's face as he spoke.

"And what have I done?" Talon responded to the accusation.

"Forcing your ways on this defenseless woman, forcing her to have your child, and now you're forcing her to marry you." Venom flowed through Dean's voice. I stood flabbergasted by the accusations. For a moment it seemed as if Talon's eyes were turning a darker shade of yellow in his frustration. I tried to squeeze in between the two men, but the doctor's grip on Talon's shirt was too tight and I also had to be mindful of the life inside me. So, I couldn't help but feel useless physically.

"I beg your pardon Doctor, but Talon did no such thing!" I crossed my arms defensively over my chest. Dean chose to ignore me, keeping his focus on Talon.

"Sweet Jessamine was going to give up that baby until you probably stopped her!" Dean said way too loud and began to gather more attention. Though people were starting to stare and talk again, nothing scared me more than the look Talon had on his face as he turned to me without a word. The look was between disbelief and unforgivable anger, his eyes said everything. As much as I wanted to bury my head in the dirt and wallow in my shame, it was not the time.

What a bloody mess I've gotten myself into, and the day started off so well.

Talon took an audible intake of breath and turned his attention toward the doctor.

"Sir I have no idea what you assume, but I'm going to have to ask you to let go of me." Talon deepened his voice along with a familiar snarl I saw him do when the Dans came to the farm.

"Doctor, let my fiancé go. I don't know how long his patience is going to last." I warned.

"What's going on here?" Jonah asked pulling his horse behind him. I made a sigh of relief at Jonah's arrival.

"This imbecile thinks I'm being held against my will by Talon!" I exclaimed. Jonah looked from me to Talon, to the doctor, and then back at me.

"Umm. I'm confused." Jonah scratched his head with his free hand. I rolled my eyes.

"There's nothing to be confused about, this savage-." Suddenly Talon's big right hand was around Dean's neck.

"I've had about enough of you..." A growl emerged from Talon. I can see him begin to add pressure. I hurry and try to grab at his arm which was draining the life out of the doctor.

"Talon he isn't worth it honey," I said, tears already welling up in my eyes. I have never seen Talon so angry that I couldn't reach him. Then again, I've only seen him upset, not furious. Jonah had shown up on Talon's left side.

"Talon! Buddy, let him go buddy he's not worth it." Jonah pleaded.

"Savage is all I keep hearing..." Talon said in an almost whisper.

"You're not a savage, but you'll be proving him right if you pop his head off right now, I guarantee." Jonah tried to loosen Talon's grip. The crowd around us was starting to get bigger, and I already hated the unwanted attention we were already getting. The doctor's eyes started to flutter as his eyes rolled to the back of his head, a clear sign Dean was about to die or go unconscious.

"Talon, you have to let go!" I said pulling his arm along with Jonah, but he was too strong. There was only one thing I could do. I looked behind me. "Rachael your awake!" A thud on the ground made me turn my attention back and found Dean on the ground coughing and gasping furiously. Dean was too weak to pull himself up, so he stayed on the floor trying to steady his breathing and the utterly shocked look he wore.

"Thank God." Jonah let out the air he was holding. After releasing my own breath, I looked up and met Talon's yellow eyes.

"You tricked me," Talon said still in his deep voice. In my relief, I didn't even notice that he looked to see if what I had said was true. I placed hands on both of his cheeks to make him look only at me, not at the many people around us that Jonah was thankfully trying to get rid of.

"I need you this Sunday in order to get married, if you're in a cell how will I do that?" I rubbed Talon's cheek with my thumb.

"Our marriage-."

"That's not the point!" I stopped Talon before he could say something that would upset me. "Our marriage is important to me." Talon's features softened.

"I'm sorry... and thank you for stopping me." Talon pulled from my grip and then kneeled to the floor; he sat Dean up by pulling on his now dirt-filled white shirt. "I don't know what someone told you, I don't know what you people gossip about amongst yourselves, and I damn sure don't know what hero you were trying to play. All I know is you better stay away from my family." Talon said in a growl before he let the doctor go, causing him to fall on the ground again. Talon stood up to his full height and turned to me. "I'll meet you at the house, where we will have to talk." Then he went to unhook KoKo from the wagon, mounted him, and left nothing but a dust trail and me chasing after him to wait. Jonah stopped me before I tripped or caused an accident.

"Talon will be back by your side in no time, just give him some space." Jonah patted my shoulder.

"Why do people keep telling me that?! Just give him some space Jessamine, just let him go off to where bloody ever Jessamine, Jessamine just let him wander for nearly a bloody fucking month! He'll be fine. What about how I feel?!" I shouted at Jonah. Jonah raised his hands in surrender.

"Missus I barely know you and I'm fearing for my life right about now." I sighed at his plea.

"I'm sorry, I just wish he wouldn't run away." Though I was dreading the conversation that we were going to have when he arrived home.

Me and Jonah turned toward the sounds of grunting, Dean finally had enough stamina to get up off the ground. Jonah helped him off the floor and when Dean shook out of his dizzy state, he rushed toward me grabbing my hands into his own.

"Oh, sweet Jessamine! I'm glad you're well I-."

"Hold on a minute buddy, you need to tell us something. Who told you these stories about Talon?" Jonah moved Dean back from me as I pulled my hands from his grip. The doctor started to blush instantly.

"Well... Dan Jr. passed me a note that came from Jessamine, stating she was in love with me and needed my help. I had thought if I spoke to her in private while the savage wasn't around, we could come up with a plan, I thought about going to the savage's lair but got busy with patients. I did not expect that big thing to be so strong." Dean rubbed his neck. "But now you're ok and we could leave now Jessamine, together." Jonah shook his head, still acting as a barrier between us. There was nothing I could do but stare at this delusional man.

"Jessamine don't take this personally, this doctor has been like this for a while now, beginning with the whores." Jonah said, trying to comfort me in front of this maniac. Dean pushed Jonah from between us.

"You're too far along to abort the child, but I'll make sure to take care of it like my own." Dean declared. A searing heat engulfed me, I was so mad I couldn't take it. I balled up my left fist and punched Dean in the jaw as hard as possible. My hand throbbed in pain as Dean fell onto the floor. Speechless, he cupped the spot where I had hit him.

"You are psychotic... You don't know me or anything about me, you don't know what you're bloody talking about, and most importantly I would never be in love with you. My fiancé is all I need." I said, glaring at Dean. My hand throbbed and I felt around to see if any bones were broken. "Bloody hell that hurt!"

"You ungrateful bitch! After I stood against that savage!" Dean scrambled onto his feet, but Jonah quickly made himself into a barrier in front of me. I could see Dean's cheek start to swell accompanied by the huge purple and blue bruise around his neck.

"Go on and be on your way, there's nothing here for you," Jonah said, pointing toward the doctor's clinic. Dean peeked above Jonah's small stature.

"Let this be a warning, don't ever come to me for anything! Not even for the birth of that savage child!" Dean stomped away from us with his final word. I rolled my eyes, but they stopped on Dan Jr. who smiled a wicked grin at me. I scowled deeply. I felt a hand on my shoulder, I looked to find Jonah also staring in Dan's direction.

"I see him too. I'll find out what's going on later missus, he's always been one to be up to no good. Until then let's get you home and have Uncle Tao check on that hand, I'm sure y'all's daughter will be hungry by then." Jonah led me back to the wagon. So many things were running through my mind. I was worried for Talon, trying to ignore the pain in my hand, and how did Dan Jr. set this whole thing up? The doctor couldn't be that daft to follow a story he didn't know was true, but then again Jonah said he had done something like this before.

"Hey, Jessamine." Jonah's voice pulled me out of my thoughts. "That was one hell of a punch."

TALON

Chapter 26

I lay in silence next to a river with my eyes closed. To me, there was nothing more calming than the sound of moving water and the sound of it crashing into itself, with KoKo snacking on grass nearby. I let my hair sprawl out on the ground, from the anger I felt earlier my braid felt too tight against my head. *I really need to work on my temper.* But the thing is, I was never quick to get so angry. Yes, in the past I never let anyone get away with things they tried to do to me, but I wouldn't strike first. Now, my emotions were like whirlwinds, I found myself more defensive than usual. I thought more about what happened and what was being said to me. The doctor said that I had 'forced' Jessamine. The statement alone made me wonder if that was how Jessamine really felt about our situation. She did see the doctor the day I had gotten into a scuffle with Dan Jr. I calmed myself after I reckoned that my proposal happened after the fact. So why was the doctor acting like that? I never did anything to him despite the rumors of his behavior. I couldn't ponder long before I could hear steady footsteps heading toward me. I still held my eyes shut but propped my right foot closer to my hand for easy access to my knife. I waited.

"Talon, before you draw that knife it's me, Bill" I heard a voice say before getting too close. I sat up quickly and looked toward the direction of the voice. To my surprise it was Mister Kale accompanied by the captain of the militia. *Great, that's all I need.* The captain was a pale man about fifteen years my senior, with black shoulder-length hair tied back and a fit figure dressed in a red militia uniform. This was rare because the militia didn't have much to do during the day but break up a few fights here and there and play cards at the whore filled ale house. "Now Talon don't have that look, the captain only wants to hear your side of the story." Mister Kale tries to assure me. I sigh a breath and rise from the ground. The captain put his fist on his chest and bowed his head, I showed the same respect.

"Mr. Thomas, it has been a while. I haven't seen you since you were eighteen, preventing the taking of a whore in the alley by six men in the middle of the night." I shrugged at his statement trying hard to avoid scoffing.

"Get to the point. What do you want to know?" I asked, raising a brow. Mister Kale came up beside me and placed his hand on my shoulder.

"I know not to cross you, Mr. Thomas. You would make an experienced opponent. Also, I respect your father and will abide by his wish for you to be left alone and to lessen your repercussions in any matter." The captain replied.

"My Father is dead; you don't have to abide by anything." I snapped back.

"Not to me, your father has done much for me that I can't repay. So, I need to know what happened."

I told him everything he wanted to know including what I had done and when I finished the captain nodded his head for a moment. "I see. The good news is that Doctor has an imagined obsession when it comes to women. It was justifiable what you did in order to protect your family. The man is not dead, so it would be easy to say you used enough force to render him a non-threat. Thank you for your time." The captain repeated the same salute and turned away.

"Wait, that's it?' I yelled after him, confused. The captain turned to me again.

"Yes, that is all, you did what you must to ensure your family's safety. No one will fault you for that." The captain explained.

"But what about the rumors the doctor said he heard about?" I asked concerned, I needed to avoid an angry mob as much as possible.

"Yes, I have also heard. People will talk, buts that's all they can do. You live on a very large piece of land far away from the people of this town and their prying eyes, no need to worry." The captain then turned and walked away without another word.

"That should give you peace of mind my boy." Mister Kale said finding a rock to sit on. I went and sat next to him on the ground bringing my knees to my chest, resting my arms on them.

"I don't have peace of mind. I will be married at the end of the week, nowadays people act like they don't know me, like I am some stranger strolling in town. Other days before Jessamine, it wouldn't bother me. I had you, John, Jonah, and a few others, that was all I needed. Then she arrived and now everything is… a mess." I explained, staring toward the river. I heard a match strike, and when I looked Mister Kale had his pipe in his mouth lighting the contents inside.

"Is this about Lisa?" He asked blowing out smoke. I stood silent pondering an answer. I know she hurt you-…"

"Yea, she did. I think that I'm afraid of losing what I have, other than that, it has nothing to do with her. With Jessamine it's different." I cut Mister Kale off before he could open an old wound. Mister Kale shook his head in contemplation.

"Why is she so different?" Mister Kale asked another question that made me ponder more, which is the opposite of what I wanted to do. Mister Kale waited for my answer still smoking his pipe, we stood in silence as the temperature dropped due to the setting sun.

"She was a woman broken, incomplete, and fragile. But every day she grew a little stronger, found pieces that were missing and became unbreakable. I find myself amazed, proud, and intrigued at her growth in such a short time. Qualities I wish I had." I answered solemnly.

"I've seen you answer hatred with a calm nature, I've seen you defend the worthy and unworthy, I've seen you grow into the type of man that many wish to be. You have those same abilities. When the time is right those abilities will show." Mister Kale took another intake of smoke. I wish I could see what Mister Kale could see, the only reason I acted peaceful in the face of hate was because there was no point to fight. I knew I could beat them; I was taught as a warrior to help those who couldn't help themselves, and sadly I'm not a man. I didn't dare share my thoughts out loud, they were too deep and personal even for Mister Kale to know.

"The sun is going to leave the sky soon, I should head home," I grunted, getting up off the ground and dusting my bottom. "You coming Mister Kale?"

"No son, you go ahead and comfort that little lady of yours. I'm just going to sit here till the sunset." He responded and added more tobacco into his pipe. I gave a quick bow and went to Mount KoKo, I stared at Mister Kale for a moment.

"Thank you for your words." Mister Kale waved a hand and with that, I clicked two times for KoKo to head home and fast. I rode atop KoKo feeling the wind travel through my hair. I felt like an eagle ready to fly as I spread my arms wide into the air. This was when I felt mostly free to be myself. When I was alone. Just me and KoKo and no one else in the world would matter. "You're a monster! I hate you!" Lisa's words entered my head echoing loudly, I clutched my head in pain and closed my eyes tight. It was as if hundreds of bells were ringing all at once, my back slammed on something hard and when I opened my eyes, I found myself on the dusty ground. "I should have known you were nothing but a savage! An impure thing!" Lisa's echo was louder than the first time. I stayed on the ground with my hands pressing against my ears. KoKo appeared above me pressing his nose to my cheek in concern. For once I allowed myself to cry, as the echoes of the past taunted me.

JESSAMINE

Chapter 27

"That bloody scoundrel!" I yelled, but then placed my hand over my mouth forgetting Rachael was sleeping. My blood boiled at the thought of Dan Jr.'s dirty smile.

"Well, that was sudden." Jonah quipped. I placed both my hands on my face in frustration.

"I need to know his agenda. He's-..." I felt that wave of dizziness that always reminded me that I needed to calm down. "Let's stop talking about this for now. That man only infuriates me." Jonah nodded his understanding. I decided to focus my mind on something positive, I turned to Jonah. "Pardon the suddenness but may I ask, how are you and my betrothed so acquainted? Talon seems awfully determined to keep to himself." Jonah smiled deeply.

"That sounds like my buddy, always keeping to himself but not afraid to lend a hand to those who need it," Jonah answered, not losing his smile. "That's how we met, him helping me out in my time of need."

"Really?" My intrigue piqued.

"Mhm. I was having a run-in with some guys; they took every chance to whip on me." Jonah's smile finally faded.

"Why is that? You seem like a nice guy." I mean, I knew nothing of the man but from what time I did spend with him he had been rather nice. *Another male that is helping to shift my thoughts of the opposite sex.*

"Because I was different. One day they hurt me bad. I didn't know if I would recover once they were done. Then here comes Talon! Doing some strange fighting I later found out was Kung Fu." Jonah's smile reappeared on his face. "I learned a little myself after, it served me well. But missus that day Talon gave them guys such a whippin' they couldn't figure out their head from their behinds!" Jonah let out a loud laugh slapping his knee. "I was 16 and Talon was 15 back then and I didn't know anything about anything, but I knew from that day on as soon as Talon threw me on his back and walked me home, that I could trust him even with my life." Jonah nodded his head in agreement. I sat and absorbed Jonah's words and wondered if I had felt the same initially. At first, I was confused and scared, but a feeling of safety and security emerged after I had knocked Talon over the head, and he showed nothing but compassion. That was when I saw what Jonah saw as he carried me to my room. I huffed.

"He has that effect on people I suppose." Silence ensued, leaving me to my thoughts.

We had reached the farm shortly after, I noticed it was early in the evening and Rachael slept for way too long and was going to be a pain to put to bed. I was exhausted from today's tribulations and the pregnancy, all I wanted to do was sleep. Jonah stopped the wagon in front of the house where John sat on the porch with a slightly confused face. "Howdy, old man! It's been forever!" Jonah jumped out of the wagon and ran into John's embrace, that's when I noticed Jonah was only a few inches taller than John.

"It's been too long Jonah. You haven't grown much but you've aged into a man." John said now, holding Jonah at arm distance.

"Ha ha ha... Very funny Tao." Jonah rolled his eyes playfully. John's smile fell as he looked over Jonah's shoulder and at me, I was enjoying the interactions but still trying to figure out how I was going to get down.

"Where are Talon and KoKo?" John asked, brows furrowed. I sighed heavily and tried to get off the wagon. I guess John saw my struggle because all I heard was a slap and when I looked up Jonah was rubbing the back of his head.

"Owe! What I do?!" Jonah whined.

"The lady needs help," John answered.

"Oh, damn it! Jessamine, I apologize, hanging around a bunch of men at war made my manners lacking." Jonah rushed toward me. It took some time but eventually, I reached the ground. I didn't say it out loud, but Jonah's height was something I wasn't used to compared to Talon who very easily helped me in and out of the wagon.

"We should talk inside; you know, where I can rest my feet," I said walking past the men and up the porch stairs. I groaned out loud. "Bloody hell I forgot Rachael."

"Jessamine, go inside. I'll get Rachael." John interjected. Before I could walk back down the stairs. I didn't argue and continued my journey.

Jonah and I explained the events of the day, and how the Doctor accosted Talon with name-calling and accusations. John sat quietly as he listened. Though he didn't look upset his body told a different story. He was stiff and his left leg bounced in a steady rhythm. "Uncle Tao, everything is going to be fine. The wedding will go off without a hitch... I wanted to ask if it would be a problem if I bring Charles. I don't want to add to any more problems y'all have on your shoulders." Jonah seemed shy suddenly.

"What kind of problem could inviting a person bring?" I asked. Jonah had a look of dread, he looked toward John, and he returned a look of discern. I looked back and forth between them; they were communicating with their eyes. "I'm waiting." Jonah was the first to make eye contact with me, fear in his eyes.

"Well, Talon and Uncle Tao were the only people that never judged me..." My brows furrowed waiting for the next sentence. "Since we are all going to be family... well, I just... prefer the company of men." Jonah confessed then slapped his hands over his face to cover it. I didn't know what to say at the revelation. I eyed John for a moment, and he returned a questioning gaze. I turned my attention back to Jonah who still had his hands covering his face.

"Is that all? I thought you would tell me something more... demeaning." I said indifferently. Jonah dropped his hands from his face revealing a look of shock and confusion. I shrugged with a smile.

"There's nothing more you want to say about it?" Jonah asked me dumbfoundedly.

"Jonah honestly there's nothing to worry about. I've seen and respected bachelor marriages before, they are more common than you realize. Of course, not everyone thinks like me, but I don't really care, it's none of my bloody business or anyone else's what you do with another person. It took me too long to learn not to care what people think and I suggest you do the same." I was caught off guard by the smiling faces John and Jonah were giving to each other.

"She's a keeper." Jonah quipped.

"Indeed." Replied John.

TALON

Chapter 28

I finally made it back to the house but didn't want to be bothered. My tears had finally ceased and dried. My hair was a messy puff, I was dirty from head to toe, and for some reason, my body ached. I sneaked quietly past the horse and climbed my favorite tree. I always sat in this tree to clear my mind of painful memories and I always went at night. It was something about being closer to the moon that made me feel calm and at ease. I finally made it to the top and sat on a strong branch that would hold my weight and rested my back against the tree. I waited. A moment felt like hours as I waited to feel calm. I even closed my eyes, but it was fruitless. Though the moon bathed me with its glow I could not feel calm, instead, I became more anxious as if I needed to do something or be at a certain place. I opened my eyes in urgency, I looked around as if I was being hunted. My breath came rapidly, and I wasn't sure of what to do. I began to climb down; one of the branches broke from my weight and fell. My stomach caved in when I slammed onto a thick branch. Usually, my body could take that type of hit when I was ready for it, but I wasn't ready for it. I ended up falling the rest of the way down landing on my back. I was beginning to wonder if I was cursed to fall on my back for the rest of my life.

"Talon!! For God's sake are you alright?" I threw my upper body up from the ground at the sound of Jessamine's voice. A calmness swept over me in an instant the moment I laid eyes on her. She was kneeling in front of me with a concerned and fearful look. "Talon, speak to me?" I stared into her grey eyes speechless. Her warm hands caressed my cheeks moving my head from side to side examining me. "Talon, I saw you fall; I need to know if you are all right." I stared at her lips wanting more than ever to taste her again. *Snap out of it you fool!* I let my eyes fall toward the ground.

"I'm fine Jessamine, don't worry about me, just a little battered." I got myself up from the ground, but I had to stop myself from staggering. I was in a lot more pain than I realized. I reached my hand out to her to help her off the dirt, but instead she rejected my hand and got up on her own. I ignored the prick in my heart. "How'd you know I was out here?"

"John told me, so I decided to sit on the porch and wait for you, despite how tired I am." Jessamine had crossed her arms in front of her chest.

"Well, I'm glad you and Rachael made it home safe. You should get some sleep." I avoided eye contact and tried to walk toward the barn but was stopped when Jessamine hurriedly stepped in front of me.

"Talon, stop, we need to talk, and you look like hell," Jessamine said placing her hands on my stomach to push me back.

"You're tired, you should rest," I said, avoiding eye contact and trying to avoid the conversation.

"No Talon don't brush me off! I have something to say." Jessamine's tone became more demanding. I dropped my head toward the earth.

"Look, if it's about today-..."

"No, it's about us! Bloody hell Talon just let me talk." She cut me off with furrowed brows. "I was gifted with the privilege to be told something intimate to Jonah, about Jonah. I even know some things about John. But you, I know nothing." I could hear her holding back tears. I finally looked up at Jessamine and the calm energy flowed through me once more.

"When you find the man you really want to be with, knowing me won't matter."

"Are you fucking dense?!" Jessamine yelled, my eyes wide at her loose language. "All of this is as lucky as I am going to get; the best Rachael and this child are going to get!" Jessamine took a deep composed breath. "There are people after us, after me. In order to combat this, we need to know each other and trust each other, or they will win."

"Who are you to tell me this when you kept your pregnancy away from me?! And then you tried to get rid of it!" I shouted unable to restrain myself.

"That was before the proposal!" Jessamine shouted back.

"Either way! I had figured you at least trusted me enough to know what's going on with you after knocking me on the head!"

Jessamine scoffed. "What does that have to do with anything?"

"I had to hear it from someone else, not from you," I said, my chest rising and falling rapidly in my own anger. Jessamine did not say another word while absorbing what I said. "My father abandoned me as a baby, then my tribe abandoned me as a child. John saved my life, he raised me, and he trained me. When I finally saw my father again, he was dying, he felt so guilty for leaving me that he gave me his land and business." I gave myself a chance to collect myself. I had let tears fall earlier and I forbade them to fall now. "I don't like talking about myself and if you keep digging, you'll find a monster."

"Talon, why don't you let me be the judge of that?" Jessamine pleaded.

"I'm trying to spare you pain! I told you the basics, isn't that enough?!" I shouted in finality.

"No!"

"Enough!" Both Jessamine and I turned to the sound of John's voice. I turned around to walk off. "Come back here Talon," John called after me calmly but sternly. I hadn't heard that tone of voice since I was a kid, so I decided it was best for me to turn back. Jonah stayed silent behind John. I think he was even more unnerved by the tone. John stared me and Jessamine down. "Both of you are acting like children. You will be married soon, so to solve this, every day you two will tell one thing about yourselves. It's non-negotiable." John stared both of us down before turning around and walking back to the house. Jonah stared until John was gone.

"Ooooo y'alls is trouble," Jonah said before I gave him a death stare.

* * *

As each day went by Jessamine and I told each other things about ourselves. I learned Jessamine had a sweet tooth, she always wanted to learn to use a sword, she wanted to run her father's business, she's always hated dresses but wore them anyway because it was the ladylike thing to do, and she loves to read. She also apologized for not telling me of her attempt at termination, she had told me John had stopped her and suggested that she tell me but never got around to it. I really did not want to participate but I had little to no choice since the internal war between my heart and head was getting out of hand. So, I kept it vague; I told her my favorite color, which is blue, that my goal in life was to make my body stronger than anyone I know, that I wanted to become a master of martial arts, I like my hair out whenever I can, and I like to go on short adventures to discover new things. I couldn't tell if the facts about myself satisfied her curious nature, I doubted it. But that was all I could share with her, anything deeper would be my downfall. Lisa once told me I'm an exotic person that everyone wants to know or own and that I should be careful who I get close to. She should have followed her own advice. I had to wonder to myself if it was the kiss that opened the door to the turbulence between us. I couldn't ponder longer because before I knew it, it was Sunday morning.

A knock sounded at the door, and I groaned inwardly. I had gotten no sleep at all as I lay on my stomach with the pillow covering my head. Between the farm work and trying to keep a balance of what to tell and not to tell Jessamine I was completely worn. Summer was approaching, the canning season came after that, and we needed to prepare. Most importantly the baby was estimated to arrive in the fall or winter months, like there wasn't enough on my shoulders. I can feel my body becoming more tense day by day. The door to my room opened suddenly and then closed. One of my wall lanterns was lit, casting a small glow that wasn't too bright. "John, leave me alone..." I said with a muffled growl.

"I can't do that, it's time to get up Talon," John responded calmly.

"The sun is not even out!" My yell was muffled.

"Out of bed." John retorted. I jumped out of my bed heaving.

"This is your fault!" I said out loud. All I had on were my night pants and the binding that held down my chest.

"Stop acting like a child, you did this to yourself. Which I think was the best spontaneous thing you have done." John said, placing his hands behind his back. I looked at him puzzled, that was the only way I could explain it because I was shocked, mad, and confused.

"What do you mean? I'm-..."

"You're getting older and need something to live for other than yourself. I know how it feels to have no one, and when I did, I was too selfish to go back to fix it. You like her, don't you? If you didn't, you wouldn't be making the plans you are making for her." John sounded nonchalant.

"Quiet old man! You know nothing, I'm not ready for this." I began to pace.

"Talon, no one is ever ready for change, but change comes to everyone. There's nothing we can do about it." John took a seat on my bed.

"This isn't about change John! It's about me." I leaned my forehead against the window glass, staring out into the misty morning. "When she finds out, what then? She'll think the marriage isn't valid, she'll think I deceived her."

"Then tell her who you are and trust in good fortune," John replied, startling me when he placed a hand on my shoulder. I wanted to embrace the comfort, but I moved away toward the closet.

"I will get married today, nothing more."

The sun finally made it into the sky shining its beautiful glow across the land, unfortunately, I could not enjoy its warmth. I walked out of the house with the front of my hair in a ponytail complimented by an eagle's feather and left the rest of my hair out. I had put on the cleanest clothes; I haven't worn them since I was nineteen. I started to roll up my sleeves to feel more comfortable in the tight shirt, I tried not to move too much in fear of ripping the fabric. Being this enclosed was making me crankier than this morning and more nervous than I had ever been in my entire life. I heard a galloping horse in the distance approaching the house. When I looked up, I wasn't surprised at Jonah's arrival. I readied myself for the 'pep talk' I was going to receive from Jonah, though it might be more entertaining coming from him. Jonah jumped off his horse in his most fashionable attire of a matching black vest and pants with a white buttoned shirt. He walked up to me with open arms for a hug. Afraid to move I kept my hands to myself as Jonah wrapped his arms around my stomach, "It's your big day! I'm so excited!" Jonah said enthusiastically. Jonah's smile was wider than his face and his sea blue eyes sparkled.

"It seems you're more excited than I am," My voice was grim shrugging the small man off of me.

"Really Talon? Smile! It's not every day my best friend in the world gets married. I'm so glad I made it back home from the military just in time to enjoy this, and unlike you, I'm free of guilt." Jonah leaned his back against the porch beam with both of his brows raised in question. I stared at Jonah making my gaze hard, piercing, and sharp. Jonah instantly put his hands up in surrender.

"You know, them yellow eyes are hella scary when you're mad. You do know that right?" I ignored Jonah's attempt at being funny and walked down the porch stairs to look up the road, but something caught my eye. I saw Jonah had his belt holster hooked onto the horse saddle.

"Why are you loaded, Jonah?" I asked. Jonah was never the type of man to resort to violence, not even in the military according to the letters he sent me.

"Why else buddy." Jonah joined me at the bottom of the porch. "To make sure everything runs smoothly today. You know I never got the hang of those knives, swords, bows, and whatnot. A gun though I mastered with ease, especially a rifle." Jonah made pistols out of his fingers and blew on the tips before he started to laugh, and I couldn't help but chuckle a little along with him.

"Well, I'll have to see how good you really are, maybe we'll go hunting. I'll show you true accuracy with my archery." I nudged Jonah on the shoulder. And we continued to laugh. I had to admit with all the stress this week, it felt good to laugh. I felt just a little lighter.

"By the way, why in the hell are we standing here and not on our way to town?" Jonah put his hands on his hips looking up at me. "Scared?" I shot him another one of my intense looks and he looked down toward the ground.

"I'm waiting for someone," I said, looking up the road to find a wagon coming over the hill. I chuckled to myself. "When you speak about the devil he will come."

"What?" Jonah went for his gun, but I stopped him.

"It's from my company. Why are you trigger-ready?" I said a little annoyed and curious.

"I'm sorry man, Tao got me jumpy, he said he had a bad feeling that I should stay on guard."

"Guard, not shoot anything on sight geez." I retorted trying to keep John's warning from getting to me.

I can only imagine what that means.

The wagon stopped a few feet short of the porch, but I couldn't miss the chubby man climbing out of the wagon in a hurry to greet me. He grabbed my hand with both of his hands to shake. "Master Thomas! It's so good to see you again, it's been too long!" He continued to shake my hand for longer than was necessary.

"Nick, it's good to see you too. You can let go of my hand now." I greeted, placing a smile on my face to cover up that I was annoyed. Nicolas Keegan was my father's right-hand man and best friend; he had been working in my father's company since it began, and now even after he was gone he's more than happy to work for me. I allow Nick under my signature to be the face of the company and its dealings, if my signature is not on it, he's not allowed to do anything. But mostly I went along with whatever business plan he had since he was more educated in it than I was. Nick collected himself from his happiness, turning from a man that was overjoyed, to a man of business.

"Sorry sir truly, I got a little overwhelmed with emotion to see you." Nick hummed a chuckle.

"Nick this is my dear friend Jonah Kale, Jonah this is my assistant Nicolas Keegan." I went on with the introductions. Both men tip their hats at each other.

"Now, Mr. Thomas I got the things you wanted and asked for, including the ledger and the incoming and outgoing reports. I also was able to acquire that last-minute paperwork, are you sure you're ok with doing this?" I gave him an amused look.

"I haven't been sure of anything since I got into this mess, but I'm as sure as I'm going to get."

"Very well then sir, here you are." Nick passed me a leather-bound package tied with a thin ribbon. I untied it and read each document carefully, making sure there were no hidden clauses. I knew I could trust Nick but it's best to cover my ground.

"Nick, did you bring a quill?" Nick went immediately to his task and looked into the bag that he had lying on the floor of the wagon. When he came back, he handed me a quill-like contraption.

"What's this Nick?" I asked, staring at the odd thing. I heard Nick snicker a bit, when I looked up at him instantly he stopped just as quickly with a cough. "Glad you think it's funny I don't know things."

"I'm sorry sir, truly. With all your wealth I would think you would at least give yourself a fountain pen." I stared at him still holding the fountain pen with two of my fingers. "The ink is already inside sir, just start writing." Nick went on.

"I'll never be used to this kind of stuff. All I ever used were quills and brushes."

"Well, that's kinda fancy," Jonah commented, looking at the fountain pen very interested in its design.

"I don't care what it is, turn around so I can use your head to write."

"What?" I turned Jonah around and laid the papers on his head and began to sign them.

"I know I'm shorter than you but I'm going to have to draw the line on you making me your personal table." Jonah quipped. I smiled to myself not saying anything, knowing Jonah was only fooling with me. When I was done, I placed the papers back into the leather wrap and handed them to Nick.

"Sir, are you sure about this? You've only known this woman for a couple of months." Before he could say more, I held my finger up.

"I'm sure. Anyway, on to other business, do you have my package?"

Nick looked upwards as if he would find his answer in the sky then snapped his fingers. He wobbled back to the wagon and reached into his bag again. He came back with a small box.

"Sir, as you requested you did not want me to take a peek, but I must say I'm quite curious." I made a cheeky smile as the small box was placed in my hand. I wanted to open it but couldn't shake the feeling of being intensely watched. I looked to my right and Jonah was trying to peak over my shoulder, I looked in front of me where Nick stood, and he stared at it. I opened the lid slowly, while Jonah sunk lower to see under the lid, Nick went higher to see over the lid. I opened the box and all I heard were gasps.

"You both sound like women," I observed as I held the ring in the box in my hand. It had a large diamond in the middle, with smaller sapphires around it, and even smaller yellow gems around the sapphires.

"Well, I'll be a monkey's ass, that is something. You know for a person who is not happy about today, you sure did come prepared." Jonah chimed in, letting out a light-hearted chuckle. I shot out a look toward him making it more frightening than before, and even Nick had gulped.

"This was not something I had planned to give her. One day I was just staring at her and felt inspired to make something that contributed to her beauty. I never wanted to give it to her because I knew I was a coward. And I could not express certain feelings, not without both of us getting hurt." I responded. "I just sent Nick a letter of a design for a jeweler from France that I had heard moved to the union and that was it." I went on.

"Are you asking someone to wed you, sir? Nick asked, still looking at the ring. I closed the box to get Nick's attention.

"No, I'm getting married. There was no time to really ask."

Nick gave me a confused look.

"It's complicated." I shrugged him off putting the box in my pocket.

"Oh, man! Talon, we got to get to the church! Daylight is wasting." Jonah said hurriedly. I nodded my head in solemn understanding.

"Mr. Thomas if you don't mind, may I attend your wedding? I love weddings and your father would want me to witness his son create a future to pass down his legacy." Nick smiled deeply. I wasn't sure if Nick knew how deep his words cut me, but it was far deeper than any wound or broken bone I ever had in my life.

After collecting my weapons and Stetson, Jonah, Nick, and I set off toward town. I thought deeply as I swayed with KoKo's strides, listening to Jonah and Nick become more acquainted. "Talon!" I snapped my head in the direction my name was being called from.

"What?!" I lashed out a little too harshly. Jonah flinched back and I instantly regretted it. "I'm sorry my friend, I'm not myself today." Jonah nodded his head in understanding.

"I was just asking how did that design come to you? It's different."

"Yes, indeed different," Nick added to Jonah's comment. I turned my attention back to the road ahead.

"While I was away from the farm due to anger and stress, I went out just to explore. One day I was lying under the stars, and I remembered John telling me about a beautiful phenomenon called an eclipse, where the moon covers the sun in the middle of the day. I've never seen one before, but as much as I was mad at her I couldn't help but feel that we were a beautiful phenomenon. So, I imagined what an eclipse would look like, I drew it out... and everything else you already know."

"That must have been very difficult to make." I hummed in agreement with Jonah's statement.

"She deserves the best," I responded absent-mindedly. When I realized what I had said I turned to Jonah to correct it. Before I was able to defend myself, I was greeted with one of Jonah's cheeky grins with his shoulders to his ears. With that, I knew I already had lost and thought it best to stay silent.

"Your father would be proud; he never had those types of feelings for the madam," Nick said quietly.

"We going to be late!" Jonah said out loud before I was able to ask Nick what he meant.

"Nick, are you able to keep up with us if we hurry?" I yelled behind me.

"I'll be alright sir, go on." Me and Jonah set off our horses into a sprint. Jonah was slightly ahead of me as his horse was born for speed, mine he was born for power. KoKo was a full horse head taller than Jonah's horse. I embraced the breeze I was receiving, the day had been humid and hot, not a good mixture with my mood but quite accurate.

"What the hell?" Jonah said pulling on the horse's reins, making his horse neigh in a screech, standing on his hind legs to stop. Jonah managed to stay on his horse despite the sudden thrust. KoKo slid to a stop next to them when I clicked my tongue once.

A row of eight men blocked the entire road, they stood with guns and rifles at their sides. One of the men who stood in the middle took out a paper, he looked at it before raising his head to look at me, then back toward the paper. He folded the paper back up and stuffed it back into his pocket. I assumed he was their leader. Nick arrived right behind us.

"Is there a disturbance sir?" Nick asked, I could hear his concern.

"You!" The man in the middle pointed at me, "cannot pass here." My brows creased inward deeply.

"Who are y'all to tell us who can and cannot pass?" Jonah yelled out.

"Well, that's none of your business now, is it?" The man in the middle replied. Jonah's face scrunched up in anger and he pulled out one of his two pistols. In reaction, the line of men raised their guns in unison. Just as quickly I drew my bow with three arrows ready.

"John was right." I heard Jonah whisper to me. I shook my head trying to send the message that now was not the time. I pulled harder on the bowstring, but before I could release, a gunshot flew by me.

"I's don't feel like killing today, Mr. Red Man, don't tempt me!" The man said with his revolver smoking. I could already see Jonah about to lose his calm, I pointed my bow down and loosened my grip. I put the arrows back in their quiver.

"They're mercenaries sir," Nick whispered from behind us. I looked at Nick, then I looked at Jonah. We exchanged understanding glances.

"Fine, you win, have it your way, we're turning back!" I yelled toward the line of men trying to keep my anger from showing. We turned back to where we came from.

"I thought he was dangerous?" one of the men in the line said whispering to another. My superior hearing caught it.

"So did I with all the rumors, turns out he's a scared little kitten." The voice belonging to the man in the middle responded and ended with a laugh coaxing the others to laugh with him. I let out a growl.

"Sir, we're not going? What about your Bride?" Nick sounded a bit disappointed.

"No worries, Talon has a plan, he always does," Jonah assured, and I gave a nod.

We weren't far from the line of men, but they couldn't see us. I had to find my sense of calm after I heard them mock me, I wasn't used to people talking so frankly about me. Everyone in town, except recently with the doctor and Dan Jr., tried their best to talk kindly to me despite what they thought about me. I jumped off KoKo.

"When you hear me call, I'll need the both of you to rush the men and keep going," I demanded.

"How are we going to show up to the church without the groom?" Jonah snapped. "You must want John to kill me."

"There could be more of them out there than just the eight and I don't need them chasing us. I also don't want either of you to get hurt." I said sternly, wanting to end the debate.

"Yea! What about you!? Jessamine needs you there! We both know who's up to this, you're just being stubborn. You don't have the fight the world alone Talon!" Jonah's chest rose and fell rapidly. "You are going to be... no, you are a father and soon-to-be husband. It's not just about you, believe it or not, you matter. If something happens to you, we'd be lost and the people you wanted to protect the most will be defenseless. Let me help you." I stood for a moment after Jonah was finished talking, I thought about what he said. He was right in certain aspects and the rest I didn't want to hear, I had to stay focused so I could make it to the church alive.

"Not today my friend, do as I ask and charge them. They'll be ready to fire but let me take care of that. You will head to the church and inform Jessamine of my arrival. Nick, stay with him." I started to climb a tree close by ignoring Jonah's searing looks of anger toward me. I knew I would hear it later but right now I had to protect my friends. I reached the top of the trees and casually walked the connecting branches. I reached the man-made blockade and not much to my surprise there were extra men on both sides of the road. *Figures.* I calculated and planned my next steps, and I thought of the different ways I could handle this situation. All leading to someone either seriously hurt or dead, the last things I needed were blood stains.

"How long are we gonna have to stand here boss?" One of the men asked the main guy doing all the talking earlier.

"I don't know but we're being paid to stand here and make sure that savage doesn't get through, so that's what we going to do, and I don't want to hear y'all bitching!" The main man shouted adjusting his grip on his gun. I clasped my hand around my mouth and made a call of an eagle, loud enough to echo through the woods for Jonah to start the charge. The men below seemed unmoved by the bird sound, keeping their positions. I could hear Jonah's horse and Nick's wagon approaching fast, meaning I had to create an opening. I pulled my bow out with two arrows and steadily aimed for the two men in the middle. A scary yet satisfying feeling emerged causing my heart to race, I was going to make the men pay for mocking me and I was more than happy to end them for it.

'You are beyond killing, you must rise above and use what I have taught you to save lives, not end them.' John's voice echoed through my head. Jonah and Nick were very close, and the men were ready to fire.

"Sorry…" I released the arrows, and, in an instant, they struck the two men. The remaining men were caught off guard by the arrows sticking into each man's chest. Jonah flew by in their confusion and one of the men was hit by Nick's wagon. I hopped down branch by branch until I reached the ground, the extra men fled from their hiding spots and aimed their weapons at my friends. I equipped another two arrows from my bow and took aim.

"Hey! It's me you want!"

JESSAMINE

Chapter 29

    I stayed in the room above the church getting ready for my big day. I looked at myself in the mirror, my hair was neat and wavy going down my back. When I first arrived at the farm my hair was only a few inches past my shoulders, now it was hitting the middle of my back and for the first time since I was a young woman, it was shiny and healthy. Due to the pregnancy, my grey eyes were brighter, and in them, I could see something that wasn't there before. Something that was growing in beautiful ways, I didn't recognize the woman looking back at me through the mirror, in a good way. I smiled at myself. I never imagined getting married again, to be frank, I didn't want to get married at all. In my heart, however, Talon was someone I needed to have, to claim. I got up from the chair I was sitting in to look at myself in the full-body mirror, I was in a white dress that was slender but loose so it could fit around my belly. I let out a small yawn, I had gotten up earlier than Talon for the first time to be ready and to get Rachael ready. Rachael gave me less of a problem than usual to put on a dress, which was a relief because she could be quite adamant when she made up her mind. There was a window in front of me giving me the chance to see Rachael and John playing with a paddle and ball, I also saw a negro helping Rachael swing. I had no problems with anyone with a darker skin complexion than my own, but it was the fact that I didn't know him. Though I knew I could trust John, my protective nature kicked in and I wanted to know who this person was to ease my mind. I turned around toward the door and my body went cold and rigid.

"Aww you ruined my view, but the front is not all that bad." Dan Jr. said with a toothy disgusting grin. It seems like he tried to put an effort to dress nicely though his stomach peeked out the hem of his shirt. I swallowed multiple times to keep the light breakfast I had down. Dan Jr. gripped his belt and started to walk closer to me, "I thought my Pa and I's asked for an invitation, that's awfully rude not to send one." Dan Jr. said, holding his grin. I became visibly angry.

"I want peace on my wedding day, so, please leave," I demanded still trying to keep the tremble from my voice. I tried to keep my distance from the fat man but ran out of space when I hit the wall.

"Peace, that's ironic." Dan Jr, chuckled, "You like things rough and wild, being with a savage and all, I bet you get no sleep."

"Get away from me..." I slapped him across his face when his grubby hands got too close to me, I had hit him so hard that not only my hand throbbed, but his face was red. Dan Jr. turned his face toward me, eyes filled with rage, he also revealed a bloody lip. Dan Jr. lunged at me, I felt his hand grip my throat and my feet not touching the floor.

"I'm preg... pregnant." I managed to say with my air supply being shortened. I tried hitting him in his arms to break his grip, but it was becoming a futile effort.

"You think I give a damn about some savage's child? Hm?" Dan Jr. said with venom. I tried to keep myself calm between worrying about myself and the baby it wasn't going to be an easy task because as flashes of my former life with Elias filled my mind, I became more manic. I started to remember how weak and helpless I was, I refused to be that kind of woman anymore and tried to hit harder even though I was already feeling my body go limp. Dan Jr. yelled out in pain at the same time I was released from his grip. I fell to the floor, avoiding falling on my stomach.

It took a moment to gather myself and fix my blurry vision, when I was finally able to see clearly Rachael stood in front of me with a paddle in her hand and Dan Jr. was on the floor clutching his right knee.

"Mommy ok?" Rachael asked, her voice so small and shaky. She nearly brought me to tears. I stretched my arms and hugged Rachael, gathering her small body into me, thankful for her bravery.

"You little bitch!" Dan Jr. yelled out, ruining our mother and daughter moment. He struggled to get up from the floor, but he didn't have to wait long before the burly negro, who was playing with Rachael helped him up but kept a grip on him by wrapping one of his arms around Dan Jr.'s neck.

John entered the room with his hands behind his back. He was holding prayer breads moving to each bead as if he were counting them. He stopped in front of the restrained Dan Jr. "Do you have no shame in a house of a God?" John asked Dan Jr. but by the look on his face, I doubt we were waiting for an answer. Dan Jr. took a deep breath as much as possible before spitting in John's face. I placed one of my hands over my mouth with a gasp, Rachael's sudden movement made me look down at her to find her covering her eyes.

"Ya's just as bad as that fucking savage, walking around acting like you belong here..." Dan said trying to recover some air. John reached into his pocket, pulled out a handkerchief and wiped his face, he stuffed the handkerchief back into the same pocket. He moved closer to Dan Jr. moving his head in a yes motion, he then made his hand open and flat and started to thrust slowly into Dan Jr.'s abdomen. John kept pushing his hand deeper and deeper. Dan Jr. screamed in pain; John's four fingers disappeared into Dam Jr.

"You hurt this woman. How does it feel? Having your life slowly drain from you. Feeling the pain travel throughout your body." Dan Jr. suddenly went quiet. "The pain is so bad you have no control over your body anymore." Blood starts to drool out of Dan Jr.'s mouth. "Then finally you see the light that greets you when you're fading." Dan Jr.'s eyes started to flutter closed, John twisted his hand causing Dan Jr. to wake up. "Finding it will not be heaven that awaits you," John said in a deep growl voice that I never heard from him before.

"Let my son go, right now!" a voice boomed. I looked toward the doorway; Daniel Senior stood there with two other men holding rifles. Both men walked closer to John placing the barrel of their firearms close to John's head.

"As you wish…" John responded retrieving his hand from Dan Jr.'s gut. Daniel approached John with heavy breaths like he had been jogging several sets of stairs. "I ought to lock you up! Let my boy go!" Daniel pointed his finger in John's face. John looked toward the negro.

"Charles, let him go," John lightly demanded. Charles released Dan Jr. and he fell to his knees coughing. When Dan Jr. tried to get up, his legs were uneasy, and he struggled with a grunt. When he finally was able to get up, he was hunched over walking step by step toward his father's side. Daniel senior assessed his son while also trying to help him stand straighter.

"I should have you charged Tao!" Daniel Senior yelled out pounding his finger on John's chest.

"Of course, Daniel, right after Jessamine charges your son first." John turned to me with an amused look. I guessed that was my cue to start talking.

"Your son nearly killed me and my baby, if it wasn't for my daughter, I wouldn't be alive," I said sheepishly. Rushed footsteps coming up the stairs made me turn my head toward the door, I didn't know if everyone else could hear it through the thick tension, the whole room was in a standoff. Jonah rushed in with his pistol in hand and the priest chasing him. One of the riflemen tried to stop Jonah by aiming their gun but Jonah knocked it away and finished him with a kick in his sweets. By the time the second rifleman could aim his gun, Jonah already had his pistol against Dan Jr.'s head. Dan Jr. ceased all movement.

"Pa..." Dan Jr. whimpered.

"Put that gun down, son!" Daniel Senior shouted at Jonah. The able-bodied rifleman kept his gun pointed at Jonah, but Jonah seemed unfazed. I turned Rachael toward me so she wouldn't bear witness, it had seemed the situation was getting more and more out of hand as even more people showed up. The priest walked into the room flummoxed, followed by another heavy-set man.

"Have you all lost your minds in the Lord's house?!" The priest shook in anger as he waved the holy book around.

"You going to pay, you son of a bitch," Jonah said through gritted teeth.

"What I's-..."

"Shut your filthy mouth!" Jonah yelled out, cutting off Dan Jr. before he could fully get his words out. "You're going to pay you fat poor excuse for a human being!" Jonah's eyes were slowly turning red, then a tear slid down his face. "You hired those thugs to block the road so Talon couldn't get here."

"I'm surprised you were able to get through." Dan Jr. said with a chuckle.

"What the hell is he talking about Dan?!" Daniel Senior shouted at his son. I could only imagine what was going through Senior's mind.

"Your pig of a son hired men to block the road from Talon's land to the town. We were only able to get through when Talon made an opening for us to get by. He stayed to ensure Nick's and my safety." Jonah's voice trembled. My ears started to pound as I took in the words Jonah said, panic flooded through me. The possibility of Talon's demise was too much to bear. We were supposed to get married, and though I would have wanted a lengthy courtship before we reached this stage, I would not have changed it or had it any other way. My heart pounded painfully in my chest.

"Jonah… where's Talon?" My voice cracked due to the tears I was trying not to shed. I couldn't hide the fear in my voice even as I tried to ignore the slow breakage of my heart while I waited for the answer.

"I… I don't know… he told me to leave him behind. I tried to make him reconsider but trying to make sure me and Nick were safe was his priority." Jonah responded solemnly.

"What the hell do you mean you don't know?" My voice started to change from sadness to anger. "Wasn't his first priority supposed to be being here?!"

"Yes, but this ass ruined it!" Jonah yelled back. I could see Jonah slightly adding more pressure to the trigger.

"Jonah, he's not worth the kill." The general store owner emerged from the stairs. They stared at each other intensely, an unspoken conversation between them. Jonah slowly removed the gun from Dan Jr.'s head, though Dan Jr. was putting on a brave face I heard the long and loud exhale come from him.

"Son let's get our asses out of here, you've done enough for the day," Daniel said with authority. With Dan Jr. still clutching his stomach he exited the room without another word, his father and riflemen close behind him. There was a prolonged silence that followed, I guess everyone wanted to make sure the Dans were gone before speaking freely.

"So, what are we going to do?" Jonah said, being the first to break the silence. John turned around and walked toward the window with his hands behind his back.

"We wait…" John responded as he stared down at the town. Seconds went on to minutes, minutes seemed like hours, and yet nothing. John and Rachael stood perfectly still at the window, Jonah and the rest of the men stood leaning against the wall making small talk, and as for myself, I sat in a chair to rest my feet and mind. All the worrying I was doing was taking its toll on me and draining my energy.

"Talon! Talon! Talon!" Rachael shouted, drawing everyone's attention other than John's. I quickly got up from my chair instantly regretting it as the dizzy spell took over. Everyone rushed down the stairs, leaving John to help me follow behind. I couldn't blame them for their excitement and relief. As soon as I reached the worship room Talon came through the open door. My smile diminished slightly as I took in the state of him. Talon clutched his bow, his shirt ripped at the shoulders and covered in blood, strands of hair fell in front of his face amongst speckles of blood, and he had swollen knuckles. Rachael ran up to Talon despite all of this and gave him a hug, Talon kneeled on one knee to deepen the hug. Everyone except for John and myself gathered around Talon giving him hugs and pats on the back with gleeful smiles and well wishes.

"I need to get married now guys," Talon said with a smile, warming my heart.

"I'm glad you made it child," John said to Talon. Talon nodded his head then focused his attention on me, he engulfed me in his arms and tears streamed down my face.

"Let's get married..." Talon whispered in my ear, sending shivers down my spine and a tingle in other places. I stepped back from him and stared into his beautiful sun-kissed eyes and nodded in agreement. We aligned ourselves in front of the pulpit and the priest opened his bible.

"May you join hands." The priest instructed and we did what we were told.

"Sorry, I couldn't come better dressed." Talon quipped.

"You're here, that's all that matters," I replied with a smile. The priest went on with his words of love a devotion, my attention was drawn away when I witnessed for a second a painful expression on Talon's face.

"Not to be a bother." Talon interrupted the priest, "But can we move to the important part, you know me being late and all." The priest looked at Talon with a hint of confusion but decided to comply with a nod.

"Talon Edgar Thomas, would you take this woman to be your wife, to have and to hold, through sickness-..." Talon motioned with his hand for the priest to hurry up.

"I do," Talon answered without the completion of the question. The Priest looking slightly annoyed cleared his throat.

"Jessamine Lunetta James, will you?" The priest asked almost sending me into a laughing fit.

This is it girl, no turning back now.

"I do." I replied with a smile that I couldn't contain. The priest placed his hand over ours.

"You two are now, and forever more, husband and wife. You sir may share a kiss with your bride." Talon leaned forward and kissed me, it was a simple kiss but one that was filled with so much hope and promise, it did not fail to light a fire I thought I never had. It was forceful, it was soft, and deafening. As we parted I finally noticed all the clapping and cheering that was coming from our family and friends, but the happy faces soon turned into faces of fear. When I turned to look back Talon was falling to his knees. Panic roared through me; Talon had fallen so hard that the wooden floorboards cracked beneath him. John caught him and eased him down onto the floor so he wouldn't fall harder. I carefully kneeled next to Talon grabbing his hand to show I was there for him. I had no idea what was wrong. John felt around Talon's body.

"Here... and... in my back." Talon said in exasperated breaths, he pointed toward his lower abdomen. "Get... me... home."

"Charles!" John yelled out. The burly Charles hooked his arms around Talon's upper body and knees and with some effort lifted

Talon off the floor.

"We need to get the doctor!" The man named Nick yelled out.

"Forget about that Nick, that ship has long sailed," Jonah replied.

"Put him in my wagon and let's hurry!" The man named Nick yelled out. Everything was happening so fast that I wasn't sure if I could keep up. My heart was pounding and the dizziness I got every time I was under too much stress was creeping in. The only thing I was able to do was to hold my crying daughter and fight the will to shed tears, I was not accustomed to seeing Talon this way. He always seemed like he was undefeatable, I mean I only saw him truly fight once and he nearly killed a man just by choking him with little effort, but those times gave me the impression that Talon was no ordinary man. I managed to gather myself and tail everyone else who was following Charles, John stood by my side. When we exited the church, people were gathered around to see what the commotion was. When I looked past the crowd, I saw Dan Jr. and though he was a little battered he had a smile on his face. Daniel on the other hand, who was standing next to his son, did not look so happy. He looked genuinely concerned. I shook my head and refocused my attention on Talon, nothing else mattered at this point.

The ride back to the farm seemed longer than usual. All I was able to do was hold my new husband's hand and watch as he took ragged breaths, fighting for his life. I could see one of the wounds in Talon's lower abdomen, John was trying to treat the wound even as the wagon bumped around, and Jonah was applying pressure to the wound on Talon's back. I fought all my tears, but some still managed to slip through. Charles volunteered to hold Rachael and keep her preoccupied in the front of the wagon with Nick as he manned the wagon. Suddenly the wagon came to a jerking halt. "My father in heaven...." I heard Nick say.

"What is it? We need to hurry!" John shouted.

"Mr. Tao sir... look!" Charles said. When I looked up, I saw that Charles was covering Rachael's eyes, in my own curiosity I sought out what had had us delayed. A gasp escaped me as I took in the horrible sight. Men lay across the road dead each having a different type of wound, some left with arrows in their chests. Splatters of blood were everywhere, I nearly became sick.

"Don't feel too bad for them, they are the ones that did this to your husband," Jonah said rubbing my shoulders.

"I don't care if a dragon came from the heavens, move it!" John shouted louder than we ever heard him, startling Nick out of his disgust at the grizzly scene. He snapped the reins for the horse to gallop, neither of us looking back for another inspection.

When we finally made it to the house, minute by minute Talon was becoming more and more unresponsive. "I'll grab everything that is needed, get Talon to his room!" Tao shouted orders hopping out of the wagon and briskly walking into the house. Charles handed Rachael to Jonah, Charles was the only one strong enough to lift Talon alone and I was thankful he was here. There was no telling how long it would have taken us to get Talon into the wagon let alone out of it without hurting him. Before I was able to follow Jonah and Charles into the house, I was tapped on the shoulder by Nick.

"Pardon me Madam, but I will not be able to stay. I pray the master will be well, but I must report the situation about those men to the barracks to protect your new husband. I will return in the morning with paperwork for you concerning the business and how you play a part in it." I gave Nick a nod just to say I understood what he was saying, and he tipped his hat in farewell. I decided to play with Rachael while the men saw to Talon, not only for her sake but for my own as well. My mind was frantic with worry, and it was becoming harder and harder to smile genuinely.

"Mama, is Talon, otay?" Rachael asked hugging her doll. I tried to give her a reassuring smile.

"Talon will be fine my love." I managed to say, trying to sound believable and failing, but Rachael seemed to accept it either way. She looked tired, so I decided to lay her down for her nap. In only a few minutes Rachael was asleep, but the worry didn't leave her face, her brows furrowed as she held on tightly to her doll. When it was safe to leave the room without waking her, I headed straight for Talon's room. I was about to open the door when a small revelation stopped me. *I've never been in Talon's room before.* Renewing my strength to handle the situation I readied myself and turned the knob, but it wouldn't budge. Perplexed, I knocked on the door wondering why the secrecy. A few short seconds John opened the door but not in a way to invite me in, the door was cracked open, only allowing me to see him. I started to become vexed.

"John, I want to see my husband." I said, putting authority in my voice. John made a long sigh; he looked like he was in deep conflict.

"I... I can't let you in." John hesitantly said in a near whisper. I was starting to get more worried and angrier; I steadied my breath so my voice wouldn't shake.

"I am his wife now. Step aside." I said, pushing the door open and John let me. When I walked through the door Jonah jumped to his feet rushing over to me blocking my view of Talon, and Charles obstructed my view further with needle and thread in his hands. I looked at everyone suspiciously, I felt they were keeping something from me. Something they didn't want me to see. From what little I saw Talon had his shirt off revealing a muscle filled abdomen, but I was puzzled by the dirty used bandage that was cut underneath Talon.

"What's with the bandages around his chest? Was he hurt there as well?"

"Now Jessamine-...." Jonah started but I placed my finger in the air cutting him off.

"Jonah... move." I demanded.

"Jessamine it's nothing on you, in fact, we are doing this for you-..."

"What YOU can do for me is move out of my bloody way, so I can see my husband." I cut Jonah off once again. Jonah still stood in my way timidly.

"Jessamine..."

"MOVE YOUR ARSE!!" I shouted, pretty sure I was startling everyone in the room.

"Jonah let her by, I believe it's time she knows the truth," John stated quietly and exited the room. Jonah's shoulders fell in defeat.

"All I ask Jessamine is that you try to understand," Jonah said stepping aside.

"Understand what?" I asked but he didn't respond. I walked slowly toward Talon; Charles and I hadn't had the chance to speak to one another yet, but his dark brown eyes were pleading with me. Charles moved out my way as well and when I saw Talon's chest, I gasped out loud, moving backward and hitting the wall. There were small breasts marked by the old bandage. I covered my mouth, I couldn't believe it, I must have been in shock because I couldn't breathe, I couldn't speak. When I looked around at Charles and Jonah all they did was hang their heads low, not looking me in the eye. I suddenly felt anger, an anger I never felt before in my life even after everything I had gone through. "You all kept this from me...?" I asked, tears falling down my cheeks. Jonah tried to move closer to grab my hand, but I snatched it away, I felt betrayed beyond measure, I wanted no one to touch me. I glared at him, warning him with my eyes. Charles grabbed Jonah by the shoulders, pulling him further away. My anger turned into rage. I wanted to shake Talon out of his unresponsive state and get answers, but I couldn't. So, I decided to go to second best. I walked out of Talon's room slamming the door behind me.

Somebody is going to give me answers.

I thought as tears fell continuously.

JOHN

Chapter 30

I pulled out the strongest white wine I owned that I kept hidden away in the cooking room, it was Talon's gift for me from my homeland. I thought I would never taste its sweetness again, I vowed to save it for my last drink before my death or something else very serious. Something serious came first. I grabbed a teacup for my wine then sat at the table and waited. I poured the wine into my cup after I heard a thump upstairs. I looked up for a second and sighed, swallowing a big gulp of wine. I let out a long grumbly exhale as the liquid burned down my throat.

I only hoped that Jessamine had fainted. I shook my head in slight disappointment pouring more wine and taking a drink. *I tried to avoid this. Why didn't Talon listen!?* I heard the slam of a door and footsteps getting louder as they got closer to me. I sighed again pouring more wine, waiting for the storm to come. Hands slammed on the table in front of me, my teacup fell over. "How could you... no, all of you, bloody deceive me?!" Jessamine said viciously. I looked into the cold grey eyes of Jessamine, I saw hurt and pain, old and new. I picked up my teacup and poured more wine.

"We did not want it to be this way, I told Talon many times to be honest. I begged Talon to tell you, in fear of what you might think but Talon didn't." I took another drink; I was starting to feel the effects of the wine too fast.

"What fear John?! What could I possibly think that would cause him... I mean her, to not be herself!" Jessamine shouted. I got up from my chair in one swift movement and with such force, the chair fell from behind me. I slammed my hands on the table just as she had done, meeting her eye to eye.

"The fear that you may think Talon a monster! And you will not call Talon she, Talon worked hard to rid of his feminine features, respect that." I snapped, trying to calm my tone. I could see the battle raging inside her looking through the window of her eyes, so many emotions all at once. Jessamine let out a huff before crossing her arms in front of her chest.

"Fine, but what about me? Didn't I have the right to know, I mean for God's sake we're bloody married!" Jessamine's voice cracked a bit from holding back tears and she pinched the bridge of her nose. "Well, I guess not since it is not valid." My brows creased inwards at her statement.

"Your marriage is what you want it to be, no one can make it invalid but you. As I said earlier, I tried to make Talon tell you before you two were married." I said softly, trying to calm the situation. Jessamine was pregnant and I could not have her over-stressed. I watched Jessamine begin to pace back and forth the length of the cook room, tears emerging again from her eyes.

"Why didn't YOU tell me?" she asked, still pacing. I sighed again, pouring the last bit of wine into my cup, I knew the answer I was going to give her was not one she wanted to hear.

"It was not my secret to tell, just like it wasn't Lisa's secret. You said it yourself." I responded then took another drink. "Talon has been hiding, not living life to the fullest in fear people will find out," I spoke walking to the pantry and back to the table with another jug of wine.

"No! If I must deal with this sober, you're not going to have another drink in front of me!" Jessamine demanded, grabbing the jug away from me and putting it beyond my reach. I stared at her for a moment before shrugging knowing that I wouldn't win against an angry pregnant woman. I picked up the chair that had fallen from under me and sat in it, again stroking my long chin beard as I watched the young woman pace some more. "Bloody hell is that what that Lisa girl wanted to tell me?" I bobbed my head yes in agreement keeping steady stroking motions. "How did she find out?" Jessamine asked sitting in the chair across from me.

"Talon thought Lisa could be trusted, that Lisa's love should be enough to accept Talon for who Talon was. As you can already guess, it wasn't." I answered with a bit of sadness recalling that day.

"John, how can I accept this? I trusted Talon, you, and everyone else, I feel so betrayed. And what about Rachael? She admires Talon and loves everyone that has entered her life, it was so hard for her before we escaped. Now that she is here, I can only imagine that she does not want to leave, how could I possibly tell her about Talon? What would I say?" Jessamine said wiping a stray tear that escaped her eye. I reached over and grabbed Jessamine's hand giving it a small squeeze.

"Child, children don't see the world the way grownups see it, all they care about is who loves and cares for them. People are going to raise their children however they want, but you don't have to make Rachael be like this ugly world or the next little ones-..."

"Bloody hell, what did you just say?!" Jessamine shouted in confusion, cutting me off. I giggled at her surprised expression.

"You are bigger than a woman with just one child inside them," I responded.

"Or maybe a big baby."

"For your sake, I hope not." I quipped. I got up from my seat feeling the sharp pain that plagues my heart more and more each day, though I kept my face as neutral as possible. "Jessamine, forgive us for keeping such information from you, but I beg that you'll try to understand. Lisa destroyed many chances for Talon to trust another woman with his life."

"Lisa hasn't told anyone yet; wouldn't you say that Talon trusts her just a little bit?" Jessamine asked with caution.

"You call someone being torn apart by a secret trustworthy?"

Jessamine shrugged at my question. "You don't see Talon being attracted to women strange?"

I shrugged at her question. "I call it love, nothing more." I placed my hand on her shoulder as the pain flowed in large waves throughout my body. "You need time to think it over. Jonah will take care of Talon along with Charles. You don't have to understand everything now." I gave her an assuring pat and left the room.

"I'm still angry!" Jessamine yelled after me. I couldn't help but laugh.

"I know."

JESSAMINE

Chapter 31

I was sorely mistaken if I thought waiting for Talon to come home was hell. Waiting for Talon to wake up was an inferno. Talon had not been unconscious since we arrived home, and it's already been six days. Six days since my wedding, six days since I found out Talon was a woman, and six days I've been mad and worried all at one time. I wasn't sure I could take on any other stress while I was with child. There was a lot of thinking I had done in those six days; I had come to terms with the idea that no one was trying to hurt or deceive me, and that John was right. It wasn't his secret to tell. Though I was still mad, I understood. The question was what I was going to do about the situation. And the answer, I just didn't know. It seemed all the good outweighed the bad, there was only one bad. Everything about us was good, Talon took care of both me and Rachael without asking for anything in return, accepted the fact I was pregnant, defended me to no end, and kept us warm and fed. But could I really be with a woman? I never thought too hard about it until now, and I didn't want to run away, but I'm not sure what to do either.

Jonah tried talking to me about it, but I ignored him. I could tell I hurt him a bit, but I wanted to stay mad. Of course, I had to see him around, he and Charles had been practically living here to help around the farm and take care of Talon. At night I sat stroking Rachael's head as she slept, she was another who was also worried sick about Talon and the worry wore her out more than usual. "Should we leave?" I asked, knowing I wasn't going to get an answer, and if I was to get one, I knew she would probably say no or ask why. With much still on my mind I left Rachael's room. It was way past midnight and the moon showed itself beyond the trees. For some odd reason, I felt very different at night, like I was stronger, more healed. I couldn't really find the words to describe it. Before I knew it, I was in front of Talon's door. I stared at the knob, frozen, my mind told me to go back to my room and call it night. But my heart had made me twist the knob and enter. Four candles dimly lit the room, I was able to see Talon's silhouette lying on the bed. Talon's hands were placed on his stomach, his hair braided in a single braid, his chest barely rising and falling with shallow breaths. My heart broke seeing Talon like this.

John had been right about one thing, Talon succeeded in ridding herself of nearly all her feminine characteristics. Without a shirt on, I could see the muscles that seemed to flex on their own with little effort. In this ruthless world, women had a hard time holding their own. *If Talon would have lived as a woman, I don't think Talon would be the person I...* "No, I will not think that way. Not yet. You still lied to me, I have no room for such emotions right now." I loudly whispered, stopping myself from admitting the impossible. I knew I was not going to get the answer I sought, not when Talon was like this. I exited the room more conflicted than when I entered.

* * *

"Morning good people!" I heard Nick coming through the door shouting. I wasn't familiar with Nick or his role in Talon's life, I didn't appreciate him just strolling into the house like he owned it either. I was sitting at the table sipping tea before I had to take care of the work on the farm. "Madam it is good to see you again, I have everything you need and will give you a brief lecture on what your duties are now that the young master is unavailable," Nick said pulling out stacks of paper from his side bag.

"What do you mean duties?" I asked, taking another sip of tea. Nick sat in front of me setting up his ink and fountain pen on the right side of the stacks of papers.

"Before the master married you, he had set up papers if anything happened to him, he would leave you in charge of everything as long as Sir John doesn't object. The money, business, and the farm are under your control until the master is able to resume his duties." Nick finished passing the ledger for me to see. "This book here is-..."

"The shipment details, dates, departure, arrivals, how much cargo, and our gross earnings and loss. Am I correct?" I cut in studying the book.

"Well madam, I'm impressed not all women are as enlightened as you. I was worried that our young master had made a mistake." I looked up from the book at Nick with a perked brow at his comment. When Nick finally looked at me, he was quickly startled.

"No offense madam, just not used to women being well educated in business. Not like I never heard of it before, I just never seen it with my own eyes. But I should have trusted the young master to know better. He really knew what he was doing when he chose you."

"Nick, shut it please," I said continuing to read the ledger.

"Very well madam," Nick said clearing his throat and organizing the rest of the papers. From what I had read business was good for the most part, but some things troubled me.

"Nick you still haven't explained who you are or better introduce yourself to me since my wedding day. I know it was hectic." I pointed out grabbing his readied fountain pen and starting to mark on the ledger. "I figure that you handle Talon's business but what role do you actually play?"

"Well, madam-…"

"Please call me Jessamine, how many ships does he have?" This was not how I pictured my morning; I was supposed to relax but doing something I was actually familiar with piqued my interest more. Talon was still not awake and everyone including myself was becoming nervous. We did our best to make sure he was hydrated and chopped up food so finely that he could swallow, which took a lot of effort because Jonah was trying to wake him up enough so he could swallow. It got to the point that John made a straw that was flexible but strong enough to go down Talon's throat to get food in. I couldn't watch it, so I left the room whenever he had to.

"Forty ships but now we had just added some private trains in the east in the Americas." I looked up at him amazed.

"Bloody hell, that's more than my father ever had." My father only had ten ships he was going to get more once we had moved from England to the West, but he didn't live long enough to see it fulfilled. "How could Talon own so many ships?"

"In Talon's leadership, he had only required ten ships, it was Mr. Thomas his father who established the first thirty," Nick answered with a warm smile.

"But that many?" I asked even more forcefully, feeling as if Nick was hiding something.

"Master Thomas was a well-connected man, beyond that is not in my right to say." I hummed my understanding. I laid the book flatly on the table so Nick could see.

"From what I see productivity is good, but we can gain more if we sell merchandise that hasn't been sold yet to smaller merchants. If we cut them a deal, they might take it since they could use it amongst themselves more than our big buyers."

When I finished pointing at the areas that needed work, we were left with a surplus. I looked at Nick satisfied with my assessment. Nick stared back for several seconds before clearing his throat.

"I won't have any more doubt in your abilities from this day forward madam," Nick said then walked to the stove to pour himself some tea. We worked on a few more details and plans for the shipments; Nick was ready to leave, and I was ready to take a nap.

"See to it that we also hire some men to help around the farm, I have a feeling we are going to need it," I advised Nick.

"You know the young master will be furious to find people other than the ones he trusts on his farm," Nick replied warningly.

"We don't know how long Talon will be out and with Jonah and Charles mostly taking care of Talon it only leaves me and John to handle the workload. We are not Talon, we could not get the heavy lifting done on our own." Nick gave me a nod of understanding before tipping his hat to me.

"It shall be done, madam." Nick was out the door shortly after. I stretched my arms above my head with a yawn, naps were a leisure I couldn't afford, not with Rachael running around. *Wait, where was Rachael?* I knew that John had gone out early this morning with Jonah and Charles, and though I had been sitting at this table for the last 4 hours, I did not see any sign of Rachael. I walked up the stairs slowly, with my stomach getting bigger and my ankles getting more swollen, it was becoming harder and harder to maintain my balance. When I made it up the stairs, I checked Rachael's room first and walked in to find it empty. I checked the bathing room and didn't find her. I checked my room, and she wasn't there. I was starting to panic when I thought of the only place Rachael would be. I went toward Talon's room and found his door open a bit. I opened it fully to find Rachael lying next to Talon with her head on his chest sleeping. I sighed in relief but my heart broke and it took more strength than I could imagine not to cry. She would have never laid next to her own father in such a way without it being forced upon her. A sense of finality resonated within me and at that moment I knew that I couldn't take Rachael away from all this, this place and the people had already become a part of her in a big way.

❋ ❋ ❋

It had been over 3 weeks and Talon still had not awakened. If this ongoing trend kept going, I would start to fear the worst. I was still upset but my anger's focus had started to shift from being mad about the discovery to being mad because Talon wouldn't bloody wake up. Every morning I would sit at the table with tea, this morning I decided to cook breakfast for everyone. Nothing lifts the spirits more than a good meal. In the middle of mixing eggs, I heard a knock at the door, and I turned to look. I wasn't expecting anyone, and Nicolas wasn't due for another week, though I would send him a parcel of all my decisions. I walked to the door and opened it; I hid my surprise as I found Lisa on the porch playing with her fingers nervously. "Good morning Mrs. Thomas, that is correct, right? You got married?" Lisa greeted me. I looked at her skeptically, I was pretty sure the whole town knew I was married. I was conflicted with so many emotions just by her mere presence at the front door, this was the woman that was the root of my current problem when it came to Talon's true gender.

"Yes, we are married. Call me Jessamine by the way, what can I do for you?" I spoke to Lisa through the netted door, placing my hand on my lower back to help support myself.

"There's been rumors that Talon massacred men but needed to be carried out the church. I was just wondering if he's all right?" Lisa asked timidly. I couldn't help but raise a brow, tilting my head to the side slightly.

"Why so concerned Lisa?" I couldn't hold back my irritation. Lisa began to fiddle with her fingers which made my irritation grow.

"I was just worried, sometimes Talon seems as if nothing can stop him, and other times, I feel like he is in over his head," Lisa said shyly.

It was at this moment my temper boiled over; I roughly pushed the net door open stepping out of the house and closing the main door behind me. I was so aggressive with my actions that Lisa stepped back a couple of steps. "How rude!" Lisa placed her hand over her chest appalled. I scoffed. "Rude? You want to bloody talk about rude? This comes from the woman that sat on her high horse and called Talon a monster for who he is, now you have caused him to hide from the people who care about him!" I began to shout; it made sense for me to close the door if I didn't want the whole house to know. But the small smirk Lisa gave me made me even more angry.

"So, you know. You know your marriage is invalid." Lisa turned her back on me, facing the tree line. "That's why I couldn't be with her, my whole entire life wouldn't be valid. No children, no family, just her and that was not the life I wanted.' Lisa sighed to herself. All the nonsense she was spewing was making me go cross-eyed.

"At least you had honesty, you had peace of mind to know he will always tell you the truth." Lisa whipped her body to face me.

"Why do you keep calling her a he, if you know she is not a man!" Lisa sounded frustrated. I shook my head and laughed.

"Are you daft? I'm going to respect what Talon wants to be called."

"Don't feed into the lies Jessamine, the sooner she can conduct herself as a proper lady the better," Lisa said as if she was having the last word turning her back on me once more. I grabbed her shoulder and twisted her around hard enough so she could face me. At this point, I was sick and tired of her standing around with her nose in the air.

"Are you blind or are you just bloody mad? Have you seen the sheer size of Talon? Talon will never be a proper 'lady' and if he was, no man would survive a day!" I said, seeing that I had hurt her a little, I crossed my arms across my chest unapologetic. Silence ensued between us as Lisa rubbed her shoulder. "Why do you want so badly for Talon to be a proper 'lady' anyway?" I asked.

"Don't you see? Talon is hurt because people think she is a man! She is fragile just like us." Lisa solemnly. I couldn't help but laugh and walk the length of the porch, I gradually pondered why I was having this ridiculous conversation when I knew I shouldn't be.

"May I ask what's so funny?"

When I turned to face her, her face was scrunched up in frustration, and I laughed more. "Just thinking it was good Talon didn't get duped into marrying you. Not only are you small-minded, but you're also daft as rocks. I could never think of Talon so lowly. Talon is stronger than any man I know, he is kinder than any man I know, I have gotten more care from Talon than I ever received from my ex-husband!" My lip started to tremble from unshed tears and anger.

"Your-..."

"I'm not done! I was the one that was fragile, broken, and I thought I was irreparable until little by little I began to heal. The only thing that makes Talon fragile is what you've done to him." I pointed my finger at her chest. I stopped myself from revealing too much of my feelings, she didn't need to know, and I wasn't ready to admit it on my own. Lisa's jaw dropped.

"You're in love with that monster?! It's a moral sin!" Lisa screeched.

"I don't have to explain anything to you, you twat! You only want Talon to be something he's not because you're still in love with him and you can't deal with your own sin!" I stormed past

Lisa and her face of disbelief, opening the doors to get inside my house. I took one step in. "Good day, Lisa." I said without eye contact and closed the door behind me, I leaned against the door for support taking breaths to calm myself. I was filled with conflicting emotions that I couldn't deal with right now. Lisa had angered me beyond reason, mostly because she made me face something I wasn't ready to face. I was in love, and no one could convince me that it was a sin. I huffed at myself, "Bloody hell."

* * *

Five months had passed, and the baby was due soon. Though I tried to do the housework and other tasks, it was becoming more and more difficult with this protruding belly in the way of everything including my line of sight. During the months Talon was still unresponsive and each day more it was breaking my heart. I had forgiven him for the lies, all I wanted was to hear his voice again. Nick came by from time to time to help with the business aspect, he did hire help with the farming, which I deeply appreciated. There were some days I asked myself, 'Who am I to be running things that don't belong to me?' But John would come around like he already knew what I was thinking.

"Everything that is Talon's is now yours, remember that Talon trusted you with it even before I did." John would say, ending all my doubts but still leaving me with more to think about. I couldn't enjoy my new marriage, and a deep hate for Dan Jr. festered because of it. I never really got the chance to get to know the Talon underneath the shield of fear. I sighed to myself as I finished the sewing of the baby clothes I was mending; it broke my heart that Talon was missing the baby kicks and movements and most importantly I feared he'd miss the birth. Rachael sat next to me on the porch just looking out amongst the trees, I had her with me instead of playing with her toys in Talon's room.

This was worse than the time Talon was gone. Rachael wasn't the only one who would find their way into Talon's room, there were nights I'd sit on the chair next to Talon's bedside even though it was bad for my back. John would come in and make sure I made it into my own bed.

"Come on Rachael, time for a nap." After putting Rachael to bed, I went to the kitchen to make myself a pot of tea. Jonah and Charles had gone out to hunt while Rachael, John, and I stayed behind to keep watch on Talon. Being that it was the middle of the day the workers already had their orders. I sat at the table while I waited for the water to boil, there was paperwork that I was taking a break from and decided to sew for a little while. Our income had increased, and we were able to rid ourselves of the surplus making room for new products. Footsteps coming from the weapons room stole my attention, it sounded like the person was staggering and the only other adult was John. I made the effort to get up from my seat and walked toward the kitchen doorway. When I peeked out into the hall leading to the weapons room, I found John leaning against the wall with blood coming from his mouth.

JOHN

Chapter 32

I heard Jessamine's voice shouting my name but soon she was overshadowed by the flaming pain throbbing throughout my whole body, "John! John! what's happening?!" My vision was able to clear just enough to see Jessamine propping me against the wall so I wouldn't fall. I could tell she was panicking by the sound of her voice. I felt the blood coming from my gut up to my throat, I spat out the iron-tasting substance and tried to focus my energy to speak.

"Take me.... to my room." I managed to say. I could already feel my lungs working over their limit. Jessamine placed my arm over her shoulders and supported my weight by wrapping her arm around my lower back. I tried to walk along with her, but my body was slowly betraying me, we stumbled side to side before reaching the stairs.

"John listen, I'm the only one here and I'm pregnant, you're going to have to help me help you," Jessamine said still holding me up. I raised my head so I could see where I was going and with what little strength I could muster, placed my free hand on the stair rail. With each step I took, more blood seeped out from my nose and mouth. Seeing this, Jessamine worked harder to pull me up. We made it up the stairs and to my room, which was next to Rachael's. Jessamine twisted the knob and kicked open the door. We stumbled in and Jessamine threw me on my bed, even my soft bed caused immense pain. When I was finally able to turn my body around and look at Jessamine, she seemed as if she was bewildered looking around my room. Then I figured out on my own that this was the first time she was ever in my room.

"Jessamine…" I managed to speak past the pain, and she promptly snapped out of her daze and left the room. I struggled to sit up, "that's not what I needed her to do." I whispered to myself, Jessamine came back with a couple of towels and a basin. "Jessamine… the top… drawer," I said setting up my legs to sit cross-legged. Jessamine quickly put the basin on the floor and did what I told her, pulling from the drawer a pouch. "And the scroll on the wall."

"What am I supposed to do with this stuff?" Jessamine asked frantically.

"Follow the picture…. on the scroll… use the needles, hurry." Jessamine opened the scroll.

"You want me to stick needles in your back?!" Jessamine asked, I shook my head yes trying to keep myself from spitting out more blood. Jessamine sat behind me, and I could sense her unsureness; she lifted my shirt till it was up by my shoulders. It was then I felt a hard prick in my upper shoulder, causing me to flinch.

"Softer….ease it in, don't just stab me," I said through gritted teeth. As Jessamine placed each needle in my back, I felt the inferno inside fade slowly.

"John, your blood." Jessamine seemed frightened.

"I know, that's what happens when you release blood that is poisoned," I responded, finally able to breathe.

"Poisoned?"

"Thank you, child, I would not have made it without you," I said feeling the needle in the final spot. My body was weak and ready for rest, if I fell asleep it would be all day. Jessamine wet the towels in the basin and started to clean me up. I could have laughed at being treated with such care, but it would be too much right now.

"What happened? Why are you like this and does Talon know?" Jessamine interrogated. "What did I just do to you?"

I held my hand up at the assault. "One at a time, I'm healing," I exclaimed trying to have a peaceful moment. "First give me the rest of the needles." Jessamine did as I asked and I added a few more needles around my chest, abdomen, and one on my forehead. I let the relief wash over me. "You almost got me you wretched thing."

"Um, what wretched thing? You're not telling me anything?" Jessamine sounded frustrated. I looked up at her, and Jessamine's full-moon eyes glared.

"You're very impatient," I grumbled.

"What do you expect?! You're bleeding everywhere and you were half-dead a minute ago, I need an explanation!" Jessamine scolded me.

"All right, all right." I conceded. I realized that Jessamine wouldn't be so easy to get rid of after all this. "I need more needles in my back and while you do that, I'll tell you the story." Jessamine held her hand out and I placed the pouch in her hand. "Just follow the picture." I waited for her to situate herself and when I felt her start, I used it as a cue to the begin as well. "I was poisoned as a young man. I was traveling with my fellow comrades during the last trail of our training. We were tired and hungry; so low on our supplies that we were very close to fighting each other to eat. But then some alluring ladies captured our attention, they promised us food, drink, and a good place to rest. To us hungry souls it was a blessing, we didn't think much of it." I relished a few breaths before continuing, "We ate and drank like kings, I had to convince my best friend Ting Ping just to relax and enjoy himself. He had his doubts and for good reason, but after a while, he started to enjoy himself. I should have followed his warning."

"Warning?" Jessamine asked curiously.

"Yes, Ting Ping felt that it was too good to be true and they gave all they offered without asking for anything in return. To him it didn't make sense, I should have trusted his words. But I was young and the little bit of freedom we had under the thumb of our master felt good. We were sleeping until a loud gong went off frightening us out of restfulness. It was a master standing before us, I remember what he said like it was yesterday. 'Like pigs waiting for slaughter.' We sat confused at his statement, we were all trying to sober up and his presence meant only one thing. We had failed. He had informed us that we had been poisoned and was disappointed that all his students were going to die. He stared at both me and Ting Ping when he said it. My other comrades squealed their apologies and begged for their lives, but all our master did was grace them with a smile that spread fear among them. He slayed them for being cowards, but Ting Ping and I did not beg or cry. We stood before him vowing we would not die, vowing we would live and continue as his disciples. He just stared at us, as if he saw our very souls dwindling, then he walked away. Me and Ting Ping made it back home, looking day in and day out for an antidote. We tried using less strength and energy to stay alive. Six days later I was fading, and my body started to self-destruct like how you saw today, Ping was in the same condition. I couldn't hang on any longer and I accepted my fate to die, I had lost consciousness. When I woke Ping was already dead." My shoulders shook as the tears flowed. "He traded his life for my own. Instructions on how to coexist with the poison inside me were left behind, I was to live to find the antidote. For the first time in my life, I begged my master to save him, but it fell on deaf ears. I blame myself every day for his death. If I could have held on a little longer, he... he would still be alive."

JESSAMINE

Chapter 33

    "Two questions. Why do you blame yourself?" As much as I was enjoying the needle thing I was doing, I couldn't help but be bothered by the self-loathing John was having. I kind of felt guilty having a good time while John was in sorrow. But this needle thing piqued my interest.

"If I had been stronger, if I had been wiser, he would still be alive," John responded. I looked at him callously.

"John everyone is responsible for their own bloody actions, and Ping decided that your life was more important than his own, Ping decided that."

"I had accepted my demise while Ping held on to hope, he was like a brother to me, and I failed him. Now I failed Talon as well and I can't do a thing about it just like I couldn't with Ping Ting." Suddenly my hand slapped John's face as if it was beyond my control. John looked at me after my hand had connected, it seemed as if he was trying to register what happened. My hand throbbed in pain.

"I'm sorry. No, I'm not sorry. My husband has been half-dead for months! You don't think I feel helpless, confused, afraid? I can't even scream at him for all the heartache." I covered my face with my hands wiping the tears away.

"Jessamine I-..." I held up my finger to stop John from speaking.

"You are not going to sit here feeling sorry for yourself, you are going to get up and help me with this bloody farm, be Uncle Tao, and make sure I don't combust when I have this baby."

"Babies…" John said quietly.

"Oh whatever, do you understand what I'm saying?" John looked down in defeat. "I'll take that as your admission to concede. Now, next question… what is this needling thing I was I was doing to you?" John made a loud sigh.

"What you did is called acupuncture, you can use it to heal and or kill. The needles can touch the nerves in the body and manipulate them."

"So, you used one of those needles to make me vomit that night, yes?" John shook his head, hiding his face. I pinched the bridge of my nose, fighting the urge to slap him once more. My chest suddenly tightened at the sudden realization. "Can acupuncture help wake a person?" John looked up at me with the same realization. "Perché non hai provato questa merda prima?!" I yelled with my hands on my hips. John gave me a puzzled look.

"Did you just speak Italian and profanity?" John asked.

"What's with all the blood on the floor? Why do you look so upset?" Jonah asked peeking into the room.

"This old man might have a way to wake Talon and hasn't tried it." I answered. Jonah walked into the room further to look at John.

"Why are you acting like a pin cushion?" Jonah asked John with more confusion on his face.

"Jonah shut up. John, get dressed, and meet me in Talon's room," I demanded.

"Jessamine, we don't know if it'll work." John said.

"If you don't want to try, then teach me how to do acupuncture properly and I'll do it myself." Jonah looked back and forth between me and John. John and I stared at each other until he relented.

"I will do it. I will try acupuncture on Talon and teach you after you have your babies," John said with his head down.

"Will you stop saying there's more than one?!"

"I wouldn't be surprised; you look like you about'a pop." Jonah added. I left with the thought that being in Talon's room was much better than being around them, at least in Talon's room it's quiet. I looked out the corridor's window.

"It's only some time past noon and I already want to sleep for three days."

The next day, Charles, John, and I gathered in Talon's room while Jonah entertained Rachael much to her dismay. "I need to remove the bandages. Will you be alright with this Jessamine?" John asked, staring at me.

I was apprehensive for a moment before nodding my head yes, I turned around to respect Talon's privacy.

"You know Talon is your husband right, you can look at him." John teased.

"Ha, ha, very funny," I said, rolling my eyes. Soon curiosity took over and I looked over my shoulder. John had set the needles on his arms, chest, neck, and head. When he was done, he gave a satisfied nod.

"Now we wait," John said packing up the leftover needles. He looked at me with doubt in his eyes as he exited the room.

"Don't worry, Talon is strong, he will make it through." Charles said, which was surprising to me because Charles never spoke a word to me. I figure with all that was happening there was not much for him to say.

"Thank you, Charles, I think I'm going to go check on the men. Please stay with him." Charles gave me an understanding nod, then I wobbled out of the room with a heavy heart. I sat on the porch, deciding to immerse myself in the newest reports and financial statuses. To my delight, our sales went up 3 percent and I couldn't be any prouder of myself. Apparently, I had my father's brain for business which my mother would dread, but I had my own mind, and it was about time I saw that and used it. Being with Talon and everyone else had given me something I never had before, choices. I was so busy in my former life trying to be what my husband and society wanted from me, that I had forgotten I was my own person with dreams and goals of my own. But now, I was able to use my knowledge and do something instead of being pretty and present. Currently, I had the helpers making a boulder wall around the bottom of the house using thick mud and stones to keep the cold at bay during the winter. Using what I had learned made it all possible and like water off a duck's back I felt myself slowly emancipating from the chains of my past, I too had power and it was time for me to assert it.

I glanced into the barn to see if Rachael was alright, you could find her in either of two places nowadays, the barn or Talon's room. I could see Rachael feeding KoKo carrots. When the help first arrived, I was very fearful of them being around Rachael, I did not trust other men except those living in the house. One day one of the men named Robbie tried talking to Rachael but was chased out by KoKo in an instant. KoKo walked freely around the barn so there was nothing stopping KoKo from chasing him away from Rachel. Robbie was a man with dark brown hair and eyes the same color, a very fit man who had an obvious problem because every time our eyes met, he always winked at me. There were a few of the men who eyed me, but none were like Robbie, always smiling and trying to strike up conversations with me. I truly think he ignores the fact that I'm married, pregnant, and too busy to care about anything to do with him. I tried to pay attention to the work in front of me when a shadow blocked the sun I was using, I could see who it was in my peripheral but ignored it. "Howdy Miss Thomas, I-…"

"Mrs. Thomas, I explained that to you more than once Robbie." I kept my eyes on the paperwork resting on my rather large belly.

"You know all this time I haven't seen your husband? I see your daughter in that barn all the time though. She's very pretty, just like her momma." Robbie threw compliments while leaning against the house. I could tell he was searching my face to see if his compliment did anything, it hadn't.

"My husband is sick at the moment; don't you have work to do?" I asked, hoping he would leave.

"Can't a man be friendly?" Robbie quipped. I shrugged indifferently, keeping my eyes on my papers. "It's not every day you see a lady boss, controlling a bunch of men. You-..."

"Is there a point to this talking? My feet are swollen, I'm exhausted, and I'm hungry. Does that sound like a person who wants to talk right now about nothing?" I snapped cutting Robbie off. I finally looked at him in the face, he didn't seem at all disturbed by my rudeness which further frustrated me.

"I just want to get to know you, is that so wrong?" Robbie whined, giving me a smaller smile than before.

"Why do you want to get to know me?" I asked without missing a beat. Robbie looked bashfully toward the ground.

"I never met a woman like you before." He said quietly. "Some of the men that know your husband say he's not a man to mess around with, but no one really pointed him out." The netted door opened as Jonah stepped out onto the porch. He had his Stetson on, with his clothes all covered with dirt and blood, probably from skinning an animal. He was chewing on a long piece of wheat hanging from his mouth. Jonah had his revolver dangling in his left hand, he stared between Robbie and me before only fixating on Robbie alone. Jonah waved his hand in the air before slapping his thigh, obviously wanting Robbie to leave. Robbie didn't seem intimidated, but he understood the gesture, "I best get back to work." Robbie said backing up and flashing me one of his smiles before heading to the fields. I watched him as he trotted away, shaking my head. I felt Jonah kneel next to me.

"That man-..."

"I know Jonah and I'm not interested." I stopped Jonah before he could rant. Jonah just nodded before heading inside without another word. I had a feeling the situation with Robbie was going to cause a problem, I just didn't know how. I worried a little for Jonah, I could see in his face that he had less and less hope for his friend, and in a way so did I.

I had taken my work inside after all the events today. I was fighting my sleepiness and decided it was better I ate something so I could concentrate better on the paperwork. I went to the cold box we installed in the storage room. I had the workers make one for the inside of the house instead of always going outside to the underground one, I couldn't risk going down the narrow stairs and end up falling because I couldn't see over my belly. I cut myself some cold meat with cheese on the side and returned to the table with my work. I absent-mindedly nibbled on the food as I read more budget plans and incoming goods. I felt a piercing pain in my pelvis but shrugged it off as mere pregnancy struggles. It was sometime later that I stretched my arms out and yawned deeply. I was finally done and started gathering the papers and putting them together neatly. When I was able to get up from my seat a wave of dizziness overcame me, I tried to shake out of it, but it stayed. The pressure pressed against my pelvis, and I tried to walk but it felt more like falling. Clearing my vision at the last second, I caught myself on the wall. Suddenly the sound of water hitting the floor echoed in my ears and wetness hit my feet. "John!!" I yelled as loud as I could, sliding down to the floor using the wall as an anchor. I could hear John coming down the stairs. When he finally appeared, he was holding Rachael in his arms. His mouth formed an O as he fully understood what was going on.

"You're... in labor," John said in a shocked yet astonished way.

"Isn't it too early?" I asked, my voice strained. John put Rachael down on the floor and came down to my level, he grabbed my right arm and tossed it over his shoulder.

"You're having twins, it was destined you'd be early." John struggled to help me up grunting all the way, Rachael was pulling on my other arm to try to help. "I'm still too weak. Charles!!" John shouted. Charles must have known it was urgent because within seconds he was right in front of me.

"Come on Missus we got to get that baby out of you," Charles said before lifting me into his arms.

TALON

Chapter 34

It felt good to walk freely in the forest, the moss-covered trees and the scent of rain in the air made me feel unanchored. I did not know how I got here, and I did not care, all the worry and fear were now replaced with feelings of liberation and excitement. I've longed to feel this way for many years not knowing when this day would come, with this newfound energy I begin to run. My hair flowed behind me as I jumped over logs and rocks, the grass crunching under my feet, and fresh air filled my lungs. No more worries of acceptance, no more fighting, no more worries about love. My sprint slowed to jogging and then nothing at all. "Love?" I said to myself out loud, and at that moment the ground shook; my surroundings fell to darkness. A bright light shimmered in the distance, uneasy and unsure of where to go I followed. As I got closer, I had to shield my eyes until they adjusted, I could feel this light held great power. It was peaceful yet had such an overwhelming force, and then I realized what the light was. The scenery changed again, the light was still there but bamboo trees and flush grass stood in place of the darkness. Instead of a forest I was on a cliff. I looked back toward the light ready to cross over, I took a deep intake of air trying to calm my nerves and I stepped in, fully embraced by the peace. A force hit me directly in my chest, knocking me back more than my own height. I had reached the edge of the cliff, nearly falling over. I rushed to my feet. I was surprised I was not in pain, but I didn't dwell on that fact too long searching for the source of the attack. The bright light began to shine brighter as another human came through.

The light dimmed as a young Asian man stood before it, he seemed the same age as me, he had long hair in a ponytailed braid, and he wore a blue Chinese robe with matching trousers. With everything I noticed what was most prominent was the way he stood, with his hands behind his back and a slight smirk on his face. Like John.

But that could not be possible because John was in his sixties.

The man walked closer to me, I kept my guard up not knowing his intentions, and he stopped a few feet away. I had fixed my hands like tiger claws and made a defensive stance. What I did, seemed to amuse the young man because he began to laugh. "Tiger style, Jin Tao is very predictable." he said in Chinese. I relaxed a bit so our conversation could go smoothly.

"Nǐ shì shuí? Jin Tao Shuí shì?" [Who are you? Who is JinTao?] I hoped using the same language would make me seem friendlier than when I was more defensive. The baby-faced man smiled at me.

"Ping Ting, but that's neither here nor there, what is important is that you need to go back to your life." He said so casually still speaking in Chinese.

"Ping Ting? Go Back? To what? I don't even know who you are and you're telling me what to do." I yelled fiercely pointing hard at my chest, but the yelling fell on deaf ears as Ping Ting stood there as if he was staring at a child throwing a tantrum.

"Jin Tao raised a weak disciple." He said unamused, his face was now very serious, and disappointment lingered in his eyes. That was the second time he mentioned that name in that the context he was using it in, and I figured out who he was talking about.

"Jin Tao? Are you talking about John Tao?" I asked, suddenly feeling my anger starting to boil. Ping Ting said nothing but nodded unfazed, watching me with what seemed like contemplation. As I milled over what he had said, I became angered beyond reason. I gave him a look I saved for people who didn't know they were in deep shit with me. I walked a little closer to Ping Ting till I was about two feet away.

"Repeat what you said about my mentor."

"Jin Tao raised a weak-..." He couldn't finish my sentence before I whipped around to do a back kick. I stood shocked at the smaller man holding my ankle inches from his head. I stood standing on one leg trying to take my foot back. I was about to flip to use my other leg to hit him in the chin but before I could, Ping Ting wrapped his arm around my leg locking it in. "Your soul is weak, which makes your body weak. Go back and allow her to mend your broken spirit, your master requires it."

"You know nothing of my spirit, and I am my own master!" I yelled, frustrated that I couldn't get my leg out of his grip.

"So be it..." Ping Ting said before pulling my leg in extension to pull me toward him and his fist slammed into my stomach. There was no pain, but I still felt the air leave me as I fell to my knees. "Go back, not only does your soul need mending but you are needed. Your master requires it." Ping Ting circled me like a predator scouting its prey.

"What master are you talking about?!" I stood up to my height calculating what to do next.

"I can't say." he responded solemnly, "All I can say is you are more than you think you are, it's in your eyes."

I stared, confused at his statement before shaking myself out of it. "Listen I don't know what you're talking about but I'm not going back," I said with finality.

"You must!" Ping Ting shouted so loud the bamboo trees rustled.

"How can I be needed huh?! I lied to the woman I cared for and when she finds out... she'll leave." I retorted before throwing a punch, but as if he foresaw it, Ping Ting grabbed my wrist twisting it and over his shoulder. I went slamming onto the floor. He held my wrist in a lock where I couldn't move it. Tears left my eyes as I laid on my back on the ground.

"How do YOU know you are not needed? How can you be the judge of that? You don't know what others think. You think you could just die, and everything will be all right? What about that little girl?" Ping Ting said in a near growl. I struggled against him to free my hand, but he held on tighter, further twisting it to keep me in control.

"Leave Rachael out of this!" I yelled, trying to twist my body but Ping Ting twisted me back.

"Listen!" He demanded. I could suddenly hear Rachael's tear-filled voice echo around me.

"Talon, wake up! wake up!" Rachael's voice repeated it as her voice faded. Ping Ting let go of my wrist, allowing me to get up.

"Why you have to bring her into this?" I asked, feeling my wrist to make sure nothing was broken.

"Don't make the same mistake Jin and I made. I gave my life to save Jin, so he can have something to continue our legacy. You have everything you need in your life, your master made sure of it." Ping Ting finished, ignoring my question.

"WHO IS THIS MASTER?! I am my own master, me and only me!" My voice echoed loudly as I pounded my chest.

"Then act like it!" Ping Ting said sternly before sighing. Ping Ting casually walked toward the edge of the cliff, bending a finger for me to follow. "You will get your answers in time, I'm sure of it, and as for Jin..make sure you tell him the secret to life is taking the purest of what life can give to fight inner corruption. You can learn from that as well, now go." Ping Ting looked at me and went on, "You need to take that leap of faith." I peeked over the cliff to look down.

"It's dark down there, I mean I'm not afraid of heights, but I can't see what's down there," I said pointing down the cavern.

"Everyone has to make that leap for different reasons even when they can't see those reasons." Ping Ting said.

"I'm not ready..." I said in a near whisper.

"Talon she will die if you don't go back!" Ping Ting shouted. Suddenly I jumped off feet first. Before I could wonder how he knew my name I was engulfed by darkness.

"Talon, wake up, Talon!" Rachael whined. I felt Rachael shaking my left arm trying desperately to wake me. I was having a hard time opening my eyes, but I could feel my body trying to awaken itself. When I was finally forced to open my eyes after struggling for some time, the light burned, forcing them shut again. I was slightly disappointed that when I opened my eyes Rachael was not there and had maybe given up on me. Jessamine's screaming throughout the house startled me to open my eyes again, this time I was able to take the burn as I tried to decipher what time of the day it was. I was trying to lift my body off the bed, but it wouldn't work yet so I decided to roll off the bed. I hit the floor with my back and hit the back of my head. Through the ringing in my head, I was still able to hear pattering feet and some large ones heading toward me. "Talon! Talon! Are you okay?" Rachael asked, falling to her knees next to me. I tried to answer but nothing came out.

"Holy smokes, little princess was right!" Jonah sounded at the doorway. He placed his forehead against my own. "Hey buddy, you shouldn't scare people like that you know?" When he finally lifted his head to look at me, I spotted the thing I wanted most. I kept staring at the glass of water so Jonah could follow my gaze. When he noticed what I was staring at he grabbed the glass and forced my head up so I could drink.

"Jonah there's no time to linger, I needed those towels-..." John said walking through the door before taking in the scene. Jonah, Rachael, and I staring at him. John then dropped to his knees, "Child, you're awake..." John then rose back up and rushed to my side. "There's no time, Jessamine is in labor and having complications, seeing you will give her strength."

"Where?" I asked, my voice raspy and dry, trying to gather energy to get my limbs to work and get up off the floor.

"Hold on y'all. Talon you just woke up. We will take care of Jessamine." Jonah pleaded. I ignored him and tried grabbing at the small drawer. After a few minutes, I finally was able to support my weight with my arms by leaning against my bigger dresser with Jonah helping me.

"Jonah is Charles here?" I asked.

"Yea, he's in the room with Jessamine. Why?"

"You're too small, I need his height," I answered.

"You lucky this isn't the time, or I'd let you fall," Jonah said before running out of the room. I chuckled inwardly.

"It's good you found your way out of the abyss and back to us," John said patting me on the back. Another gut-wrenching scream flowed through the house, making me feel very nervous. It was then I saw myself in the mirror, and I looked horrible. My hair was dry and frizzy without the usual care of my oils and creams, my skin seemed paler than normal, and instead of the deep sun-kissed honey, my eyes were the color of corn. I had to say I was quite startled at my appearance.

"I was going to go into the abyss until someone stopped me," I responded. Looking at John I could tell he wanted me to say more but was interrupted by the presence of Charles.

"Talon, sir, you're up," Charles said engulfing me in a hug. I pulled away from him with a smile.

"Hurry and help me, I need to see my wife," I said tossing my left arm around Charles's shoulder. I was only a tad bit taller than Charles which made it easy for me to lean on him. Charles had his hand around my lower back holding me up, while Rachael held my right hand on her shoulders to help. I almost fell a couple of times during the walk to Jessamine's room, making me very frustrated and annoyed. I've never been this immobile before and it was something I never want to experience again. John stopped in front of Charles, Rachael, and me when we were only a couple of feet away. I stared at him with a brow risen.

"Before you go in there you need to know something." John had a serious look on his face.

"John, I need to be in there."

"She knows Talon, she knows about you and what you are," John said before I could speak any further. I contemplated turning around and going back to my room and pretending to fall back into the darkness I came from, but Jessamine's screams of anguish quickly allowed me to discard my thoughts.

"It's not about me right now, it's about her," I said tapping Charles to help me move forward and enter the room.

John entered the room before me and sat in the seat that was between Jessamins legs. "Come on child you can do it!" John said encouragingly but his words fell on deaf ears. I didn't think Jessamine noticed me yet. I watched in awe and in horror at what was going on, I could see the struggle in Jessamine's face. She was sweaty, red from the pain and pushing, and visibly tired yet I had never seen such beauty. Charles walked me to Jessamine's side; he steadily sat me on the stool, so I was able to grab Jessamine's hand into my own. Her eyes were closed as she breathed in rapid breaths.

"Hey there…" I said, trying to keep my tears at bay.

Jessamine turned her head to look at me, I smiled deeply as I began stroking her cheek. Gray-silver eyes stared at me with uncertainty, "Am I dreaming?" She said with a strained voice and like the river breaking through a dam, my tears flowed.

"No… you're not dreaming." I responded with a knot in my throat. "But I know one thing, you need to fight through this," I said giving her hand a small squeeze.

"I don't think I can… I'm so tired." Jessamine said in a near whisper.

"No, you can. I know because you're strong, stronger than me. I had to find the strength not to give up, you already had it. I didn't come back to lose you." I lost some of my voice due to my failed attempt to withhold my tears. Jessamine suddenly propped herself up on her elbows, I could see in her eyes a new resolve.

"When I survive this, you owe me a bloody explanation," Jessamine said, her thicker accent than usual. She took a couple of deep breaths before a screeching growl emerged from her lips as she pushed with all her strength.

"I see a head!" John yelled with excitement. A few more screeching growls filled the air as Jessamine squeezed my hand for support.

"He's out! It's a boy!" John exclaimed as he pulled the baby into his arms. John's face went from ecstatic to concerned in an instant.

"He's not breathing..." John lifted the baby and slapped him on the behind, but nothing happened. I released Jessamine's hand as I could already tell that she was beginning to panic.

"Give me the baby..." I said holding out my hands. Charles helped me get closer so I wouldn't hurt myself since my legs were still weak. John did as I asked of him with near tears in his eyes. With the baby in my arms, I begin to work quickly. Sitting against the wall, I could see Jessamine's tear and sweat-stained face, I could tell she didn't want to lose hope. "I won't let him die," I said out loud for her comfort. Through a raging storm of worry and panic, I kept calm. I felt Rachael sit next to me and with her strength, I wiped the baby's mouth and blew inside. I rubbed his chest upward; due to his small size, I could not press hard.

"What's going on?" Jonah said upon entering the room, but John and Charles shushed him. I kept going, trying to bring back life to the baby, but still, there was nothing. I was able to hear Jessamine starting to cry and everyone except myself and Rachael bow their heads.

"One more time…" Rachael said to me holding on to my right forearm, I nodded gathering a good amount of breath, and blew into the baby. Suddenly a coo and then a cry filled the room, and everyone cheered, Jessamine's tears of sadness became tears of relief. Rachael hugged me around my neck and the sudden embrace gave me warmth. Jonah frizzled my hair earning a side eye, and I was able to catch John smiling at me over Rachael's shoulder.

"Well Jessamine, time to get that other one out," John said, pulling his sleeves up his arms after he wiped his eye from a stray tear. I hid my smile as Jessamine groaned inward, but then I looked at John in bewilderment.

"Another one?!"

JESSAMINE

Chapter 35

    I opened my eyes in darkness. Ever since having the twins I've done nothing but eat, sleep, feed the babies, and more sleep.

By God, why did I bloody have to have twins?

It had been a week or more since they'd been born. Due to the sleep, I had lost some track of time which explains why I'm up now. My healing process had also been hell on earth, I had been ripped a bit when the first twin was born, and I needed to be stitched up. I wasn't used to a man being down there other than my ex-husband which was a horrid experience, but John seemed to know what he was doing and was very gentle. I didn't even notice I had stitches till I woke up in pain one night. I still felt the pain, but it was duller than at first. The more awkward thing was that the babies weren't the only ones that had to wear a nappy, but me as well. I couldn't hold anything long enough to reach the bathroom. I lay in bed, still in my thoughts, a smile slowly emerged on my face as I thought of Talon. I wouldn't have made it without him, he had woken up and was by my side when I felt like giving up. I wanted the anger to emerge, I was ready to flare up and it never happened. Though I was happy I was worried about the soundness of Talon's mind and body. His body because in a matter of days Talon had made his legs work for him, allowing him to start doing work again around the farm and I worried he would strain himself. His mind because he had awoken to chaos and a near-death experience, not only for himself but for one of the babies. Talon had not yet been able to really heal from everything.

My little Rachael had acted bravely throughout the whole ordeal. When I was first going into labor, I was having a hard time when suddenly she disappeared. I was worried, she had been afraid, but Jonah helped me fill in the blanks about what happened. She had run off to get the only person she trusted to help and that's when Talon had emerged from his long slumber. I had to wonder how deep Talon and Rachael's bond was. As quickly as that thought came, it was replaced with another.

How can I make Talon and I's relationship stronger and deeper?

A soft knock at the door sounded and it slowly began to open. I tucked my last thought away to ponder later and pretended to be asleep. I heard the floorboard creak under the weight of the person inside, I already knew who it was that had entered, and I tried not to smile. Usually, it was John or Jonah who would come in and check to see if I and the babies were all right. The smell of mint, pine, and herbs filled my nose as extra weight on my bed had been added. Talon's hand stroked my head in a soft rhythm, "I'm sorry..." he whispered. I sighed inwardly.

"You couldn't talk to me while I was awake?" I said, keeping my eyes closed, I instantly felt Talon's hand stiffen and moved off my head, the warmth it created gone.

"I should go..." Talon said getting up from the bed.

"Talon, sit. I'm not going to chase you." I said low but commandingly, opening my eyes from my fake sleep. Talon was near the door with his hand on the knob, I could tell he was deeply contemplating his options. After a few seconds, he returned to me with his eyesight toward the floor and standing next to me. I propped myself up using the pillows for support. "I want to know the truth."

"Jessamine, you already know the truth. Why do I need to say it?" Talon whined, keeping eye contact.

"I want you to tell me because it will show that you will talk to me, instead of hiding from me. I need to know you will talk to me no matter what, I honestly want to move past this with nothing but honesty between us." I could tell Talon was thinking very hard about what I was saying. "I'm not going to beg you Talon, so I need to know." I went on hoping he would concede.

"I shouldn't have lied to you, but then again I lie to everyone…"

"I am different! And I refuse to be compared to those out there." I blurted out before Talon could continue, I reached for his hand and pulled him to sit and reluctantly he let me.

"I did not think we would be in a situation that required my honesty," Talon said looking toward the window.

"You're going to have to be more specific." Talon looked at me with confusion.

"Pacific? Like the ocean?" I couldn't help but laugh at his questions.

"No darling, that is Pacific. Specific means more detail, for the most part." Talon nodded in understanding, making me laugh some more at how serious his face looked in learning the new word. A pain hit me suddenly, making me whine down my laughter. "I shouldn't laugh so much; everything still hurts a bit."

"Are you mad at me?" Talon asked staring out the window. Though it should have been a hard answer filled with confusion and pain, I had already passed it all. I took Talon's hand into my own again and sighed.

"I was very mad at you, and at myself… but not anymore," I answered clearly.

"I did not know we would be this involved with each other, a time ago I vowed to never get close to anyone anymore after Lisa. Which reminds me, I never got to ask you why Lisa was here the day of the bear attack?" I scoffed at Talon's question not wanting to talk about the woman that started this mess.

"She's not important right now I want to talk about us, don't change the subject." Talon gave me an understanding nod. Silence ensued for a prolonged time, I was barely breathing waiting for Talon to say something, anything.

"I don't deserve you..." Talon whispered just loud enough for me to hear before getting up from the bed.

"Talon, wait!" I yelled after him, but the only response I received was the click of the door shutting behind him.

* * *

I stretched my arms in the air to the new morning. It had been two weeks since the talk, and with me being bedridden, it was easy for Talon to avoid me. I was elated when John gave me the news that I would be able to get up and move around properly. *Let's see Talon try to avoid me now.* The babies were still asleep which for any mother is a blessing within itself, I've had help in the middle of the night by Jonah and John, so I was not deprived of sleep. I went toward my closet to pick out a wardrobe. My sudden gay mood washed away the moment I saw nothing but dresses in my closet. I rolled my eyes at my selections; a knock came at the door startling me as I noticed I was nearly naked. "Just a moment!" I ran toward my bed, quickly wrapping my body in my bed sheet. "Come in!" I invited the unknown visitor.

"Mommy! Mommy!" Rachael said when she opened the door and ran into my room with John behind her. Rachael gave me a hug and I hugged her in return.

"Morning child, it's good to see you up and moving," John said placing a wooden box on my bed.

"Morning Rachael, morning John, and yes it's good to be up and moving." I greeted both with a smile.

"I didn't get the chance to say thank you for saving my life." I put my hand that was not holding the sheet in the air to stop him from talking.

"You also saved my life, John, long before I saved yours. Besides, we are family now, it's what we do for each other." I responded.

"Well, to thank you I got you a gift. Something you will need when we start our lessons together." John said giving me a wide smile. "Come on Rachael, we must let your mother dress," John said holding his hand out for Rachael to grab.

"Bye Mommy," Rachael said leaving with John.

"Don't worry we will see her when she comes down." I heard John assure her before the door fully closed. I took a breath of relief and let the sheet I was holding fall to the floor, it was then that I caught a glance at myself in my full-body mirror. I was fuller in places, my hair longer and silkier than when I had arrived. I took a moment to feel up my curves starting from next to my breast to my hips, and even though I had marks on my body from carrying the babies I knew it would go away with creams and I was in fact proud of how I looked. I looked healthier and dare I say, happy. I was going to go back to the closet to pick out a dress but decided to see what John's gift was first. I removed the lid of the box.

In the box, three sets of footwear caught my attention. I grabbed the three pairs one by one and laid them out on my bed. They all had about an inch and a half heel, but the length of the boot was different. The first boot was black and looked like it could go up to my knee, made from some animal fur but shaved. The second boot was a brown leather halfway up my shin. The third boot was made the same way as the knee-high boot but went up to my ankles, with fluffy fur at their rims. They were all fabulously gorgeous, I looked back into the box and pulled out different packages. I ripped them open like a kid on Christmas. One package held shirts, the second corsets, and the third trousers. I silently thanked John and dressed myself in my new clothes. When I was done, I stared at myself in the mirror, I had put on one of the white long-sleeve shirts, with black trousers, and a black corset with white lace trimmings that went over my shirt. I put on the knee-high boots and got a pleasant surprise, on the side of my right boot was a knife sheath close to my knee. My trousers hugged my legs which was making my new hip curves more noticeable, and the corset made it no better. I let my hair loose and took a deep breath, I had one goal in mind today and that was to make Talon notice me, and with these new clothes the task should be much easier. I went to the bathing room and freshened myself with new fragrances and washed my mouth with mint. I peeked into my room relieved to see the babies were still asleep, which gave me time to handle unfinished business.

I walked down the wooden stairs hearing the click from my heel with every step. I walked into the kitchen, but no one was there. "Good heavens!" I heard Jonah say down the hall near the storage room. I looked toward him to see him covering his mouth with one of his hands. "You look so beautiful! Please tell me you're going to show Talon." Jonah squeaked as he ran up to me, grabbing my hands and spreading my arms out to get a better look. "Well, if you didn't turn heads before, you're about to snap necks now," Jonah exclaimed; his smile lighting up his sea blue eyes. His smile was so contagious it made me smile through my nervousness.

"The only head I want to turn is Talon's, but I couldn't help but wonder where Rachael is?" I said slightly concerned.

"Oh, no worries. She, Charles, and Tao just stepped out shortly, I don't know where but that's what Tao told me to tell you," John answered with a shrug. I couldn't fathom where Tao would have gone and in the back of my mind, I had a feeling John was up to something, he always is. Pushing my thoughts aside, I straightened up.

"Jonah, where's my husband?" Jonah lifted his eyebrows up and down rapidly at my question.

"Your husband thought he was not fit enough after his long slumber, so he's getting fit outside. His words, not mine." I absentmindedly bit my lip, but quickly stopped when Jonah gave me a knowing look. "How are the workers?" I asked, trying to settle my thoughts, Jonah snickered a little. "what's funny?"

"Oh nothing, the workers are fine. One, in particular, has congratulated us on our babies." Jonah burst into a fit of giggles.

"Our babies? Who?"

"You know who, he's never seen Talon, so I guess he assumes me competition." Jonah started laughing again but I didn't find anything funny. When Jonah saw how stoic my face looked, he quickly became quiet, clearing his throat.

"How was Talon's reaction to the workers?" I walked toward the front door and looked through the netted door, knowing the answer.

"You know Talon he stays away from people, I'm pretty sure though that he wants his farm back with him doing all the work." Jonah finished walking beside me.

"Watch the wee ones, would you?" I said clenching and unclenching my hands in nervousness.

"No problem, good luck."

I stepped out onto the porch, with my heels clacking against the wood. I placed my hands on my hips searching for only one person. I could tell the weather was changing, leaves were falling and most of the field had been harvested already for selling and canning. I was surprised at how my new clothing was keeping the chill away. In the distance I spotted my target, I was in awe at what I saw. Talon was lifting a log over his head using carved-in handles, he lowered the log onto his chest and lifted it over his head once more. I could have stared at this fascinating creature for the rest of the day if I hadn't caught Robbie in my peripheral walking toward me with lust in his eyes. He leaned his body on the porch stairs railing, I shivered inwardly when he licked his lips and stared at me like I was some common whore. I wasn't sure if Talon and I's relationship would be one of admiration and wouldn't go further than that, but just looking at Robbie made me question less why I liked being around Talon. At this point in my life, I was just a fish swimming in a river current hoping for the best, I didn't know what or who I was sexually attracted to, but for now, Talon was all I needed. "Why look at you Mrs. Thomas, mmm, looking like fine wine," Robbie said huskily. I crossed my arms over my chest, I felt naked under his gaze. "You don't look like you were with child at all."

"How are you, Robbie?" I asked indifferently and slightly annoyed.

"I should be asking you, having a baby is not 'n' easy thing. Hell, some women don't even make it past childbirth, and so I tip my hat to you." Robbie tipped his hat like he said he would, right after he disgustingly spat out tobacco that he had stuffed into his cheek. I walked down the stairs of the porch trying to still my shiver. Before I reached the bottom Robbie placed himself in front of me. "I have also been wanting to apologize for upsetting your husband, to be honest, I didn't know that short man was your husband for such a long-legged lady like yourself," Robbie said winking at me. I scoffed at his attempt at flattery and walked past him.

"Jonah, the short man you are talking about is not my husband," I said trying to get as far away from Robbie as possible.

"Then who is the lucky fella? Can't be the old man or the negro!" Robbie yelled after me. I whipped around to face him.

"Watch it, Charles is a man to be respected, and I think you are done on my farm and need to leave. Like it or not I am a happily married woman, I am a happy mother, and most importantly I'll be happier once you leave!" I yelled with authority, before I could walk away Robbie grabbed my wrist.

"You can't just-..." Robbie's mouth was suddenly agape; he was looking behind me with an expression I couldn't read. When I turned around Talon was staring at us still lifting the log over his head and back to his chest. Talon had made himself more noticeable. Now that I was closer the log was thicker and longer than from the distance I was at before. "Who is that Behemoth?" Robbie asked.

"How dare you! He is not a behemoth, he's my husband!" I yelled, offended. Robbie released my wrist in the new discovery. Talon threw the log on the ground with a thump and walked toward us. Talon looked between Robbie and me, Robbie flinched when Talon stared at him. Which was funny because a very opposite reaction happened to me.

"I never knew a savage could look like that! Look at them eyes." Robbie said still transfixed on Talon. While I was appalled at Robbie's words, Talon seemed to shrug at them unfazed.

"You need to leave!" I said pointing down the road that left our land, my anger was forcing me to start shouting gaining some concerned looks. "You'll be fully compensated for your work, thank you and goodbye." I finished with my hands on my hips trying to manage some restraint.

"My wife has spoken; it is time for you to go," Talon said unwrapping the linen he had placed around his hands; his voice was low yet full of power and authority. Robbie huffed, turning his gaze back to me.

"I believe you're not in this marriage 'cause ya want to, nobody would want to separate themselves from proper people. Blackmail, a debt, or maybe-."

"Just stop!" I put my hands up for him to silence. "I don't know what I've done to give you the idea that I want anything to do with you sir, but let me make it bloody clear, you are released from your duties, and I never want you on our land again. Furthermore, I am happy with my husband, I couldn't ask for a better one..." I finished looking up at Talon and to my surprise I had sun-kissed honey eyes staring back at me. Robbie's scoff broke my trance, turning my attention back to him.

"My wife has spoken twice now; leave…" Talon said crossing his arms over his chest. Robbie glared at Talon from head to toe as if weighing his options, he spat at Talon's feet before he turned away heading down the road and kicking the dirt beneath him frustratingly. I felt as if I was being watched. I turned to Talon to find him once again staring at me. This time it was more intense, a little lustful though I could have been mistaken. I looked down at my clothes and smiled deeply, before looking back at him.

"Mr. Thomas…" I made my voice as sweet as possible.

"Huh? Oh, I uh… I need to check on the log I um threw around." stumbling as he turned away heading to the barn. I rolled my eyes as I tried to catch up to him, grabbing his hand I made him stop and look at me.

"Talon, I need you-…"

"Are you feeling, okay? Are you hurt? You really should rest-…"

"Stop rambling Talon and please just listen!" I snapped, looking him straight in his eyes, which was my own undoing. His eyes were so intense; I couldn't stop my eyes trailing down his cheeks and then to his lips. I shook out of my trance by wrapping my arms around Talon's waist hugging him close and leaning my head against him. Talon's whole body stiffened at my action. "Maybe not today, maybe not tomorrow, or a month from now. But I want you to… I need you to open yourself to me."

"You could have happiness with a normal man," Talon said with a small shiver in his voice. I tilted my head up to him and smiled.

"Let me be the judge of that, for now, I want us to move forward. Moving forward means picking names for the babies, being a family, trusting, and just allowing yourself to let loose. I know who you are, and I was mad but not anymore. Think about it." I released Talon from my grasp, backing away from him. It was the worst mistake I ever will make, the warmth I felt left as quickly as it came. "I've got to find John…" I scurried away trying to hide my flushed red cheeks. I hurried into the house, shaking off the feeling of being watched. I couldn't keep the smile off my face as I walked down the hall toward the training room, I knocked and opened it without waiting for a response. I was greeted with the sight of Rachael's arms spread out wide with books on her head trying to keep balance. John was sitting on his cushion on the floor behind the low desk.

"John, what do you have my daughter doing and how did you get here without me seeing you two pass me by?"

"One, Rachael is learning about balance. Two, the child and I thought it best not to interrupt mommy and daddy time." John finished with a smirk and suggestive eyes.

"Ok darling, time for mommy's lessons." I grabbed the books from Rachael's head and kissed her on the forehead. "Go find Talon, I'm sure he would love for you to help him." Without another word, Rachael ran out the door. "John I'm here to start my lessons," I said standing straight with the books held to my chest.

"You really want to learn child?" John asked me, rubbing his beard with a curious stare.

"I want to be more than the woman I was; so if it means learning something to heal and kill, then so be it," I said firmly. John stared for a moment before nodding his head, he got up from his floor cushion with a grunt.

"We must start with the basics," John instructed walking past me to a bookcase.

"Books? I must read books?" I asked glaring at the old man.

"Did you give your teachers this amount of trouble, with that fancy education of yours?" John said with an amused look, but I didn't think it was all that funny. "You must learn Chinese, and we need to condition your body..."

"Wait, what!?"

"My books are not in English, and you have to train your body in order to train your mind..." John said removing the books I had in my hands and replacing them with a heavier stack.

"Bloody hell," I grumbled placing my new study books on the table.

TALON

Chapter 36

The moon was shining brightly outside. It was near the morning hours, a good time to practice under the moonlight. Staring in the mirror in my dimly lit room, I felt a lot better about myself than I had in the last two weeks. My clothes fit better than when I woke up from my coma, and I regained most of my strength. When I had looked in the mirror after the babies were born my hair was in disarray, my skin was pale and dry, and my eyes were a deep yellow and wild looking. I pulled my loose hair forward taking in its length, I had to soak it in multiple oils for weeks to smooth it out from the dry knotty mess it was. It grew over six inches past my bottom, and when loose it draped my shoulder in waves like a cape. The light brown rivers that course through my hair were becoming more noticeable, a trait that reminds me that I'm not full-blooded. Then I gazed at my reflection again as my yellow eyes stared back, another reminder that I'm not normal. For all my life, looking at my reflection, I felt what stared back was not my own. Lately though, when looking at my reflection I felt like myself. I no longer felt there were two sides of me battling for dominance. I felt complete.

I took a few more moments to look at myself, I was wearing dark brown trousers and a sleeveless shirt. I braided my hair leaving the shorter strands in the front loose, tying the end with a skinny piece of leather. I grabbed my white buttoned shirt, put it on, and tucked it in. The days had become colder and the wind bitter with the winter months coming, but it was perfect for me.

I tend to get overheated in training. Crying from down the hall caught my attention, I walked briskly to my door and opened it. The crying was coming from Jessamine's room, I closed the door behind me and tried to walk quickly yet lightly across the wooden floor. I was between panic and worry. Panic because one of the babies was crying and worried because he might wake up Jessamine. The last thing I wanted was for Jessamine to wake up after a long day of training with Tao. I was quite surprised that Jessamine was training. I wasn't sure of what Tao was teaching her since I watched from a distance, but it takes tremendous strength to train oneself after childbearing. I gently opened Jessamine's door and closed it behind me. I didn't dare look at Jessamine, afraid she may be indecent, and I walked lightly toward the young ones. "Shh, young ones please." I pleaded in a whisper, to no avail. I picked up the baby hesitantly, and his cries died out slowly. I stared into the eyes of the baby I had saved, and he stared back. In that instant, I did what I was afraid to do even with Rachael. I allowed myself to fall in love.

"Which one was it dear?" Jessamine's groggy voice startled me out of my trance.

"Oh, it's the survivor." I sat at the edge of the Jessamine bed, "Do you want him?" I asked, holding out the baby. Jessamine gave a giant smile that outshined the moon while shaking her head no.

"No love, too tired to hold the baby. Besides I want you to finally name them, we need to register them under our family." Jessamine said fixing herself to sit up more.

"I um, I don't know if that is a good idea. They are your children, it's not my place."

"They are our children," Jessamine said sternly, I looked at her before sighing in defeat. I sat and tried to ignore Jessamine's gaze upon me, the only living thing I ever named in my life was KoKo.

"Hania, and the other Honovi" I said softly testing the names out loud.

"Beautiful, not common, but beautiful. What do the names mean?" Jessamine asked, taking Hania from me and into her arms.

"Hania means spirit warrior, Honovi means Strong. Is that okay for you?"

"Hello Hania Willard Thomas, it's nice to finally meet you." I got up and gently picked up Honovi.

"And this one?"

"Honovi Angelo Thomas." Jessamine said with the utmost pride in her voice. "Finally, little ones, you have names." I put Honovi back into his cradle before he could wake up.

"Do you think Hania is hungry, does he cry often?" I asked sitting on the edge of the bed again.

"No, Hania barely cries. It's usually...."

"Honovi?" I snickered.

"Yes Honovi. Now that they have names, I need to get used to them," Jessamine said, trying to stifle a yawn.

"Get some sleep, I have Hania." I cradled him close to me and got up from the bed.

"But Talon, you have never been with any one of the children alone."

"I'll lea-..." I spoke too loudly. "I will learn, now rest," I whispered, creeping more than usual toward the door. Normally I would use light steps, but this time I was literally tiptoeing. Sniffling stopped me before I was able to put my hand on the knob.

"Jessamine, are you all, right?"

"Oh, it's nothing, I've just never had such support before. It's a little overwhelming." Jessamine wiped her tears with the blanket. I was stunned, unable to respond to the sudden confession.

"I really don't know what to say, except I will always be there if you want me." I went to touch the knob again but then the sudden urge to say something more held me back. "I should also say thank you."

"For?"

"For giving me a family and making my world bigger." I smiled, hoping it was enough to forget her worries and pain, if only for a moment.

"You're welcome..." Jessamine returned the smile, making my heartbeat gallop.

"Rest..."

"Oi, one more thing Talon. It's Rachael's birthday today."

"What?!" I asked in shock.

"Yes, and she loves you enough that she would like anything you give her," Jessamine said tucking herself in her bed. "Now darling, Tao is going to work me to death. Mentally and physically. I need sleep to deal with him, goodnight." Jessamine finishes with another yawn. I left the room with more things on my mind than when I entered, but at least they were good things.

"Dammit!" I shouted, after tripping over one of the dining table chairs and dropping the pot of rice I was holding. I got up fast and kicked one of the table legs out of frustration, no surprise I broke one of the legs, though the table wobbled it stayed up on its left-over legs. After getting Hania settled in his basket and back to sleep, I grabbed a bunch of food and started making breakfast. I didn't even know what to make, I just started to cook things. Bacon, fish, steam buns, eggs, and more. I had forgotten about the training I needed to, which probably explains why I was so clumsy.

"Talon?" Rachael's worried voice startled me from my tantrum. Rachael stood in her night clothes, wiping the sleep from her eyes.

"Everything is all right, just made a mess. Happy birthday little cub." I greeted her, nervously kneeling on one knee and opening my arms for a hug. Rachael wrapped her little arms around my neck with no hesitation, closing my arms around her. "Daddy is planning a special day for you," I said, testing out the new title.

"Daddy?" Rachael questioned pulling away from me. Her green eyes stared into mine, they seemed to be filled with uncertainty. I did not want to push the little cub into anything she didn't want to, but I also couldn't help but want her to acknowledge me as such.

"I would like to be a father to you if you let me." I wasn't sure she could understand my words and meaning, but my heart begged her to try.

"Daddy!" Rachael shouted, giving me a tighter hug around my neck than before. In that moment I felt complete and fulfilled. Like my past and all its pain was slowly washing away. I looked up to find Jessamine hiding behind the wall peeking in. I did not know how long she had been standing there, but tears were streaming down her face and her hand covered her mouth.

"Jessamine, what's wrong?" I asked, letting go of Rachael and standing at my full height. "Why are you crying?" I asked with concern.

"Mommy...?" Rachael also sounded concerned.

"Hey! Why don't you get dressed for our birthday adventure." I said to Rachael patting her head. Rachael hugged my leg, then hugged Jessamine before leaving to go upstairs. I waited till I was sure that Rachael was gone but before I knew it Jessamine's lips were upon my own. I can feel her arms circle around my neck, her fingers tangling in my hair, her tears falling on my cheek, and a sensation I haven't felt in a long time. Jessamine's lips moved against me, and as if my lips had a mind of their own, they moved along with hers. I wrapped my arms around the small of her back, keeping her as close to me as possible. I jumped slightly when I felt her tongue graze across my lips. Her kiss started light and sweet, but it was starting to grow with hunger. I greeted her tongue with my own, deepening the kiss further. I felt strange pricks all over my body and heat growing below. I had little control over myself as I lifted Jessamine above my waist, sitting her on the strongest part of the three-legged table. I started to trace Jessamine's neck with my lips.

"Ahem..." I jumped away from Jessamine startled, but quickly caught her when I saw she was falling backward due to the missing leg. Jessamine was pressed against my chest as the table fell to the floor. I looked down at her and was greeted with a smile.

"Nice catch..." Jessamine said in a whisper, close to my lips.

"AHEM!" I sighed as I turned to the small Asian man, whom I wished was not in here at this moment. "I apologize for the interruption, but I do believe it's time for your lessons," John said with a smirk forming into the biggest smile. Jessamine and I stepped away from each other, we exchanged looks before Jessamine fixed her corset to its proper comfort and left the kitchen. I shamelessly watched as she went. When Jessamine was out of sight, I laid my eyes on John with a glare. My glare scared him none for he went into a fit of laughter. "Fix your shirt," John said in between breaths, I looked down to find three of my buttons were ripped off.

"When did that happen?" My question seemed to make John laugh harder as he slapped his knee repeatedly.

"Stop laughing old man, so I can talk to you..." I said with a growl.

"I cannot help you in that department my son, you're going to have to discover that on your own," John said with his laughter still present. I was stunned to silence only for a moment hearing the word 'son' come out of John's mouth. I wasn't used to that endearment.

"What...-" I stopped at the sound of small feet coming down the stairs. "Me and you tonight old man," I whispered before turning my serious face to a smiling one as Rachael approached. I crossed my arms over the opening of my shirt. "You ready to have an adventure?" I said chuckling at Rachael's messy hair, lop-sided shirt, and untied boots.

"Ready!" she replied in laughter.

"Come here little one so I can braid your hair," I said, turning Rachael around and lightly using my fingers to straighten it out before braiding it and binding it with her own hair.

"Change your shirt boy, I'll finish her up," John said patting my shoulder. I nodded and skipped steps going up the stairs. I stop in front of Jessamine's room first kissing my fingers and placing them on the two sleeping boys.

"Let the spirits protect you and give you good dreams while I'm not around," I said before leaving and heading toward my own room for a shirt.

By the time I made it back downstairs Rachael was ready to go, wearing one of the fur coats John had made for her. I looked toward the training room contemplating whether to get more weapons or just go with my doubled harness knives and bow I left on a hook near the door. "Alright, I'm ready." Thinking maybe I should avoid Jessamine for a while, I grabbed the harnessed knives and hooked them around my shoulders.

"What about your mess?" John asked, handing me my long fur coat.

"Howdy family!" Jonah shouted coming through the door with baskets of goods in his arms.

"Have him do it, I'm off; come on little one," I said putting on the fur coat and wrapping my quiver and bow around my chest. I opened the door letting Rachael walk out first.

"Wait, what I do?" Jonah said obviously confused at the situation. I closed the door behind me without answering, knowing it would only piss the little man off. I grabbed Rachael's hand and we walked together to the barn.

I opened the door to the barn and a warm heat washed over Rachael and me. It was a vast difference from the chill morning air. The fire was going for the animals, keeping them warm during the cold times of the year. A small fence was built around it as a precaution so the animals wouldn't accidentally roast themselves or panic. After retrieving KoKo and closing the barn door to keep the warm inside, I hoisted Rachael up and then myself on KoKo's back. I wrapped my arms around the little one as I loosely held on to the reins, and we started our steady ride through the woods. It had been a while since I fully explored the land I owned in its entirety. We stopped in different spots in the woods, crafting spears and throwing them into trees, showing Rachael the amazing animals around us, and skipping rocks across the river. I looked at the sun. I was having so much fun, time had slipped, and it was already past noon. "Hungry little one?" I asked Rachael, taking off my long coat and covering her with it. She gave me a pouty nod yes that made me smile, "Me too. I'll get some fish, but first, let's get a fire going."

I started to pick up dry sticks, twigs, and heavier pieces of wood. I arranged the bigger pieces of wood in a circle. Sticks dropped beside me, and before I knew it Rachael started to arrange the sticks right alongside me. I held in my tears of love and pride I felt for this little girl, it took more effort than I realized. Before I knew it, a tear left my eye and landed on the little one's hand. She looked up at me with curious eyes. "Daddy, why you cry?" Rachael asked, wiping my eyes with her small hands. I took her hand onto my own.

"Daddy... is just happy to be able to call you daughter, that is all." I said, trying to swallow the choking feeling in my throat. The little one smiled wide and lovingly, tossing the rest of the sticks on the ground and charging into me with a hug. We stood there in each other's embrace, tears flowing silently down my face.

Two growls emerged from below us, when we pulled apart all we could do was laugh as our stomachs begged for food at the same time. Rachael wiped my tears before gathering the sticks again and trying to set them up the way I had. After starting the fire, using stones and a bit of my hair, I took off my boots and rolled up my pants to my knees. I placed my socks into my boots to keep them warm from the chill. I looked sideways to see Rachael doing the same, "No, no, little one, you cannot do this with me." I said as I kneeled next to her.

"Why?" Rachael responded pouting with her bottom lip. I couldn't help but smile at her defiance, her nose scrunched up to her eyes and her eyes communicated her anger.

"Because, it is cold out here, very cold; and the water feels like ice. You are small and will freeze a body part off or get sick. Wait that's not right."

"I want to help you," Rachael said with near tears in her eyes. I rubbed my chin trying to figure something out, wanting to kick myself for not being more prepared.

"Give me a moment little one." I got up from my knee and went to KoKo, who was grazing and minding his business. I reached under the saddle where I kept my emergency knife, it was a simple knife, with nothing much to it but sentimental value to me. It was my first knife and I always kept it sharp and ready, and now it will no longer be my job to do so. I looked around for some thin but sturdy sticks and returned to the child, sitting beside her. "This will be your everything. It will be your friend, your protector, your savior, even your resource; but it is all in how you wield it." I informed Rachael, handing her the sheathed knife with some hesitation. It was not unusual for a native child to possess their first weapon, but where Jessamine comes from, girls learned to be proper and dainty. *If these will be my children, I will not allow it.*

Rachael took the knife from me cautiously, inspecting it with curiosity. I laid the sticks down next to us leaving one in my hand. I unsheathed the knife on the left side of my shoulder harness, I started to shave up the stick until it was sharp. "I need all of them to look like this, just like this one. Can you, do it?" I held the stick to show her my work, after looking long enough she nodded, unsheathing the knife carefully. She grabbed a stick and started to repeat what I had done, with corrections here and there she got the hang of it quickly. I was sure to teach her to always hold the sharpness of the knife away from her body.

"Daddy, why you need it?" Rachael asked, holding up the stick, I grabbed the sharpened stick from her hand with a smile.

"Watch." I walked barefoot into the river up to my knees and held the stick, with the sharp end pointing down. I waited with utter stillness in the water.

"Daddy?"

"Shhhh..." I hushed. Then I inhaled.

SPLASH!!

I pulled the stick out of the water just as fast as when I plunged it in, with a skewered fish at the end. Small claps and cheering could be heard as I gave a hardy laugh at my victory. *Wait, when did I become boastful?* Rachael ran and grabbed the sticks she had carved into spears placing them near the river, where I could reach them. I gave Rachael the fish and picked up another spear and waited.

JESSAMINE

Chapter 37

"LI4?" John asked pacing back and forth behind me as I study the medicine meridian poster on the wall. I held the small needle between my thumb and pointer finger, twisting it between them trying to remember what the pressure point was that I had studied over a hundred times. "Concentrate!" John said firmly.

"I'm trying, you bloody slave driver!"

"Not hard enough, you said you studied." John still paced behind me at the same speed, but his voice showed his impatience. I bit my lip in frustration.

"Lie Que!" I said confidently with a huge smile, placing the needle indicating the location above the wrist on the inside of the arm.

"Wrong..." My smile faded with John's response "He Gu." John said picking up the needle and moving to the dot location between the thumb and pointer finger on the chart. "Large intestine channel, LI Jessamine. I thought you would get it, considering you are rubbing the needle with your thumb and first finger."

I scoffed at his remark. "I tried and got it wrong, no big deal." I waved my hand dismissively.

"Life and death are no big deal?" John retorted with a hint of anger.

"You know what I mean. I think I'm way over my head with this." I started to walk out of the room, but John cut me off.

"Acupuncture. Healing or killing is not in the mind. It's in the body. It's understanding the body, and then eventually controlling it." John said, looking me straight in my eyes. A knock sounded at the door. "Come in," John responded. The door crept open, and Jonah popped his head through before opening it all the way.

"Ya'll want some lunch?" Jonah asked, letting the door open fully and leaning against the frame with his forearm. Jonah looked between me and John, most likely sensing the tension between us, "Everything aw'right?" Jonah's eyes moved back and forth between us. John gracefully placed his hands behind his back, he gave me a visual inspection.

"I'm going to get tea," John told me as he was walking out of the room passed Jonah and disappearing into the kitchen. I let out a frustrated huff of air. I haven't been in the house long, but I've come to learn that John underlines the meaning of his words. He meant, "I'm going to cool down but when I get back, I expect you to do a lot better." John was officially worse than my own father. I thumbed through the pages of the medical books, trying to figure out what I was missing through the Chinese-English translated pages. My thoughts lingered on Rachael and Talon; how I would rather be enjoying her birthday with the twins, lavishing in the love of my husband. Baby cries sounded, pulling me from my daydream. I sighed deeply wondering how I am going to become better than my former self.

TALON

Chapter 38

Rachael and I were full like a predator after enjoying a fresh kill. We rode on the back of KoKo lazily, Rachael was occupied looking over her new knife. She traced the wooden handle with her fingers, feeling its carving of the sun I placed there. "The Father," I stated, wrapping a bit of my fur around the little girl.

"The Father?" she questioned looking behind her. "Like you?"

"No, no. More important and grander than myself." I replied giving a smile. I looked down and was greeted by a puzzled face. The Earth is the Mother; the spirit and heart of the land. The Sun is the Father who brings life and light." Rachael lowered her head staring at the carved sun on the blade. I assumed she was contemplating the words I spoken and their meaning. A bang and a loud howl on my far right paused the words I was going to speak; I unsheathed the knife from the left side of my holster with my right hand, staring in the direction the sound came from. I went to look down to comfort Rachael in case she was startled. To my amazement and pride as a father, Rachael held her knife unsheathed looking in the same direction. Smiling to myself and giving a light tug on KoKo reins, we were off in a gallop with two clicks of my tongue.

KoKo's hooves thundered through the forest under his full weight. I drowned out the sounds, relying on my senses of sight and smell. Gunpowder and blood became stronger the closer I got, fueling me with anger as I reached two men with rifles in front of an animal's den.

Hunters? On my land!

The men turned around fast. One aimed his gun toward me, and in reaction, I threw my knife toward him knocking the rifle with force out of his hands. I gave a sharp look at the other armed man; he dropped his gun without hesitation, shaking in his boots with fear.

"Oi! You a fuckin' coward Patrick!" The first man shouted toward his partner. I dismounted KoKo and pulled my second knife from its sheath; pointing it forward. The first man had a grizzly beard and red hair under a raccoon fur hat and an all-black fur coat; it looked like a black bear. Patrick on the other hand, had a clean face but black hair coming from beneath a fox fur hat. and he wore a thinner coat, which seemed to be made from deer. I kept my knife pointed at the more aggressive man as I walked closer to see where the smell of blood was coming from. "Look lad we don't want any trouble, we'll just..."

"Silence!" I shouted, my voice echoing among the trees. My lip quivered as rage heated my blood like fire. A wolf mother lay dead in the shallow den, her two pups pleading for her to wake. The way the wolf lay; its mouth closed, and restful eyes told me one thing. The wolf was sleeping. "Cowards!" I shouted, charging at the red-haired man and tackling him to the ground.

"Lad! Be easy, we are only hunters!" The man blurted out as I placed my knife to his throat.

"NO! You are not hunters! You have no honor, no respect for the beings of the earth! The desecration on my land!"

"We fur men, sir. We didn't know we were on your land." Patrick stammered. I whipped my head toward him while keeping my knife firmly pressed to the man I had pinned down.

"Oi! Why would you tell a savage that?!" The man under me shouted loud enough for his partner to hear. I added pressure to his neck to quiet him, and to my satisfaction, he yelped at the threat. The black-haired man ran toward me. I replaced the knife under the man's neck with my hand, collapsing my fingers over the vital points to choke and or snap his neck. With my free hand, I pointed the knife toward the second man ready for an attack, but the black-haired man put his hands up.

"Sir we apologize for everything, and we have no intent to harm you. God, your eyes are not normal…" I narrowed my eyes hinting I was losing my patience in response to his assessment of me. I increased tightness around the pinned-down man's throat, ignoring his struggling hits against my arm to free himself.

"I will kill him…" I growled.

"Okay! Okay! We can resolve this without people dying right?! What about the kid…." The drumming in my ears drowned out the rest of what Patrick said. I went from killer to worried father in an instant as I looked where KoKo once stood, and he was not there. "She is right there sir, right next to the dead wolf." Patrick pointed behind me obviously seeing the worried look on my face. I released the man from under my grasp so I could stand up. The red-haired man coughed lifting himself up slowly, only to be slammed back down by my foot across his neck. "Hey was that necessary?" Patrick whined. I raised my knife toward him in warning and he backed away with his hands up.

I watched as Rachael petted the dead wolf's head. KoKo stood next to her in his protective stance and my heart mourned the creature as its murderer struggled beneath my foot. Rachael then grabbed one of the pups and cradled it to her chest, after securing one of the pups, she used her free hand to gather the other pup. I could hear the pups still mourning their loss. Rachael placed the pups in one of my side saddles that hung low enough on KoKo for her to reach.

"Daddy, home now?" Rachael asked with no fear in her voice. I gave her a smile and a nod, then turned my attention toward the men.

"Thank the great spirit I was merciful today. I never want to see you on my land again, now go." My tone was low and threatening. I lifted my foot up letting the man go, it took him a few seconds to regain himself as the air rushed back. His partner helped him up to his feet; done with the situation, I was ready to go home.

"Can we have our guns and the fur?" I heard Patrick say behind me.

"I know you didn't ask me that." I hissed without turning to face the men.

"Right, sir we will be on our way then." The men began to walk back from where they came. But I heard their whispers.

"I saved your ass back there." Patrick praised himself.

"Oi shut up! The boss ain't going to be happy about this." The red-haired man replied still stumbling here and there.

JESSAMINE

Chapter 39

The gunshot did not escape my ears as I laid Hania down to rest after his meal. Fixing my blouse and corset, I headed downstairs to investigate the situation. Reaching the bottom of the stairs I saw an empty space, no one in sight. I walked hastily toward the front door, opening it with a sense of panic. Thoughts of Rachael and or Talon getting hurt made my heart ache. "Where the bloody hell did that come from?!" I blurted, nearly stumbling down the porch stairs in my haste. John, Jonah, and Charles turned to me with concerned looks on their faces. Jonah held his pistol in his hand, his finger nervously on the trigger.

"We don't know, but I'm gon' go out there and find out." Before Jonah could walk toward his horse John held his hand out to stop him.

"We are the last defense for the babies if anything has happened to Talon."

"Talon is not the only one that can do something, John!" Jonah countered frustrated.

"It's not what I said." John retorted.

"Rachael is with Talon. They both could be in danger." I said pleadingly, standing beside Jonah.

"Silence!" The word echoed in the distance.

"Talon." I huffed a sigh of relief. It was quite visible that everyone relaxed, just a bit.

"Cowards!" Talon echoes rang out among the trees once more.

"It seems Talon has it under control." John soothed. "He should be fine." John pressed his hand to the small of my back to usher me toward the house. I shrugged off his touch, marching to Jonah's horse. I stumbled the first time trying to swing my leg around, but after the second attempt, I sat on top of the beast. (It has been far too long since I've ridden on a horse.)

"You sure about this?" Jonah looked up at me nervously. I gave him a determined look.

"If it was Charles...?" I asked, raising a stern brow. Jonah getting my meaning flashed me a grin of understanding.

"To the ends of the world, I guess," Jonah said looking at his mate filled with love and turning his gaze back to me.

"Be careful..." Jonah sighed, handing me his pistol with the holster. Wrapping the holster around my upper body, and straightening myself up, I gave the horse a little kick to usher it forward.

I trotted the horse toward the direction I thought Talon's voice was coming from. I shivered a bit, cursing myself for not bringing a coat with me in my haste to find my husband and child. A sinking, disturbing, and very fearful feeling settled in my stomach. I felt the world spin at the possible realization of the situation. I pulled the reins to stop the horse, my breathing was heavy and unsteady. My lips trembled as I fought through tears. *Elias has found me.* "Kya." I kicked the horse hard in the ribs, snapping the reins to set the horse into a fast gallop. *I must hurry.* "Talon!!! Rachael!!!" I frantically screamed through the woods. I hadn't heard Talon's voice for a while now, and my mind was envisioning the worst.

"Jessamine?" The familiarity of the voice froze me in place, tears flowed a steady stream down my face. A warm hand caressed my back startling me to look up. Warm bright yellow eyes met mine along with small green ones.

"Hi Mommy!"

"Are you ok?" Talon's voice was filled with concern. I sniffled wiping my eyes.

"Yes, I was just so... What in the bloody hell happened?!" When I looked down at Rachael's hands, they were covered with dried blood. I frantically searched her body, but it seemed she had no wounds. I turned to Talon still waiting for an answer, when I noticed his shirt was covered in blood as well. Before I could commence my search, Talon grabbed my hands gently into his.

"It is not our blood Jessamine."

"Ouch!" Talon squealed as he rubbed the shoulder I punched. My hand hurt more than his arm did, but I was unwilling to reveal that.

"Whose blood is it, Talon?!" I snapped crossing my arms in front of my chest. The horse under me began to sway nervously feeling my angry energy.

"A wolf," Talon said nonchalantly. I was stunned by his cool manner.

"A wolf?" I chuckled in hysterics. I grabbed the reins to the horse I was on and pulled him in a direction, any direction just away from Talon. *He went wolf hunting, with my daughter. I can't believe this.*

"Jessamine, I don't understand why you are angry," Talon said aligning KoKo with Jonah's horse.

"You went hunting! Possibly putting Rachael in danger!" I shouted, still not looking directly at Talon. Silence grew, forcing me to turn in his direction. Hurt yellow and green eyes stared back at me.

"Mommy don't be mad..." Rachael whined.

"You can at least ask, and not assume." Talon spat as he leered at me. "There were poachers on our land. They cowardly killed a mother wolf in her den as she slept. Me and Rachael buried the body respectfully."

"What are you doing facing poachers with Rachael around? Rachael's safety always comes first, the possibility that my husband's men are still out there looking for us is high." I informed.

"You have me and the others to protect you and the children. She did not get hurt in my exchange of words with the men, they paid her no mind. And he is your former, not current husband." Talon retorted.

"That is not the point!" I countered, not wanting to be bothered by any excuses. Talon didn't say much and neither did I. Rachael was quiet as well, and in place of our voices, nature spoke.

We reached home before the sun had set, Talon had unmounted himself and Rachel and was heading inside the house before I was done tying Jonah's horse to the hitch. Rachael was still with KoKo digging in the saddle bags. I couldn't help but be frustrated. It was I who felt he had betrayed my trust in putting Rachael in a dangerous situation, I should be the one stomping into the house mad. I made it into the house but found Talon was nowhere to be seen. Jonah, Charles, and John all sat at the dining table, Jonah and Charles holding each of the twins. As if they read my mind, they pointed down the hall. I looked in that direction and all I heard was metal slicing through the air from behind the training room door. I rolled my eyes as I walked down the hall to find Talon. Opening the door, I was greeted to the site of Talon's long hair loosely draping his shoulders and a large sword in his hand. I breathed in deeply to readjust my thoughts. "Can we talk?" I didn't get a word in response. Instead, Talon continued to swing the sword with elegant precision. "I want you to understand why I acted as such." This time Talon stopped and looked at me, I could barely see his face with his hair draping it.

"What you have made clear is you don't trust me." Talon said with a breathy huff. I was stunned by his words.

"After all the secrets, I'm still here. I married you. All I'm saying is that I would like you to be more mindful, you're a father now."

"I am mindful, today was the most I felt like a father. But I also know that Rachael is not going to be a child forever. She wants to learn and do new things. She is not tied to societal norms here. I will be more careful of her safety, but do not stunt the person she wants to be."

I let out a sigh unsure how to take his words. Looking at his perspective I could see why he would feel that way, in his culture children learned things I wouldn't have, being from a "civilized" upbringing.

"Daddy, Mommy they need baths." Rachael's voice said behind me. *They?* Talon looked past me with a smile. I turned around and Rachael was holding two wolf cubs as best she could in each of her little arms. My eyes widened as I turned back to Talon.

"No! Absolutely not! We have babies! They can try to eat them!" I bellowed, thinking of all the possibilities.

"It will be fine," Talon said trying to be reassuring.

"Everything is always fine with you. What if-."

"You have been living your life on what ifs instead of living!" Talon interrupted. "We will fight, and we will adapt toward a better future. You must start living. Rachael is trying to live. And our babies deserve to live fearlessly." I was stunned again by Talon's words. Tears fell, and Talon engulfed me in a hug. I wrapped my arms around him in return and just let it out.

"Rachael let's go and give you all a bath. Your parents need time alone." John said. I turned around to see John smiling, directing Rachael toward the stairs. When I turned back Talon kissed me.

www.ingramcontent.com/pod-product-compliance
Lightning Source LLC
Chambersburg PA
CBHW030406020726
47493CB00003B/959